Praise for One Shade of Red

"So well-written that it flows easily, hooking the reader right from the beginning. I had real problems to stop reading it." — Cinta Garcia de la Rosa, author of *A Foreigner in London* and *The Funny Adventures of Little Nani*, and reviewer of <u>Indie Authors You Want to Read</u>.

"How *nice* it is to see a dude lit-style book! And well-written at that!" — Lisa Jey Davis, "<u>Ms. Cheevious"</u> <u>blog</u>

"A great escapist read." — Jesi Lea Ryan, <u>Diary of a</u> <u>Bibliophile</u> and author of *Arcadia's Gift*

"Deliciously sexy!" — Dawn Torrens, author of Amelia's Story

"The sex scenes are explicit, relentless and often hilarious ... Deliciously erotic with something extra." — Frederick Lee Brooke, author of *Doing Max Vinyl*

"So hot, you'll want your own pool boy." — Charity Parkerson, author of *The Society of Sinners*

ONE SHADE OF RED

By Scott Bury

Cover design by David C. Cassidy

Edited by Gary Henry, Roxanne Bury and Cinta Garcia de la Rosa

Proofreaders: Bruce A. Blake and Benjamin X. Wretlind

Quality control by iAi Independent Authors International

Published by The Written Word Communications Company, Ottawa, Ontario, Canada

www.writtenword.ca

ISBN 978-0-9879141-5-6

Library and Archives Canada Cataloguing in Publication information is available.

To Roxanne, and everyone who loves.

Contents

Chapter 1

Falling Down

As if it's not hard enough living with a genius, I had to do his work, too.

It was just SO Nick.

You know about Nick, right? 180 I.Q., thinks up business solutions in a flash that IBM pays thousands for.

Meanwhile, I struggled to maintain a 6.0 GPA in Economics.

So what does he do? Not help me through Professor A's class. No sir.

(We all called him "Professor A" for Asshole. But that's not part of this story.)

No, Nick set up a pool-cleaning business. Not worthy of a genius, but then, back in university, he had NO money. More precisely, his parents had no money. That was just the first thing that set him apart from all the other students. So, unlike all of the other geeks in the BComm program, Nick had to come up with business start-ups that didn't take ANY capital.

Hence PoolGeeks.com. All it took was about fifty bucks for a pool skimmer and water vacuum, and an ad on Craigslist, and he was in business.

For all of two days, before he got whisked away on some intense business management internship or something.

In Europe.

Damn geniuses.

"Come on, Damian, you have to take this for me!" he said as he was packing his suitcase. For London. The lucky fucker.

"Take a bullet for you? No thanks." At that moment, I resented *everything* about Nick: his thick black hair, his pouty lips that girls, apparently, like to bite, the symmetrical planes of his cheeks, the way he could grow a beard in, like, ten minutes if he wanted to.

"Oh, come on! Look, you'll get paid. Fourteen bucks an hour." He didn't even look at me as he spoke, just kept folding clothes.

"Big deal. It's worth more to me to study."

"What good does it do you to study? You'll be a lot further ahead with some real business experience that you can use to impress Professor A-hole."

"Thanks a lot. Not all of us are geniuses, Nick. Some of us—"

"Have to work for a living. Yah, I know. Suckers."

"Okay, so *this* sucker has to study to get passing grades. Look, it's not everybody that aces every exam without ever opening the textbook."

"Is it my fault the professors put the answer in the question?"

"No, and it's not my fault that I can't see the answer in the question, and therefore, I have to study. So sorry, no, Mr. Skinny Genius, I cannot do your dirty work for you."

"What dirty work? It's cleaning a pool! Come on, I promised the lady I would clean her pool regularly. She's depending on me! How can you say no to a poor old widow? It's not like she can do it herself! And now, I get called up for this co-op in the UK. It's not my fault!"

"You said that already. It's not my fault, either."

"You said *that* already. Don't be a selfish asshole. Think of that poor lady. She's a widow. And you're going to make her clean her own pool? Come on, I'll make it worth your while."

"How?"

"How about 50 percent ownership of the company?"

"Half ownership in a shit-ass start-up service company that hasn't even issued its first invoice, yet?"

"Look, it's a solid concept. Complete, turn-key pool maintenance in the wealthiest neighbourhood in Canada—"

Nick's phone rang— that is, his ring-tone went off: Bon Jovi shrieking "we're half-way there-ere."

"Yes?" He paused, listening, but being Nick, he never stood still. He walked to the window, glanced outside, walked over to me, took the Mad magazine out of my hands, flipped to the back and handed it back. "Well, that would take about 16 and three-quarter hours," he said to whoever the hell it was on the phone.

I went back to Mad magazine. It was pretty lame, but it was better than listening to Nick negotiate with some poor asshole on the phone. They should put him in charge of negotiating the mideast crisis. Or oil prices — then maybe I could afford gas.

"Okay, I'll be there in an hour," Nick said and tossed the phone into my lap. "Gotta go."

"What! Where?"

"The airport. The flight's been moved up. See you in a quarter." He shrugged a backpack on, picked up his nerdy, hard-sided suitcase and opened the apartment door.

"A quarter of what?" I asked, but my gut knew the answer. I could tell, because it was dragging my balls down to the floor.

He shoved a torn scrap of paper into my hand. "A quarter of a year. Take care of the little old lady for me, okay? Tell you what: you keep all the money you make through the company until I get back. Fifty percent ownership, one hundred percent revenue. You can't beat that."

A horn honked. "That'll be the limo."

"They sent you a *limo*?"

He opened the door. "Gotta go. Be good to the customers, 'kay? Gotta go."

And he was gone.

I sighed. I had known all along it was inevitable. As soon as he had announced he was starting a business, I knew I would end up doing all the work. And now, it was inescapable.

So the next day, I coaxed my 12-year-old Suzuki Swift along the winding, shady roads of Rosedale, looking alternately between the scrap of paper in my hand and the numbers on the fronts of the houses. There: number 17. I pulled into the semi-circular driveway.

The house was an immense, Tudor-style pile. Or maybe Tyrolean. Whatever — it had brown beams at 45-degree angles set in white stucco. The front door was made of oak, or some other heavy-looking wood, and had a semi-circular window on top. Iron brackets reached two-thirds of the way across.

Clutching an aluminum pole in one hand and a canvas bag in the other, I rang the doorbell. I heard a deep ring from somewhere inside that echoed for seconds. Then silence. I waited for what seemed like a very long time. Sunlight burned the back of my neck.

Should I ring again? Would it be rude? I didn't want to piss off these rich people.

But—hell with it. This is Nick's business, not mine. I pressed the doorbell again, heard the same deep ring and echoes.

Then I nearly jumped out of my skin as a buzzing voice said: "Yes? Who's there?"

I hadn't noticed the little speaker, a white plastic box that blended with the trim around the doorway. I pressed a little round button under the speaker grille. "PoolGeeks," I said, loudly and clearly.

"Don't talk so loud or so close to the speaker," the voice buzzed. It was impossible to tell if the speaker was male or female, young or old. "Come around the left side of the house. I'm by the pool."

Great. The old biddy was going to watch me clean her pool. I pictured a crone in a flowered sun-dress and a big floppy hat, sipping on a mint julep, croaking "Don't miss the far corner."

I threw the strap of the canvas bag over my shoulder and followed a stone path around the house. The side yard was filled with flowering bushes and exotic shrubs. A gate with a semi-circular top that matched the front door pierced a solid cedar fence. I pushed it open with the aluminum pole of the pool skimmer to see a huge patio of interlocking reddish stones. In the middle of it, a curved pool gleamed blue and white in the sun.

"You're early," said a musical voice from somewhere around the back corner of the house at the same time that the gate closed, catching the butt of the pool-skimmer pole as I took a step forward. It was enough to yank me back, just a little, and I fell forward.

The canvas bag, loaded with accessories and supplies, vomited all over the stone walk. The aluminum pole hit the ground and bounced up, smacking me in the face as I went down. I barely got one hand under my face before it hit the stone, too.

"Oh, dear! Are you all right?" said the musical voice. Nothing like the buzzy squawk from the speaker by the front door. All I could see, though, was grey flat stone and a little green blur to the side.

I craned my head up. This can't be real, I remember thinking.

She was a dream. My dream. A tall woman with long, wavy brown hair. Couldn't be more than 30 years old.

In a big floppy hat. And a string bikini.

I scrambled to my feet. My hands and knees were scraped and my face hurt where the aluminum pole had hit it. "Ya, yah, fine," I stammered. "I'm from PoolGeeks." I yanked the pole free of the gate.

"You're early."

"Sorry."

"No, that's good. For once, my pool will be clean before all the neighbours'." She pointed at the pool. "Well, as you can see, there it is."

I couldn't look at the pool, because I couldn't stop looking at her. I felt like I was in junior high again. The only word that came into my mind was: *stacked.* There were acres of bare skin. The bathing suit barely covered her nipples and pubis, but none of those words made it into my mind at that moment.

She looked at me, eyebrows raised, and I realized that she was waiting for me to say something. My tongue felt thick and heavy.

"I'm ... um ... Damian Serr." I looked at her some more. I forced my eyes to stay level with hers, but it was so hard not to let them just fall, rest on the curves of those big, beautiful breasts ... I coughed. Choked, actually. "From PoolGeeks."

She laughed. "Yes, you said that." She bent down daintily, knees together, and picked up the little round net that fit onto the end of the aluminum pole. She took two long steps toward me, stepping carefully because she had bare feet. I held the canvas bag open, and she slipped it inside. "This is yours, I think. I'm Mrs.

Rosse. Come on to the pool."

She had a high, musical voice — oh, did I say that already? Sorry. Okay, she turned around, and I was very happy to follow her. It was a long way around the side of the house to the big patio in the back. No, I did not stare at her ass the whole way there. Not the *whole* way.

Finally, we got past the side of the house. There was a huge sliding walk-out, wide open. Bolted to the outer wall beside it was a big intercom system, the one she had used to talk to me through the little speaker by the front door. It had a small TV screen in it that showed a very clear colour picture of the front steps. It was depressing to see my rusty Suzuki in the background, too.

Even I could tell the patio furniture between the door and the pool was expensive. Just the big glass table cost more than all the furniture in my apartment. Cost more than my car. Of course, I would probably have to pay someone to take my car away, so that wasn't really a good comparison.

And the pool. It was depressingly big, at least thirty feet long and twenty wide, with a curving side. And dirty. So dirty, so early in the season. I had no idea how I was going to clean it.

"This will be the first time it's been cleaned this season. I guess I just didn't expect the weather to get this warm, this early. It's still only May, after all," she said. She picked up a tall glass from the table and took a sip of a greenish liquid through a straw. I watched the liquid go up the straw in slow motion, fascinated just to watch her swallow.

"Well, I'll let you get to it," she said. She turned and sashayed — okay, she walked like a normal person, but I enjoyed watching her ass sway as she stepped into the house.

I sighed. The spell was broken. And so was my spirit.

The place was a mess. There were leaves and branches all over the pool deck and floating in the water. And the water: a definite unhealthy green. A darker green layer clung to the side, all the way around. I walked all the way around the pool to make sure.

Did I say I had never cleaned a pool before in my life?

Behind the pool was a tool shed that matched the fence. It was probably as big as my whole apartment. I peeked inside and found a push-broom and a big rubber garbage bin. It was a start.

Sweeping around the pool took longer than I thought, filled a quarter of the garbage bin and left me dripping sweat. I kept wiping my eyes with the bottom of my t-shirt.

Then, to the water. I had no idea really how to do this, but I swept up crap using the net on the long aluminum pool. That not only filled up the garbage bin, but also turned it into a dripping, stinking cesspool. Only after I had filled it with wet, rotting leaves and garbage did I wonder what I was supposed to do with it. Haul it to the curb on garbage day? Did rich Rosedalers wait for garbage day?

Now, the layer of green slime around the pool. How do I get that off?

Why the hell hadn't Nick talked to me about this?

Why the hell hadn't I asked him?

An hour later, and I had gotten most of the green slime off the sides. Not all of it, but it sure looked better than it had when I started.

"Well! It's certainly coming along!" The musical voice startled me. Mrs. Rosse was holding out a big glass of ice water for me. She had changed into shorts and a tank top, and was wearing big sunglasses, but she was still breathtaking.

I chugged the water, surprised at how thirsty I was. "Thanks. That feels good."

"I'll get you some more. Oh, you missed a spot." She pointed across the pool to a big, stinking, horrible green blob, clinging to the side of the pool.

I held in the sigh. "Don't worry, Mrs. Rosse. I'll get it."

She laughed as she went back into the kitchen to refill the water. "Call me Alexis."

I got down to scraping the last of the slime off and throwing it in the rubber garbage bin. Then it took me twenty minutes to figure out how to connect the water vacuum. By the time I did, Mrs. Rosse — Alexis — was in the back yard again, looking slightly annoyed. "I guess this was a bigger job than either of us anticipated."

"Guess so," I agreed, wiping my face with my shirt again.

"Look, I have to go. You can let yourself out, right?" She handed me an envelope.

"Thank you, Mrs. Rosse. I mean, Alexis." I nodded in what I hoped was a grateful way.

She went back into the house. I heard the lock click. I picked up the pool vacuum and listened, but I couldn't hear anything that sounded like a garage door opening or a car driving away. The house was too big, the front yard too distant. So I switched on the vacuum and swept it back and forth, sucking up dirt from the bottom of the pool for what I hoped was long enough, even if she was puttering around inside the house. Or watching me.

Finally, I couldn't take it anymore. I pulled the envelope from my back pocket and tried as carefully as I could to open it. I just smudged slime across it. I tried, and failed, to keep the slime off the cheque itself.

Neat handwriting. Dated correctly, signed, the right amount. I almost felt happy.

Then I noticed the "Pay to the Order of" line: "PoolGeeks."

Crap. What was I going to do with that?

Fucking geniuses. Think of everything. Except paying their employees.

Fucking Nick.

Chapter 2

The Re-Do

I actually had my hand on the door to the beer store when my cell phone chirped. The screen showed "Private number." I took a couple of steps away from the store as I put the phone to my ear. "Hello?" I fully expected it to be Kristen; she was paranoid about cell phone stalkers.

"Damian, it's Mrs. Rosse." I nearly dropped the phone—a customer calling you out of the blue probably wouldn't be good news.

It wasn't.

"I want you to come over here right away and finish what you started," she said.

So many ideas went through my head all at the same time, but none of them were right. "I'm sorry?" were the only words that made it out of my mouth, however.

"You left yesterday before I came back, and I know that we had agreed to that, but on the understanding that you would do a complete job of cleaning the pool, first." Did her voice have a really bitchy edge to it, or was that just the way the cell phone made her sound?

"But I thought I had finished. I cleaned out all the leaves and grass and finished up with the pool vacuum."

"Well, if it had been the very first time that you had ever cleaned a swimming pool, I could understand it," she said. Yep, that's definitely a bitchy, pissed-off edge. "You cleaned out the easy debris, but you didn't clean off the green slime around the side."

"Yes I did!" Don't get mad, some small, wise part of my brain warned. And don't tell her it *was* the first pool you've ever cleaned. She's your only customer.

When did I start caring about this stupid job?

"Well, it's not as bad as it was, but there's still a lot of slime there. Now I've already paid you in full for the job, and it has not been done to my satisfaction. Quite frankly, it's not to anyone's satisfaction. I would have been mortified for any of my friends to see it."

"I'm sorry," I repeated. God, I sounded so lame.

"Well, it's fine to be sorry, but that doesn't do me much good, now, does it? No, I want you to get down here and finish the job properly."

"Ooo-kay," I said, holding back a lot of swear words. "When would you like me to come?"

"Right now!" She sounded genuinely surprised at my question.

"Uhh, well, it will take me some time," I started to say. "I'm at the other end of town, and with traffic ..."

"Fine. I'll leave the side gate unlocked for you. Just make sure you're finished before two o'clock."

"Two?" I would have to scramble to get my cleaning stuff together and drive over there and get the job done — if my crappy car didn't break down. "I'll try my best, Mrs. Rosse, but is there a reason it has to be done by two? Mrs. Rosse?"

Cell phones don't click or anything when you hang up, I realized.

So there I was, back at the pool under the mid-afternoon sun, scraping and scrubbing disgusting, smelly slime off the tiles. I had taken my shirt off and put it back on again when I felt my skin begin to burn, and now the cotton was saturated with sweat. Every so often, I reached into the pool and splashed my face. I thought about getting into the pool and staying cool while I cleaned, but I didn't dare the risk of making Mrs. Rosse any bitchier.

"Now even the fussiest bitch has to be happy with this," I muttered as I wiped off the very last of the gunk.

"That's much better," made me jump and I dropped the debris net into the pool.

I turned to see Mrs. Rosse in her jogging suit: tight blue-and-white top stretched across her breasts, matching tight shorts, expensive Nike running shoes with the top edge of pink half-socks peeking above the ankles. I made an effort to raise my eyes to hers, away from the outline of her nipples pushing against her top. I dropped the bucket and slimy water slopped onto my feet.

"Sorry to scare you," she laughed and stepped to the edge of the pool. "I just wanted to say that the edge looks great. Nice and clean, now. I guess it's my fault, really, letting it get as dirty as I did before having someone in to clean it."

"I didn't hear you come in," was all I could think to say. I wondered if she had heard my out-loud thought about fussy bitches.

She laughed, but carefully inspected all around the edge of the pool. I got down on my knees, face burning, to try to fish the net out without getting all wet. When I stood up again, she was standing right in front of me.

"You're awfully cute," she said. My mouth opened, but nothing came out. What do you say? I tried to smile and tried even harder not to look at her nipples. "I think you deserve a tip for your hard work," she added.

She sank to her knees and two thoughts went through my mind at the same time: This is going to be fucking great, and No, I'm mistaken. This kind of thing *never* happens.

She pulled my shorts down, and I didn't know whether to be embarrassed or not that my penis was already getting hard. She smiled up at me as she stroked it gently. Her hand was so soft.

Then she put her mouth around the shaft and I didn't think anymore. I looked at her hair and stroked it gently, letting her do what she was doing so well.

Nothing had ever felt like this to me. It was so much better than masturbating... I hesitated to even think the word, but then Mrs. Rosse sucked me in deeper and all I could see and feel was a white wall of ... good.

It was good.

No one had ever done this before. Never. Never even close.

The back yard, the house, the damned pool, all faded away. All I felt were her lips, her wet soft lips, sliding up and down as she moved her head back and forth, making sexy slurping noises.

And then, all of a sudden, I climaxed. I tried to pull away, but she leaned toward me, keeping me in her mouth as I came. I choked back a yell to avoid alerting the neighbours. Then neither Mrs. Rosse's nor my desires mattered as I fell onto my bare butt onto the pool deck, my dick flopping around.

She laughed at me. "There. Was that a good tip?" She stood.

I nodded. I could not speak. I did not know what to think. Did she do this a lot?

"Don't worry. I don't make a practice of going down on every tradesman who comes here. I just thought you're really cute and you deserved a reward for a job well done — particularly because I'm not paying you cash for today's visit."

I still couldn't speak. I could barely pull up my pants. But maybe she read what was left of my mind. "You were just finishing the job you didn't complete properly yesterday," she said. "Remember, customer satisfaction is the first requirement of any business. My late husband used to say that." She patted my face. "Now, since you've done such a good job, I'm going to recommend you to my friends who have pools. A lot of them complain how hard it is to find a good pool cleaner."

"Thank you," I managed to croak. My throat was very dry. I wasn't sure, though, whether I was thanking her for promising to recommend me and helping to grow my list of clients, or for the blow job.

She smiled again. "You're welcome. Now, shouldn't you be going?"

I nodded. She disappeared into the house, and I picked up all my gear and stumbled around to the front. The gate closed on the aluminum pole again, but I managed to extricate it without falling down this time.

I drove home in a daze; I think I ran a red light on St. Clair, but I can't be sure. In my crappy little apartment, I cracked a beer and switched on a baseball game. I heard the announcer and colour commentator buzzing about pitches and fly balls, but all I could see was Mrs. Rosse's brown hair from above.

The way it bounced as her head moved back and forth. Her brown eyes as she looked up at me and laughed with my cock in her mouth. That sound was all I heard, then, that and the slurping noises she made.

I thought of her mouth moving down, swallowing me. I realized I was rubbing my penis through my pants. I couldn't help it. Happy for once that Nick was far away, I unzipped and rubbed my cock, then regretted it as I came again, all over the couch. Shit.

I felt my pulse in my neck. I heard my own breath catching in my throat. I held it, then let it out slowly. My surroundings came back to me; I saw the baseball commentator looking at me from the TV. Embarrassed, I zipped up and went for some paper towels to clean up my mess from the couch.

I downed the rest of the beer and went to bed, trying hard not to think of Mrs. Rosse.

Alexis.

Ever try *not* to think of someone?

Chapter 3

Emergency Pick-Up

"No fuckin' way!" Patrick laughed, loud over the noise of the music, the game and the general conversation in the bar.

Tyler sat across the table from him. "Not only that, then she sort of squeezes one tit out of her blouse — you know, so no one else can see — and just about jabs it into my mouth."

"So, did you fuck her?" Patrick asked.

"Nah," Tyler guzzled down half his beer. "She just gave me a handjob in the car. I dropped her in front of her apartment."

"So, you going to see her again?" I asked, and immediately felt stupid when Tyler and Patrick laughed.

"As if! I don't even know her name!"

I hoped my buddies couldn't see how red my face was in the dim bar. Then again, I could just say it was sunburn from working outside all day long.

It was Patrick's turn, and he leaned forward. "Dudes, this new girlfriend I got — Frieda. She's some kinda freak!"

"Whaddaya mean, bro?" Tyler asked, slurping more beer. He signalled to a passing waitress for more shooters.

"I mean, you know, she takes some gettin' goin'. Like, I gotta take her to a nice restaurant, and not just the Keg, ya know? Or a movie, or she likes museums and shit, ya' know? But after that, man, she's *wild*. I mean, I get her started and she literally goes all night long!"

"You, all night?" Tyler banged down a Slippery Nipple and chased it with half a pint of beer. "You don't last moren' two minnits, I hear."

I wanted to say something about Alexis. Mrs. Rosse. I could tell a better, truer story than either of those jerks. But every time I rehearsed it in my mind, it sounded too creepily like Mrs. Robinson. Or Penthouse Forum.

"Fuck, man, I don't get any sleep till the sun comes up!" Patrick said. "Last weekend, we did it in an *art gallery.* There was an exhibit of 'erotic art' from France or somethin', I dunno. It didn't look like shit to me, but did it ever turn Frieda on! We went into a back hallway and did it against the wall! Then, when we got home, we did it again!"

"That's not, technically, all night," I pointed out.

"It's more than you're gettin', Damie!" Tyler shouted, and two guys at the bar turned and grinned at our table.

"Shut up, Tyler. What do you know?"

"How about you, Damian?" Patrick asked. "You gettin' anywhere with Kristen?"

I took a long drink. How to answer that? "You know, Kristen is my girlfriend, not just some bimbo to use for sex." I wanted to sound serious and pissed off, but it came out as a whine.

"Girlfriend, huh," Tyler leered. "More like a wife, if you ask me."

"What the hell does that mean?"

"It means, you do whatever she tells you, and you don't get any sex out of it."

"How do you know I'm not getting any sex?"

Patrick and Tyler looked at each and laughed. "From the Virgin Princess of East York?" Patrick practically yelled. "Super-Christian Kristen, President of the Church Youth League? Miss Morality herself?" Neither of my so-called friends could speak for at least a minute as they laughed.

"What did you do, pry her thighs apart with the jaws of life?" Patrick giggled. Tyler laughed again at that, eyes squeezed shut.

"Dude, her gynecologist gets more out of her than you do!" Tyler said.

"Now, you're just being gross," I said.

"No, dude, he's right," Patrick jumped in. "Go with her for her next check-up, and when she's got her feet in those stirrups, *mmhh!* Give her a bone!"

"That's not funny," I said, but I could not suppress a smile.

I never believed my buddies when they started bragging about the girls they bagged. Patrick was good-looking enough. He had bulked up on the high-school wrestling team and took pride in his muscles. He kept his dark hair cut short and his blue eyes could blaze intensity when he wanted to get a girl's attention. But he was so self-centred, it was no wonder that his relationships with girlfriends never lasted more than three months. And Tyler was not good-looking, I thought: a little too heavy, with short, curly hair and bad skin — acne had been hard on him. Nor was he particularly bright. He was usually rude, crude and loud.

And yet, Patrick always had a girlfriend; when one dumped him, he usually hooked up with another within a day. I had even seen him get dumped at a party by one girl and leave with another a couple of hours later.

And come to think of it, I remember Tyler going home from that same party with a girl that I thought was *way* too good looking for him.

And I thought I was smart. My girlfriend ... well, I had a girlfriend, I thought. Although hanging out with her wasn't particularly fun. And it was in no way sexual.

So who was smartest among the three of us?

We sat there, drinking beer and shooters and watching the game with half an eye, mostly trading bullshit. But I have to admit, I wasn't much of a drinker then. After a few more rounds, the conversation came back to my girlfriend and sex life—or lack of it.

"Gotcher cell phone?" Tyler asked. "Lemme see."

I was too drunk to suspect his motives, so I fumbled my cell phone — yes, a cheap, crappy dumb phone, not a cool phone like Tyler and Patrick had — out of my pocket and put it in Tyler's hand.

"Got any naked pix of Kristen on here?" he asked, poking at the buttons.

I just shook my head, wondering how many girls had posed nude for Patrick's and Tyler's cell phones.

Then Tyler stabbed a button and held the phone to his ear. I realized he had pressed "Call."

"Who are you calling?" I asked, alarmed.

"Your girlfrien'," he answered, grinning. Try as I might, I couldn't get the phone out of his grasp. Kristen answered on what I figured must have been the third ring or so. "Hey, baby, it's me, Damian," Tyler said, trying to impersonate me. It didn't convince me, but then, I was there; it seemed to convince Kristen. "Listen, you and me been wasting enough time, already. It's time to get naked and get it together! I'm comin' over for some booty, right now."

"Are you crazy?" I yelled, hoping my voice could overcome the noise in the bar and make it through the cell phone, somehow, to tell Kristen it wasn't me. She was going to be *so* mad.

I grabbed at my phone again, but Tyler twisted away. Patrick came around the table and grabbed my hands as Tyler said "I'm at the bar with my best buds, Tyler and Patrick. Don't pretend you don't know who we — they are.

"At the bar," he continued. "The Red Fox. Yah, that's the one." Another pause. "No, no, I'll ... awright, awright, come on over! Yah, it's on the Danforth. You been there! Okay, see ya." He handed me the phone. "Good news, buddy: she's comin' to get you."

"What?" Patrick and I said simultaneously. "Kristen is coming to pick you up for a booty call? Oh man, I never even had that much luck!" Patrick added.

Luck had nothing to do with it, I thought. At least not good luck. "Shit, shit, shit," I said. "Kristen hates it when I'm drinking."

"How many beers you had?" Patrick asked.

I had to think about it. "Three. Maybe four," I answered. "Shit."

"Like I said, more of a wife than a girlfriend," Tyler said and drank more beer.

I stood to brush peanut crumbs off my clothes and headed for the door. It would be better, a little, to meet Kristen outside, rather than in the bar.

It wasn't such a bad place. The Red Fox was also a restaurant that catered to families at suppertime. But Kristen felt — I knew this because she told me several times — that sitting in a bar drinking beer with my "dumb buddies" was a waste of time and money, something done by low-lives only. Not by respectable university students who hoped one day to be respectable professional members of the community.

I could hear her voice telling me this as I stood on the curb, looking eastward for her car. Or actually, her father's car. One part of my brain could not believe she would actually agree to come and get me at — I felt shocked when I looked at my watch — quarter past midnight. Her father let her come out this late?

Another part of my brain kept predicting what she would say. I could hear her clipped voice in my head: the way she bit off her words when she was pissed, the way she would emphasize every sentence with a "Hmmm?" that was more of an accusation than a question.

But there was another part of my brain that kept asking pesky questions. Like "Why does she need her father's permission to go out late at night when she's over 18?" And "Why does she get to dictate when and how often I go out with my friends?" Or "Just why does she get to decide what 'respectable' professionals do in their own time? Or what constitutes 'respectability'?"

And "Why is it taking her so long to get down to the Danforth from her house? She should have been here a long time ago."

"Dude, you owe me thirty bucks," said someone beside me. I jumped, literally jumped, before I saw it was just Patrick. Tyler was behind him. "You left without paying for your beer. The waitress was pissed — she thought you had burned her. So I hadda pay her."

"Can I get you tomorrow?" I asked. I really didn't want Kristen to see me giving Patrick money. She'd have something else to lecture me about: "Really, given how little money you make, should you be paying your dumb buddy for beer from a bar? And what if someone had seen you handing over money on the street like that? They'd think you were buying drugs! Yes, Patrick does look like a drug dealer."

"Okay, just don't take too long. I need to buy some shit tomorrow," Patrick said. He slapped me on the shoulder.

I looked down the street, expecting to see Kristen's father's car any minute, but even though traffic was light, I couldn't see the familiar shape of the minivan anywhere. When headlights lit up the asphalt at my feet from behind me, I was confused.

A grey Jaguar pulled up the curb, pointing the wrong way. The driver's window slid down silently and a musical voice said "Well, do you want booty, or not?"

I bent down to see the long wavy hair and deep brown eyes of my employer. My only customer. I looked at my friends, and they were staring at me and the car with their jaws hanging loose. "Mrs. Rosse? What are you doing here?"

"You called me, remember? You wanted to get naked. What's a girl supposed to do when she gets a call like that? Now get in."

I flashed my friends a grin as I walked around the car to get into the passenger seat. They still had their mouths open. Mrs. Rosse gunned the engine, cutting off a hatchback coming the other way — the right way down the Danforth. Before I could say anything, she said "Boy, you have dumb friends."

"I was just going to say, that wasn't me. That was Tyler," I stammered. "He thinks he's funny."

"I know what your voice sounds like, Damian. We have spoken on the phone."

"Sorry if he offended you."

Mrs. Rosse laughed. "Offended me? Maybe disappointed me!"

"How?"

"That it wasn't actually you making that phone call." She looked at me and I swear I saw her eye sparkle. She made a turn way too fast, throwing me almost into her lap. "Do up your seatbelt, cowboy."

"Where are we going?"

"My place. You said you wanted to get naked with me. Or your friend said it, but anyway, I'm turned on now."

I decided not to bother trying to explain that both Tyler and I thought he had dialled Kristen's number. I was so glad he had made a mistake.

How had he managed that? Or was it deliberate? I scrolled through the list of numbers on my phone, and there were at least three between Kristen's and Mrs. Rosse's entries.

"Calling someone?" Mrs. Rosse asked as she turned onto one of the tree-lined avenues of Rosedale.

"I, uh, got a text," I lied. "Just my cell-phone provider telling me I should upgrade my plan."

"Are you going to?"

I snapped the phone shut and shoved it back in my pocket. "No way. Can't afford it." My mouth suddenly was very dry. Did she really say she was turned on? "So, uh, sorry to drag you out this late."

She laughed again. I was really starting to love that laugh. I squirmed in my seat, hoping to hide my sudden erection. "I wasn't doing anything, just reading a really bad book and feeling horny. Your friend's call was the excuse I needed to get out and scare up some action."

I was sure she could hear my heart pounding, because that's all I could hear at that point. I hadn't noticed what she was wearing when I got in the car. As we passed under streetlamps, I could see that she was wearing a pink jogging jacket, but her legs were bare.

She noticed me looking at her. "That's right, Damian. This jacket is all I have on."

With that, she swung the car into her driveway. I sat there, staring as she walked, bare-assed, to her front door, the flip-flops of her sandals echoing down the street. She turned to me from the step, smiled and pulled off the jacket. She posed for a second, nude, and tossed the jacket into the house, then stepped inside.

She left the door open. I ran in after her, slammed the door behind me and took the stairs two at a time. I glimpsed her ass as she disappeared from the hallway into a room.

What an ass! Round, high, firm. I had to grab it. I was drooling.

I found myself in a bedroom lit softly by an old-fashioned table lamp. Beside it on the night table was a book, open but face down, one half hanging over the table's side. Inevitably, it was *Fifty Shades of Grey*.

The bed was the biggest I had ever seen, with four high wooden posts holding up a lacy awning. Mrs. Rosse was posing on it, sort of sitting on her side, looking at me. Her breasts hung slightly over her arms and her long hair was a wild storm.

"I thought you said you wanted to get naked with me. Oh,

wait, that was your friend. I guess he wanted to get naked. Should I call him instead?"

I shut my mouth and struggled out of my clothes. I pulled my runners off with my feet as I pulled my t-shirt over my head. Taking my pants down required a little more care as my erection was pushing them out pretty far. Mrs. Rosse laughed a little, but that didn't faze me. I jumped onto the bed, landing beside her, and kissed her mouth.

She responded to my tongue with her own, wrestling with it. I grabbed at her boobs, but she pushed my hands down and away. "Slow down, speed demon. We have all night."

I sat up and kissed her neck, starting high and working slowly down. I dragged my teeth lightly over her collarbone and she sighed. She ran her fingertips up and down my sides. That usually tickles me, but her fingers felt like they were on fire.

She kissed me again and slid her tongue into my mouth, then sucked on my lip. I copied her, then kissed her throat again. I kissed lower and lower — I had to get those red nipples into my mouth.

I licked her breasts, sliding my tongue over the top of one breast and around the outside of the nipple. Since she wanted to take all night to do this, I thought I would be creative.

Hell, no matter what I did, it would be creative — this was my first time.

So I licked around the outside curve of her breast, then underneath, sliding my tongue all the way to the other breast, up and around. She was breathing fast and shallow and her eyes were closed.

I decided to take what I wanted, and sucked her nipple into my mouth.

"Not so hard. Don't bite!" she said. She pushed her fingers through my hair. I let up on the pressure and sucked lightly, then kissed just the very tip of the other nipple as lightly as I could. I was rewarded with a deep sigh.

She put her hand behind my head and pushed deeper, so I sucked and licked her nipple, trying to remember to be gentle. I couldn't believe how soft and simultaneously firm a woman's breast could be.

She opened her eyes and smiled at me. Not a wicked smile, or a calculating smile. She just looked very happy at that moment. I came up for a tender kiss on the mouth. She pulled me close till her bare skin touched mine, all down my body — the biggest thrill I had ever known.

"You're doing very well for your first time," she said. Before I could ask her how the hell she knew, she said "Go down on me now."

What if I did it wrong? I could not bring myself to say I didn't know what to do.

She'll let you know when you're doing it right or wrong, said another part of my brain. So I took her words literally and went down, kissing her neck, her breasts, taking time to suck each nipple again. I kissed her flat belly and licked her navel, then lower. I kissed her pubic hair and inhaled her sexy scent: musky but somehow sweet at the same time.

I thought of all the porn I had seen of men tonguing women's vaginas, but none of it looked particularly appealing for either actor.

Some part of my brain gave me the idea to kiss even lower, so I kissed down her right leg to her knee. Mrs. Rosse pulled her legs up and wide apart and in the lamplight I saw her vagina, fully exposed, the lips pouting and shining a little with moisture.

I kissed the inside of her left thigh, working my way higher. She moaned, I moved up, biting the inside of her thigh until I was breathing in her musk.

Alexis squirmed and moaned. She grabbed my head in both hands and called out my name. I flicked my tongue back and forth across her clit. I moved my tongue down until the skin under my tongue burned from the stretching.

Delicious.

My dick was hard; I moved my hips, rubbing it against her sheets and thinking of thrusting into my employer.

"Oh, Damian, are you thinking of sliding your cock into my pussy?" she moaned.

How does she keep reading my mind? I wondered. "Soon, baby, soon," I said. Her thigh was shaking. Is this good? I wondered.

"Go back to what you were doing before," Alexis said. I flicked my tongue left and right. "Not so hard!"

I lifted my head a little and stretched my tongue out farther, barely fluttering it against her. Alexis was breathing like she was running a marathon. Her skin burned against my cheeks. I took a risk and licked lower, sliding between her pussy lips. She seemed to like that, like that a lot.

Mrs. Rosse grabbed my hair in both hands and thrust into my face. A shriek tore out of her mouth and her thighs shook. She rammed her hips up into me one more time and then pushed my head away from her. "Stop! Oh ... fuck me. Fuck me now, Damian!"

I didn't need any more encouragement. I jumped up the bed and onto her. My stupid dick, though, rammed her thigh.

She took charge, grabbing me by the shoulders. We rolled over on the wide bed and she grinned down at me. Her legs straddled mine. She brought her face down and in one motion bit my neck and impaled herself on me. Two simultaneous sensations: pain on my throat as she sucked the skin between her teeth, and unbelievable pleasure as her wet, wet heat slid down my length.

She straightened up and I watched her magnificent body riding me. Her brown curls swept back and forth over her shoulders, brushing the tops of her breasts. She put her hands on my chest and pushed up, then slammed her hips down again. She pushed up and down over and over until she arched back, trembling, and screamed again.

Then she fell forward, pressing down on me. I could feel her vagina clenching and relaxing. I put my hands on her magnificent ass, fulfilling the wish I had had since the doorway. I squeezed it, savouring the feeling, the way it filled my hands. She gasped and wriggled her hips — a delicious sensation. I started thrusting, faster and faster while squeezing that ass.

Alexis sat up. Then I was screaming, unable to hold back a second longer. Too late, a question of birth control flashed in my mind, but I felt my whole life was flowing through the tip of my penis into Alexis. I kept thrusting and Mrs. Rosse's legs shook, until I couldn't thrust any more. I wrapped my arms around her and held her tight. Her hair fell over my face.

I kissed her face. I could barely breathe. "Mrs. Rosse," I said, half-conscious.

She rolled off of me, laughing. "I think you can call me 'Alexis' now."

I felt so stupid. "I'm sorry for coming in you like that. Are you, you know, using anything...?"

"It's kind of late to ask, but yes, I am on birth control. But you're right. We should have used condoms. We hardly know each other. Although I did blow you the other day."

Whoa! Did she really say that? Who was this woman? How did she talk so frankly about sex, yet seem so ... *classy* was the only word that came to mind. Yes, she was classy. Sophisticated, educated, smart. She fit right into this Rosedale, top-one-percent world she inhabited. Yet in the light of the table-lamp, lying naked on this enormous bed, she looked like a porn star's dream. A face like an angel framed by wild, curly brown hair, a taut body with all the right curves, and those big dark nipples that begged to be kissed.

"Wow, you really came a lot, Damian," she said, as casually as if she were saying "You sure made a lot of coffee." She wiped her hand between her legs and held up a wet finger, laughing. She looked me straight in the eyes, as if asking me, daring me to — what?

What did she expect? What was the right answer to this unspoken question? Would she think I was a timid, prudish schoolboy if I said no? Would she think me a complete pervert if I said yes? What would she consider a pervert, anyway? What were her boundaries?

Was she testing my boundaries, or was she just playing? How should I respond?

I hate that part of my brain that goes into question overdrive.

My penis started to stiffen again.

Alexis reached for it, spreading stickiness. "Mmm, feels like someone's getting hard again," she said.

I could not have said a word at that moment if my life depended on it. There was no point, anyway. I couldn't argue when her hand wrapped around my erection.

I was amazed when she took my penis in her mouth like she

had that afternoon by the pool. I felt like the room was spinning, like my legs were evaporating, like Alexis was sucking my whole life force into her.

She let go, climbed on top of me again and engulfed me. We both screamed over and over as she rode, up and down.

Some kind of instinct took over in me. I pulled her close and rolled over, roaring as I thrust into her with all my might. Alexis screamed in response, pushing hard against me. Inspired by I don't know what, I lifted her legs up high, over my shoulders and slammed into her. Alexis rolled her head back and forth, whipping long hair over her face. She screamed and clenched her muscles, relaxed, screamed and clenched again.

I needed to come. Nothing else mattered but releasing that energy. I pounded into her, over and over, watching her breasts bounce up and down with each thrust, hearing her cry out every time.

And then the world went blank. I roared again and felt something open in me. My hips kept going, faster and faster even as I climaxed. I felt wetness on my thighs and I heard Alexis scream high and loud, and finally I collapsed on top of her, chest heaving.

"Get off me," she panted after a couple of minutes.

I tried. "I can't move," I whispered.

"I can't breathe, Damian," she said. I rolled to the side and immediately missed the feeling of her around my penis. The air was cool on it.

She touched my cheek. Her fingers were warm, soft. I could see she was panting, too.

She rose on one elbow and looked at me. "Damian, for your first time, that was very good," she said. She kissed me, gently this time. "With a little more work, you just may turn into one of my favourite lovers."

Chapter 4

What a Morning After

Sunlight streamed through the spaces between the blinds and the window frames. Mrs. Rosse breathed steadily beside me, lying on her side, covered to her chin in a light comforter.

The clock on the night-table showed 7:30. What am I doing here? I thought. My head was a little fuzzy, as usual after a night of drinking.

Memory came back: Tyler and Patrick, their tall tales, Tyler dialling Kristen. Mrs. Rosse picking me up in her convertible. Her naked ass as she walked up her front steps.

The taste of her skin. Her nipples in my mouth. Her wet heat.

It all flooded back, and the morning wood sprang up.

I looked at her in wonder. I could see less than a quarter of her face with her long brown hair disarrayed on the pillows and bedclothes. Could she be real? A woman who went down on you for cleaning the pool, who picked you up in a hot sports car when your friend mistakenly drunk-dialled her, as a joke, then fucked your brains out with no strings attached?

No, said part of my brain. This can't be real. You must be dreaming.

I remembered a cliché from some silly British books I had read as a child: "pinch myself to make certain I'm not dreaming." I squeezed together some flesh on my thigh. My situation did not change, other than now having a sore leg.

I stood up, careful not to wake her, and gathered my clothes where I had dropped them on the floor the night before.

I sat on the toilet so the sound of my peeing wouldn't disturb

Mrs. Rosse.

Alexis, I reminded myself. She said to call her Alexis.

I tiptoed down to the most beautiful kitchen I had ever seen: ceramic tile floors, dark wood cabinets and blue granite counters. The stainless steel oven was built into the wall, waist-high. I had to search for the refrigerator, though. It took me a few minutes to realize that the two full-height, side-by-side doors in the cabinets were actually one immense fridge. I could almost step inside.

It was stocked with packages of food from a gourmet shop on Yonge Street. I knew it only because my mother had once laughed when a new neighbour asked if she ever shopped there.

Eggs filled a special holder in the door. There was no margarine, but a crystal dish held butter. I opened and shut drawers until I found, not bacon, but a vacuum-wrapped package of back bacon. Superb!

I clattered around in other cabinets until I found heavy frypans. They looked brand new.

Now, the stove. I had never used a gas stove before, but I had used gas cookers when camping. The way the flame started automatically when I twisted the knob both surprised and pleased me.

Thanks, Dad, for making me help with breakfast on all those camping trips, I thought.

Alexis is a rich lady. So simple scrambled eggs and bacon wouldn't do. I rooted around in the fridge, pulled out some exotic cheese (exotic to me, anyway), a green pepper and a red pepper. I found half a purple onion wrapped in foil. In the cupboard, extra-virgin olive oil. Whatever the hell "extra virgin" meant.

I found the bread, cleverly hidden in a wooden breadbox with the word "Pane." Inside: crusty bread, a couple of rolls. Good stuff. I cut the loaf into hefty slices with a hefty bread knife that probably cost more than I charged for cleaning a pool.

I set to chopping, shredding and slicing, and by the time Alexis stepped into the kitchen, I had an omelette sizzling on the stovetop. I slid warm bread out of the oven warmer and slathered on the butter.

"Mmm. Smells good," she said and kissed me on the cheek. "I love it when a man makes me breakfast. Or any meal."

She wore a deep-red silk robe and matching dainty slippers. She had tied her hair behind her head with one of those scrunchy things, also matching red. "Did you make coffee?" she asked.

I wondered whether she wore a nightgown under the robe. "Damian?" she said. "Coffee?"

The omelette sizzled, dangerously close to burning. I flipped it quickly. "Sorry. I didn't think of it. I'm not much of a coffee drinker."

"That's all right, sweetie." From a cupboard, she pulled out an odd-shaped kettle and set it on an element, then pulled containers out of other cupboards and poured fine coffee grounds into the kettle thing.

"Is that expresso coffee?" I asked.

She smiled. "It's pronounced 'espresso.' Do you like it?"

"I don't know; I've never had it."

She put two plates on the granite counter. I slid her omelette onto one and started frying mine. She set the plates and cutlery in front of the high chairs beside the raised portion of the counter, then covered her plate with a stainless steel cover. "That should keep it warm enough until yours is ready."

That didn't take long, and as I slid my omelette onto a plate, she poured two little cups half-full of expresso — sorry, "espresso," and put a spoonful of sugar into each one.

"Mmm. This is good," she said after her first dainty bit of omelette.

I had to agree. Simple, but tasty. "This is good bread," I said. "Where did you get it?"

"An Italian bakery on St. Clair," she said. "Do you know it?"

"I don't, but my Dad probably does. He loves bread."

"You know, the sex last night was really good. I really enjoyed it."

I could not swallow my bite of omelette.

"I mean, usually, men who don't have a lot of experience just sort of fumble around. But you were quite gentle. Mind you, you still have a lot to learn. But I think that you have some natural ability. Talent." She smiled at me as if she were talking about me playing the piano or something.

Alexis blew on her espresso and took a sip. I choked down my eggs and tried the coffee. "Ugh!" I couldn't help it.

She laughed, which made me laugh along with her. "Don't like espresso?"

"Um, no, not really," I admitted.

"Not to worry. It's a bit of an acquired taste. Especially if you don't normally drink coffee. It's best to kind of ease into it."

The sunlight slanted in through the big walk-out, crossing her face from just behind her left shoulder. In the light, she was even more beautiful than the night before.

If I'm dreaming, I thought, I never want to wake up.

"So, what are your plans for the day?" she asked.

"Um, I don't have much to do, really. I thought I might read up some, get a bit ahead on my classes for the fall."

"What about your pool-cleaning business? Don't you have some work to do?"

Another occasion to choke on fried eggs. How is that even possible? "Is there any juice?" I croaked.

"In the fridge." She waited until I had explored her hangar-sized refrigerator and brought back a big jug of fresh-squeezed orange juice before she asked me again. "The pool cleaning business?"

I gulped down juice. "Well, actually ... you're my only customer. So far."

She looked at me with her head tilted on the side. "What kind of advertising are you doing?"

"I have an ad on CraigsList."

She laughed again. That laugh could cheer up Hell. "Okay, but so does every teenager with a bucket. Is that all?"

I explained that I hadn't started the business, that it was all the product of Nick, my former roommate who was now luxuriating in some shwanky business school in England.

"Like you're luxuriating right now?" she asked. My pique at Nick evaporated. She turned slightly in her chair as she used her bread to mop up the last of the omelette. The sunlight slipped in between the lapels of her robe. I could see nothing but the light on the skin of the side of her breast. Oh, yes, that was luxury.

"Nick, the supposed business genius, didn't set up any other marketing?"

"Not that I know of. I think the idea was that he would scare up customers and get other students — dweebs like me — to do the actual work. Sort of a franchise operation."

"Well, if you want to make any money this summer, you're going to have to get more customers, and to do that, you're going to have to do a hell of a lot more marketing than a free entry on CraigsList." She stood and her robe opened just a little more, letting me see just a little more of the side of her breast. Her robe parted further as she leaned to put her plate in the sink, and I got close to seeing her nipple again.

Oh, those beautiful nipples.

"The best form of promotion is, of course, word of mouth," she said. "That's what my late husband used to say. And as you can see, he knew a little something about business."

She poured another cup of espresso. "Come, let's sit on the deck. It's a beautiful day." I had to be careful not to spill my juice as I watched her ass sway under that silky robe.

The air outside was already hot, but we sat under an awning. The smell of flowers growing all along a huge hedge mingled with the chlorine scent from the pool. The pool itself glistened, perfectly clean. There was not even a stray leaf floating in it.

"Well, after two attempts, I am happy to say that your pool-cleaning expertise appears top-notch," she said, settling gracefully onto a wicker sofa. "So, I won't have a problem recommending you to my friends and neighbours who have pools. And trust me, around here, everyone does."

I smiled. Could this day get any better?

Yes, said part of my brain. You could bang her again. Okay, that wasn't my brain.

"Now, I want you to do more than just CraigsList," she said. "There's a computer you can use in my study. Look for places to put ads in for handymen and home services in the city. There are plenty enough of them. And while you do that, I'll call a few of my friends. We'll see if we can't line up some work for you this week." She looked at me. "That is, unless there's something else you have to do?"

"No, no!" I had not made any plans for the day. While I had told Alexis that I would do some reading, in truth, I probably would have spent the day playing on my X-Box.

"Do you need to go anywhere? Get anything at home?"

"Well, I could use a toothbrush."

"I'm sure I have a few spares. Or you could use mine. There's nothing on it to catch that you haven't been exposed to already, after all." She laughed again.

I loved the way she laughed.

We relaxed on the wicker sofa on the deck for a little while, enjoying the sound of birds in the trees and wind in the leaves. I leaned close to Alexis to breathe in the smell of her hair.

After a little while, Alexis said "It's getting too hot out here. I need to get into some air conditioning. And you have work to do. Businesses don't build themselves."

I followed her inside. "Oh, stop looking at my ass," she scolded as she slid the walk-out shut.

"But it's so nice!"

She patted my cheek. "Be nice yourself, and you can have a piece of it later. For now, I want you to concentrate.

"The guest suite is down that hall. You'll find toothpaste and extra toothbrushes in the medicine cabinet. And there are some clean clothes that will probably fit you in the dresser in the bedroom. Now, I'm going to get dressed myself before my maid gets here. It's nearly 10 o'clock."

The guest suite consisted of a big bedroom with a queen-size bed, light-coloured, modern wooden furniture that looked more expensive than my parent's master bedroom set, and an attached bathroom. Like the kitchen, it had ceramic tiles on the floor and a granite countertop. Or is that marble? I wondered. All very modern. Up to the minute in style, I thought. Mrs. Rosse's typical guests probably would not be impressed if the decor were a year out of date.

I found toothbrushes still in their packages in the medicine cabinet. How often does she get unexpected overnight guests, I wondered?

In a dresser, I found t-shirts in plain colours and an assortment of sizes. In another drawer was underwear, again in assorted sizes.

Just how many lovers did she keep?

I pulled on a light blue t-shirt and my old, dirty jeans, then went back to the kitchen. As I was coming down the hall, I saw her leg disappear past the doorway. I heard the sound of water hitting stainless steel.

I quickened my pace, grabbed the side of the door frame and swung into the kitchen to kiss her cheek, but I had to put on the brakes. The woman standing at the sink was five feet nothing, rail-thin with long, straight black hair. She wore a full-length floral apron and yellow rubber gloves up to her elbows. She stared up at me with wide, dark eyes and looked as though she had been backed into a corner.

I realized I *had* backed her into a corner of the counter. "Oh, sorry," I stammered. "I thought you were Alexis."

"I am Van," she said with a tremble in her voice. "I am the cleaning lady." She had a slight accent. Vietnamese, I thought. With a name like Van, that's not hard to figure out.

"Ah. Oh. Great!" She had gathered the dirty frypans and other utensils into the sink. As she stared at me, I reached over and pushed down the handle before the white, fragrant suds overflowed. "Sorry to disturb you."

"Are you Mrs. Rosse's new lover?" she asked. She started to scrub the frypan.

"Um, I guess so." How lame did that sound? "Yes." Slightly better, asshole. Geez, I hate my brain sometimes. "I'm Damian." I held out my hand.

She shook it with her wet glove on, leaving me wet. Serves you right, Damian.

Shut up, brain.

"I will wash the sheets as soon as I have finished the kitchen," Van said, looking at the sink.

"Thanks." I couldn't get out of that kitchen fast enough. But where should I go? Upstairs, to the bedroom again? But Alexis was probably in the bathroom, or getting dressed. Maybe she wouldn't want me invading her privacy.

Right, said my brain. Like there's anything you haven't invaded already.

Instead, I went down the main floor hallway and found what I assumed was her study. A window from floor to ceiling filled most of one wall. A thick, mostly red Persian carpet covered the centre of the hardwood floor. And in the middle of that floor stood a desk made of cubes of light-coloured wood, attached to a granite top by stainless steel fittings. A long credenza of the same wood, but without the granite top, stood behind the desk, flanked by matching filing cabinets. The desk chair was high and covered in dark red leather. Two matching but smaller chairs sat in front of the desk, and two more sat near a square table that matched the desk in the corner near the window.

One interior wall was a bookcase that matched the rest of the furniture, and it was nearly filled with books: hardcovers, softcovers, big picture books, magazines and more. One special case was stuffed with CDs in cases, another with DVDs.

I stepped closer to the desk and ran my fingertips across the cool, smooth surface of the granite. It seemed to have depth; the flecks and sparkles shifted as my eyes moved. The only things on the top of the desk besides my fingerprints were a wide, leather blotting pad and a sleek black cordless telephone.

Beside the desk was what I had learned to call a "secretarial return," which held a computer; the computer was not sitting on top, but rather was built into the furniture, itself. The widest flat-screen monitor I had ever seen, other than a TV, was set at an angle, like a book on a reading stand; the keyboard was tucked low and at an ergonomic angle. No doubt, it was customized to Alexis' comfort.

"You found it all by yourself. Very good," said a musical voice behind me. I jumped to see Alexis. She wore a light green top that was loose, revealing, professional, stylish and damned sexy, all at once; pearls around her neck and gold bangles on one wrist, a jewelled watch on the other. Tight dark green leggings hugged her long legs, and she wore shoes with just a slight heel. A tall woman like her doesn't need stiletto heels, said my brain.

I know that, brain.

She took out a brand-new Macbook Air from a drawer in the credenza and put it into my hands. "You can work at the side table, there," she said, pointing to the cube by the window. "Put the word out on cyberspace about — what is your pool company called, again?"

"Poolgeeks," I muttered. Damn Nick, coming up with the

stupidest possible name for a company!

Alexis smiled a little. "Get the word out. Does the company have a Facebook page?"

"No."

"Well, get on that. And Twitter, and Google Plus, too. Meanwhile, I have some phone calls to make. But I'll start on them on the deck. When you get some work done, you can join me." She took a notebook out of a drawer and a tablet computer from another one and left the study.

I had my assignment. She's the boss, said my brain.

I sat down at the side table, wishing I could use the big honkin' computer on the big honkin' desk, but I did not dare to risk pissing off Alexis.

I had never thought of making a business Facebook page for PoolGeeks. Neither had Nick, and he was supposed to be such a business genius, being whisked off to London for a paid internship. But it was a great idea — all the major businesses had one, already. Score another for Alexis: brains as well as beauty.

And money.

Nick had created a website for the company and given me administrator access so that I could update it, but the credentials were on my computer at home — that is, in my crappy apartment. I really didn't feel like going there. Actually, I didn't feel like leaving Alexis' house, ever. It was comfortable and nice to look at. Maybe I could go for a swim, later.

And maybe I could go for Alexis again.

I copied the PoolGeeks logo from Nick's website — cheesy as hell — and used that and other elements to create a Facebook page. I tried to keep it simple, so it wouldn't look too amateurish, but graphic design was not my strength. I did as much as I could until I realized that any further changes were only making it worse.

Next, on to Twitter. I had my own Twitter account, already, so it was easy to create another one. But whom to send tweets to?

What else had Alexis instructed? Google Plus. What the hell, it's not hard, even though nobody uses Google Plus. I set up the PoolGeeks account and invited all my friends into the circles.

I stood up and stretched. I had been at the computer for nearly two hours, and I was hungry, thirsty and I needed to piss. I used the "guest" bathroom again and encountered Van as she was coming down the stairs, carrying a vacuum.

"You going to have lunch with Alexis? I mean, Mrs. Rosse?" She actually was very pretty. Probably a little older than me, in her early 20s. Small, thin, she could not have weighed even 80 pounds. She had long, straight black hair that she tied into a long ponytail, big dark eyes and light-brown, flawless skin.

"Mr. Damian?" she said, and I realized that I was supposed to answer her, not just ogle her. "Lunch?"

"Yes, Mr. Damian will be staying for lunch," came Alexis' voice. I turned to see her step through the walk-out. "It's getting very hot outside, now that the sun is coming around the house. Time for some air-conditioning and something cold to drink!"

Van disappeared somewhere and Alexis took a bottle of white wine out of her enormous fridge. I looked at my watch and was startled to see it was nearly noon.

Alexis poured two very large stem glasses full of white wine — it was nearly the whole bottle in them. She drank down a healthy swallow and licked her lips. "Do you like sushi?" she asked.

"Sure. But I'll need a lot of it. I'm pretty hungry." I sipped my wine. I don't know much about wine, but this seemed good: not sour, not too sweet — and those extremes made up my total knowledge of white wine. "You got any peanut butter? Just till lunch is ready?"

"Peanut butter!" Alexis laughed. "You're going to have peanut butter after Chardonnay?"

I shrugged. "Why not? It'll hold me over."

Alexis laughed, but found a plastic tub filled with a liquidy brown goo. "Organic," she said. "I use it when I make Thai food."

I surprised Alexis by eating big globs of peanut butter with a soup-spoon. And she surprised me: the peanut butter actually tasted like peanuts. Less sweet, more oily than the commercial stuff I usually ate by the jarful. And much, much better. It dried out my mouth a little, so I washed it down with wine.

Alexis was right: peanut butter doesn't go very well with

Chardonnay. "You have any milk?"

She smiled and poured me a big glass. I chugged it down as Van came into the kitchen, sans rubber gloves and wearing a different apron now. As she bustled in and out of the fridge, making sushi rolls, Alexis took me to the study again.

I showed her what I had done so far. She nodded, thoughtful for a few minutes. "Not bad. The logo needs some work, though."

"It wasn't my idea," I told her. "My roommate, Nick, set up the whole thing and created the web page."

"Huh. Some business genius, with one paying customer. Where did you say he was?"

"He's on a fancy business internship in London."

"Oh, was he the one from U of T who got selected for the Crosfield Internship? Well, I don't know whether to be more impressed by your roommate or less impressed by Crosfield." She pointed out a few more things to correct. "But take care of those later. I have called a few neighbours. Everyone around here has a pool, some of them are even indoors. Three people are willing to interview you tomorrow afternoon."

"Interview me? What for?"

"To put you on TV." I realized that when Alexis got sarcastic, she spoke very deadpan. The only way to really tell was to listen to how low her voice got. "Did you think anyone is going to hire you without interviewing you, first? At least with me, you already have a reference."

"You hired me without interviewing me!"

She smiled, the way she did when she was about to say something she thought I should to know already. "I fully intended to interview you when you came over the first time," she said slowly and carefully, as if she were speaking to a child. "I didn't expect you to arrive in your work clothes and with all your equipment. But you were so adorable, all ready for work, I decided the best way to determine whether to hire you or not was to give you a live test. Besides, you're cute, and I thought I might end up fucking you, anyway."

I nearly dropped the laptop. She took it and put it down carefully on the table. "Come on, Van has lunch ready."

Van had set out plates and a big platter of all kinds of sushi on the table on the pool deck. There were also three clean wine glasses and a new bottle of white wine, sitting in a clear plastic bucket filled with ice water.

Alexis filled the three glasses with more wine — a clearer, lighter colour than the wine she had served earlier. "Aren't you supposed to have sake with sushi?" I asked.

"I don't really like sake. I prefer French wine," Alexis answered.

I was surprised when Van sat down with us. "Van makes excellent sushi, Damian. Go ahead, eat up."

Alexis picked up a piece and popped it into her mouth. Van followed suit after pouring some sauce on hers. "Van often joins me for lunch, especially when she makes sushi," Alexis explained.

I dug in. "Mm. This is the best sushi I've ever had," I said, and it was true. I wasn't just trying to compliment my hosts.

Van smiled and looked at her lap, embarrassed. I tried to ask her about herself, but she was too shy to tell me much. She told me, in increments, that she was a part-time student at Centennial College. She was taking culinary arts at the hospitality school. She wanted to be a sushi chef. No, it wasn't easy to find a job — all the restaurants wanted Japanese chefs, usually men. "Plus, I usually need a stool to stand on in most restaurants," she said and took a big gulp of wine. "I lost one job on the first day because my arms were too short to reach a lot of things."

"That's terrible," I said.

"Mrs. Alexis is very kind to me," she said.

"You deserve it, dear," said Alexis. "Don't worry — you finish your program at college, and then we'll see about getting you a job. Or maybe, your own restaurant. One day." She smiled, and Van smiled back. Then she stood up and hugged Alexis.

Van cleared the table and started washing up.

"Come on, Damian. I'll take you home."

I was disappointed, and must have looked it. "You need to get some clean clothes, don't you? And isn't there anything you need to do?"

"Well, sure, a couple of things."

Alexis smiled what I was starting to recognize as her indulgent smile. "Don't worry, I'm not throwing you out. In fact, I think I promised you a swim in the pool before you go, didn't I?"

I could do nothing but nod as the memory of the first time I had seen Alexis flashed before me: in her string bikini and big floppy sun hat. "I don't have a bathing suit," I said, my voice hoarse.

"Okay, Mrs. Alexis, I'm done. I'm going now!" Van called from the front door.

"Good bye, Van. See you tomorrow. Thank you!" Alexis answered.

The door slammed. Alexis smiled again. "Who needs a bathing suit? I never wear one in my own pool!" She stepped toward the walk-out, shedding clothes along the way.

"But you were wearing a bathing suit that first time I came over!"

She looked at me as she pulled her pants down. That left just her jewelry, which she put carefully on a little table near the open walk-out. "That was only because I knew a new pool boy was coming over, and I didn't know what he looked like. I had no clue that I'd end up taking him as a lover."

I could do nothing but stare at her fantastic body: long wavy brown hair cascading nearly down to her nipples, wonderful big breasts that swayed slightly with every breath she took. The curve of her breasts, of her hips ... I could barely breathe. The sight of her thick pubic hair brought back the memory of its smell and taste. She turned and stepped into the sunshine and her tanned skin seemed to glow. The way her ass moved as she walked ...

She turned and looked at me again. "Well? Are you going to swim in your clothes?"

I stripped as fast as I could, trying to keep from showing my half-hard penis. Alexis picked up a hair tie she had left on the patio table and I enjoyed the way her breasts rose as she reached up and over her head to tie her hair back.

She stepped to the edge of the pool and dived smoothly into the water, hardly making a splash. I tried to copy her, but my foot slipped at the edge and I tumbled in.

I came up, sputtering, to Alexis' laughter. She splashed me. I swam toward her, intent on a kiss, but she laughed and slipped away from me.

The cool water drained away my erection, but I still enjoyed watching Alexis' naked body slip across the pool. She swam laps and I did my best to keep up. In the shallow end, she stopped and turned and I bumped into her.

She took my chin in both hands and kissed me hard on the mouth. Her lips parted and I slid my tongue into her mouth. Her arms went around me and our bodies came together, warm and slippery.

Her legs came up on either side of me and I realized that I was hard again. She bit my neck lightly, dragging her teeth forward on my throat as I slid into her.

I wrapped my arms around her so that the edge of the pool wouldn't hurt her back as I pressed her into the pool's wall. I watched her face as she tilted it up with closed eyes and panted in time with my thrusts.

I kissed her jaw and her throat as I thrust. The small muscles in her thighs trembled. I quickened my pace, thrusting faster and faster and was rewarded when she shrieked, arching her back and pressing her pelvis into mine.

I stepped back from the side of the pool and took her hips in my hands. Now, she was floating, balanced on my pelvis. Her nipples stood above the surface of the water, heaving up and down with every thrust of my hips. "Wait!" she gasped.

I pushed into her as far as I could and paused. She paddled backward in something like a backstroke, pulling me with her. She found a pool noodle floating in the middle of the deep end and wrapped her arms around it so that went behind her. Now, she could lean her head back and easily float as I continued to thrust into her.

It was so easy now. The warm water supported us. Alexis hung on the pool noodle and I hung onto her hips. The tips of my toes barely touched the bottom of the pool, providing just a little stability. It was like being weightless, floating in space. The surface of the water churned near Alexis' thighs.

Alexis' eyes clenched shut and her mouth hung open. Her chest heaved up and down and she screamed again. I was sure the neighbours could hear but I didn't care. And then I could not hold back another second. The pool and the back-yard faded as I flowed into her.

I sank under the surface. When I came up, I saw a dreamy expression in Alexis' eyes. She was still breathing hard, but her whole body was relaxed, floating just below the surface of the pool. She shuddered twice, then tilted her head back again and blew out through pursed lips.

"Well, Damian, I certainly did not expect that kind of ... intensity. You have talent, that's for sure."

We drifted around her pool until my mind came back to my body. Alexis paddled over to me and kissed my cheek, then my mouth. "That was very nice, Mr. Serr. We must do this again, sometime." She kicked to the concrete steps at the shallow end and climbed out, water streaming off her naked skin. "Come on, loverboy. You have work to do."

Chapter 5

Shopping

If you knocked me out and woke me up in a clothing store, but still blocked my eyes, I could tell you how expensive the store was. High-end stores smell different from cheap retail outlets.

No, it's more than that: there is a pervasive feeling about an expensive store. It's probably the sum of a whole lot of little touches: more expensive cleansers, more frequently used; plus a little perfume in the air.

I think more expensive clothes smell better than cheap clothes, too. They sure feel better against your skin.

I came to these conclusions at the third high-end men's clothing store on Bloor Street that Alexis took me to. And it was still only 11 in the morning.

Alexis lay another sports coat over my outstretched arm. I started to feel impatient as she turned again to the salesman, who held out two pairs of dress pants.

"The one on the left will go nicely with that jacket," the salesman said. He was a short, bald man with a prominent belly, probably my father's age and flagrantly gay. The name-tag pinned to his blazer proclaimed him to be Wilson.

Wilson and Alexis wandered over to another part of the store to look at shirts, leaving me standing there like a tree bearing expensive men's clothes for fruit.

I thought back over the morning. I had gotten up early, dressed in what I thought were nice clothes, gathered my pool-cleaning stuff and driven to Alexis' house, ready to start meeting her friends and neighbours for pool-cleaning interviews.

"Oh, no, that won't do at all," were the first words out of Alexis' mouth when she opened the door. Not even "good morning."

"What's wrong?" As usual, she was stunning, wearing a short skirt and a loose, light-blue blouse with a lot of puffs and folds around the front of the neckline. At first glance, the outfit was modest, but every time she moved the cloth would reveal a little more smooth, light-brown skin. My eyes followed curves, wishing they could continue under the clothing.

"Damian, you're going to a series of job interviews. You need to present a professional image to offset the customers' nervousness about letting a stranger into their homes. You can't show up looking like a bum. Come on."

"Where are we going?" She led me through the house to the garage, which held four different, expensive cars.

She picked out a red BMW convertible. She looked at me, standing by the door to the house as she stepped in. "Well, come on." I shut the passenger door as the garage slid up silently and Alexis put the car in gear. A stick-shift, I noticed.

Alexis drives stick.

It was a short drive from Rosedale to Yorkville. She apparently had a monthly parking spot under one of the big office buildings for shopping convenience. It figured. Alexis would not be seen in a shopping mall, let alone a big-box outlet. No, only the high-end cachet of Bloor Street and Yorkville Avenue for her.

Alexis practically danced down Bloor Street from store to store. They were all painted mild beige and gray, and arranged their clothes in neat piles on tables placed just so. There were no "Sale" or "50% OFF!" signs in these stores. No: if you want a bargain, go somewhere else.

In each store, Alexis ran her hands over the material, admired the cut or the stitching or God knows what, chatted with the sales clerks and cooed over new arrivals. She even put a fedora on my head at one point and laughed.

Eventually, she got serious in some store with a name that didn't make any sense and started picking out things as if she really intended to buy some. Why hadn't we just come here in the first place? I thought.

Don't feel annoyed and resentful, said my brain. She's buying me clothes — expensive clothes, at that.

The best I could feel was bored. Clothes are boring. You put them on to cover up, keep warm, protect yourself. Some of my friends wear them to make artistic or political statements: Occupy Toronto, or Mumford & Sons.

But now I had to Dress for Success.

"Damian!" Alexis' musical voice carried across the store. "Try these on."

I trudged toward the changing rooms. Wilson took the jackets from me and hung them near the changing-room door, while Alexis refilled my arms with pants and shirts. "Let's try on a few combinations," she said. To Wilson, she explained, "We're looking for a confident, somewhat professional look, but also remember: he works with his hands."

Wilson smiled and picked out a jacket. I stepped into the changing room as the front door chimed. It was the biggest changing room I had ever seen: there was a rack at one end to hold up the clothes you were trying, another rack presumably for the crap you came in wearing, and a wide bench. There was even a bowl of mints.

"Go ahead, tend to the new customer," I heard Alexis say. "We'll be here for a while. There are a lot of combinations to try."

"Thank you, sweetie," Wilson said. I heard him walk away and greet someone else.

I pulled off my clothes and dropped them on the floor, and paused to look at my body in the full-length mirror. I should have gotten a haircut, I thought, and dragged my fingers through it to try to smooth out the disobedient curls.

Even with slightly neater hair, the body in the mirror was too skinny. I held my arms out and I could no longer see my hands' reflections. My legs were ridiculously long. Why couldn't I have muscular legs like Patrick? At least my chest acne had cleared up.

The door opened a little and Alexis' arm came in, holding a piece of cloth. "Here, try this, too," she said.

I reached for her hand as she pushed her way inside. Startled,

I stepped backward. She shoved the cloth into my mouth and pushed the door closed at the same time. It was wet and smelled ...

It was her underwear. I dropped it and it slid down my chest.

Alexis locked the door and pushed her skirt down. "God, shopping makes me so horny," she whispered. She practically ripped my shorts off. "Don't worry. As long as you don't make noise, we'll be fine." She took my penis in both hands and kissed me, pushing her tongue into my mouth.

I tongue-wrestled her as she pushed me onto the bench. She turned around so her back was to me, straddled my legs and reached down to take my erection in her hands again. She sank down.

She rose and fell slightly, pushing back into me. "Oohh, Damian, oh, that's good," she whispered. I pushed up into her as she pressed down. "Yes, that's right. Keep doing that," she whispered.

I reached around to grab her breasts through her silky blouse. She was not wearing a bra. I thumbed the silk over her hard nipples and her back stiffened. She pushed back again.

I grabbed her harder and stood up. Alexis gasped as I pushed against her. She reached out and pressed her hands on the door to the changing room, but as I pushed into her again, the whole wall moved.

I wrapped my arms around Alexis and turned us around, pressing her against the solid back wall of the changing room. Alexis looked over her shoulder at me. "Harder," she said, and her eyes rolled up in her head as I pushed into her.

I slammed my hips into her and pushed her up the wall. I must have grunted or something, because her eyes widened and she said "Sssshhhh."

I gritted my teeth and slammed my hips. Her legs trembled and she gasped, high-pitched yelps that she failed to stifle.

My orgasm burst out of me, draining the energy from my brain to my toes. Everything went white in front of my eyes. I let my hips relax and watched Alexis' feet come back down to the floor. She shook and gasped twice more. I thought she looked like she was going to collapse, so I pulled her closer to me, hugging her from behind.

She reached over her head to stroke my hair. "Mmm, that was good. I love fucking in a changing room."

I wanted to say, "How many times have you done this," but before I could, she picked up her wet underwear from the floor.

"Guess I can't put these back on," said. She shoved them into the pocket of one of the jackets. "I don't like them, anyway." As she pulled her skirt back up, she wiggled her hips in a way that made my jaw drop. She straightened her clothes and puffed up her hair, then picked out a jacket, a pair of pants and a shirt from the rack. "Put these on," she said. "They're the best." She picked up one other shirt and opened the door, taking care not to make noise. She peeked out. Wilson was fussing over an older man at the front, so Alexis stepped out carefully and closed the door.

My head was spinning. I put one hand on the wall and slumped onto the bench.

I had just had sex in a public changing room. This was better than any story Patrick or Tyler had ever told.

I leaned my head back against the wall behind me. It felt cool and good. When my breathing returned to normal, I pulled on the clothes that Alexis had told me to and looked in the mirror. The image shocked me: I looked older, somehow more ... trustworthy. How do clothes do that?

A knock on the door startled me. "Well, let's see how it looks," said Alexis in her normal, musical voice.

I stepped out to see Alexis and Wilson the salesman appraising me. Alexis clucked her tongue and shook her head as Wilson tugged and straightened the jacket's laps and brushed the shoulders. "Young people never know how to wear good clothes," he said. He knelt and straightened the crease on the front of the pant legs, and I felt alarmed when his hand came closer to my crotch.

"The fit is nearly perfect," Alexis said.

"Yes, a 42 Tall. I knew it," Wilson said.

"We'll take the outfit he has on, plus the blue striped shirt in the changing room," said Alexis. "He'd like to wear them today."

"The pants will need to be hemmed, madame," Wilson said with a sneer.

"Can you do it right away? He has a job interview this afternoon."

"Well, I do have a sewing machine in the back room, but we charge extra for immediate service."

Alexis smiled and patted Wilson's arm. "Put it all on my account. Come on, Damian. Leave the shirt and jacket on, but leave the dress pants with Wilson to hem. Put your jeans back on. Wilson, we'll be back in an hour for the pants. Come on, Damian, let's get lunch. I'm starving."

Chapter 6

Building the Client Base

"Good morning. Mrs. Zelinski?" A small, thin woman stood at the door, her reddish hair cut into what I thought was called a page-boy. She smiled a phoney smile, showing a lot of large teeth.

This was the address I'd put into the calendar on my phone. Mrs. Ramona Zelinski, it said. The address had led me to a big, red-brick house with a big leafy tree in the front yard, like something you'd see in a movie. The heat plastered my shirt to my back, and I regretted wearing the jacket Alexis had just bought me, even though she promised it was "summer weight."

"PoolGeeks?" Mrs. Zelinski asked and stepped aside, motioning an invitation to enter. I stepped over the threshold, wondering whether she noticed my crappy old Suzuki on the road.

"I'll show you the pool," she said, leading me through the house. I wondered why she didn't just take me around, but maybe she wanted to stay in the air conditioning as much as possible.

Mrs. Zelinski opened a walk-out from the family room. The back yard was bigger than Alexis', but the pool was smaller. I walked around, scanning the tiles and the ladder as Mrs. Zelinski told me about the pool and the pool shower and the hot tub in a tone that said "do it the way I like or your ass is out of here." I frowned and jotted notes on my clip-board and otherwise tried to look professional, but mostly I was thinking about the sun scorching the back of my neck and the sweat spreading from my underarms. I hoped I didn't smell.

I wrote the estimate on the form that Nick had made before he had left. I guess geniuses aren't completely useless. I handed the sheet to Mrs. Zelinski and held my breath as she looked at it.

Too much? Too little? Should I ask to change it? Will that make it worse? Oh, God, what do I tell Alexis when Mrs. Zelinski crumples up the estimate and laughs in my face?

"References?" she asked.

"Well, Mrs. Rosse is very happy with my work so far." Unless she takes off her clothes when she's unhappy.

"Yes, she told me that. No one else?" she read the estimate, not waiting for an answer. "This is for cleaning twice a week?"

No, you bitch. That would be for once a week. Cleaning the pool twice a week costs twice as much as that estimate. "Umm, yes," is what came out of my mouth. Wimp!

She looked at me, her face expressionless. Or was that contempt? "Mondays and Thursdays, in the morning, are good for me," she said.

Say it! my brain told me. "Uh, okay." Say it! "That will be fine. I can start this week." Say it, you wimp! "Um, uh, I'll need … need a cheque. Before I can start. A deposit." My throat was dry. "Company policy." My voice faded into a desolate scratch.

Mrs. Zelinski tilted her head back and looked at me with her eyes half-closed. A chequebook appeared in her hands. "How much?"

I forced out "Two weeks." Why are you afraid to ask for money? "Then, I'll collect a cheque every second week. In advance."

"I'll pay *after* the work is done," she retorted, but she was scribbling on the chequebook. She tore out the slip of paper with practised ease and thrust it toward me. "That way I can validate your work."

"Oh … okay." I could barely hear my own voice. I put the cheque into my inside jacket pocket, hoping that the motion looked professional. "See you on Thursday."

"Good-bye." She stepped into her family room and slid the door closed, so I walked around the house, grateful for the shade. In the car, I took the cheque out. I hadn't even looked at it when she gave it to me. It seemed to be filled out properly; the only problem was that the amount was the price for once-weekly cleaning, not twice.

I let out a deep breath slowly. Ah well, second client. And the first sale I had made on my own.

I checked my phone: five minutes to get to the next appointment that Alexis had set up for me. This was a block away, another mansion with big trees. An elderly man with a ring of messy white hair around the sides of his head had a kidney-shaped pool and a slide. "My grand-kids love that slide," he said.

I gave him an estimate for twice-weekly cleaning. "My, you boys are sure charging a lot more than you used to," he said. "This is more than I made a month in my first summer job! Maybe I should just get it done once a week. How much would that cost? Would that be enough?"

Inspired, I said "Well, that depends. How often do your grandchildren use the pool, and how clean do you want it to be for them?"

He looked at me and smiled, and I knew he saw through my ploy. He surprised me when he said, "Of course, you're right. All right, my boy, twice a week it is."

Determined to redeem myself from the idiocy I had shown Mrs. Zelinski, I took a deep breath and said "I'll need a two-week deposit, and payment every two weeks, in advance, after that." I smiled.

He gave me a cheque. This time, I read it over before putting it in my pocket. "Thank you, Mr. Hedges. See you Thursday afternoon."

Two for two, I thought as I drove to the next appointment. This business may just work out after all, I thought.

I had to drive all the way to Etobicoke for the last appointment that Alexis had set up for me. The only good thing about driving across Toronto in midday is that it's not as bad as driving during rush hour.

Another tree-lined avenue, another brick house; this one was considerably newer than the two in Rosedale. I knew it could not be as ridiculously overpriced as the mansions in Rosedale, but it was still an expensive area, close to the subway, with expensive cars and luxury SUVs in the driveways. I checked my list: Mrs.

Casales.

As I pressed the doorbell, I imagined Salma Hayek coming to the door. Instead, Mrs. Casales was a slightly overweight young woman wearing a long print skirt and a loose top. Her messy, light-brown hair was tied with a bandana.

I just wanted to step into the air conditioning, but Mrs. Casales wanted to shake my hand, first. "Ah, PoolGeeks?"

"Good afternoon, ma'am," I said in the best door-to-door salesman voice I could muster in the heat. "My name is Damian. I'm here to give you an estimate." It was now one p.m., and all I could think about was air conditioning.

Instead, Mrs. Casales led me around the house, jaws chattering and hips swaying the whole way. "I'm so glad that Alexis told me about you. We used to do it ourselves, but we get so busy in the summer and now that the kids are bigger and aren't at home as much, well, it was all too easy to get careless. And that led to the pool getting, well, a little gross from time to time. I just hope your rates are reasonable!"

Mrs. Casales kept talking as I inspected the long oval pool. After Alexis had made me clean hers twice, I got a book on pool maintenance. By this time, I knew how to recognize the signs of repeated attempts to rectify pool neglect with nothing but chlorine shocks: there were about a million leaves and dead bugs floating on the surface and yellow scum clinging all around the sides. Scratched and dented chairs were scattered among toys on the pool deck. A shaggy mutt slept in the shade of a messy looking shrub.

I made a show of walking around, looking at the pump and the filters, inspecting the ladder and the deck. I said "mmm-hmm" whenever it sounded like Mrs. Casales wanted me to and scribbled on my clip-board.

My brain kept alternating between two thoughts: that I should charge Mrs. Casales extra for being so dirty, and Alexis in her string bikini.

And then a third thought intruded: Alexis *not* in her string bikini.

"So, what do you think?" startled me.

I handed Mrs. Casales the estimate sheet. "I think I'll have to be here for most of Friday morning, and then at least twice a week after that," I said, trying to sound friendly, professional and reassuring all at once. I failed.

"Oh, my," Mrs. Casales said when she read the estimate.

How to say this without insulting her? "I'll need to do a fair bit of work just to catch up on the season," I said. I stepped closer to her, wondering what her hair would be like if I pulled off that stupid bandana.

She leaned forward to sit on a deck chair and I looked down at her cleavage. I wasn't certain, but I did not see a bra.

Mrs. Casales sighed and looked to the side, fanning herself with my estimate.

Don't get cocky, my brain warned. You got two easy sales from beginner's luck and Mrs. Rosse. You may have to bargain with this one.

But she's such a pig! I told my brain. That estimate is fair. I'll have to spend a lot of time here just cleaning up their mess.

Mrs. Casales sighed again. "Do you have any references besides Alexis? Mrs. Rosse, I mean?"

"Well, I have ... a number of other clients," I said. I tried not to lie, but it was hard to be honest and get the sale at the same time. "I'll have to ask them if they'd give me references, though. You know, use their names."

She looked at me for a moment, her head tilted to one side a little. "Are you sure there's no discount for friends of Alexis Rosse?"

Does she mean what I hope she means? I wondered.

Stop being an ass, said my brain.

"Well, maybe I can take off ... ten percent?"

She smiled a sunny smile that seemed to make the sun dimmer. It also made me even hotter. I wondered if it would be unprofessional to take off the jacket.

What the hell. I'm a pool boy. Or pool geek. Make that Pool Geek.

I slipped the jacket off, revealing huge sweat stains on my brand-new shirt. Mrs. Casales suppressed a laugh. "How about twenty-five percent off and I'll make sure to bring you nice cold drinks when you're here?"

I was mortified by my pit stains. "Okay," I said weakly.

Defeated by perspiration. I felt like the dumb guy in all the commercials.

"Wait here," she said, and went in the back door. I could see her moving in her kitchen, opening a refrigerator, and then the best sound possible in those circumstances.

She came back out with two open bottles of Heineken. "Let's seal the deal with a drink," she said, we clinked bottles.

The beer was a lifesaver. I drained two-thirds of the bottle in one shot. "Thank you, Mrs. Casales. I really needed a drink in this heat."

"It's important to stay hydrated. But beer won't do that. Wait a minute." She went back to the kitchen and came back with a tall glass of ice water. "Drink this down. You'll feel much better."

I drained it, and I did feel much better. A pressure across my forehead that I hadn't been aware of until that moment eased. "Wow. Thanks very much."

"You do have a water bottle to take with you when you work?" she asked. "They say it's going to be a very hot summer."

"Yes," I lied. Water bottle. Buy a water bottle, shmuck.

Shut up, brain.

"When can you start?"

"Friday morning," I said. I gave her the spiel about the deposit and payment. She pushed the estimate back to me to adjust the price, and I scratched it out and wrote in the 25 percent discount. She almost skipped into the house to fetch her chequebook, and as she let me out the gate, she paused to shake my hand.

"See you Friday." Then she stood on tiptoe and kissed me on the cheek.

I did not know what to do. She giggled and shut the gate, separating us with sturdy, weather-greyed wood.

What is it about women and pool geeks?

I called Alexis from my car.

"I hope you're not driving while talking on your phone," she said. "I hear the police are clamping down on that this summer."

"I have a hands-free system," I lied. "I just thought I'd tell you, I got all three customers! They all said yes!"

"Yes, I heard from Ramona. Mrs. Zelinski, that is. She said she got a really great deal from you. I hope you didn't let her take advantage of you."

What did she mean by that? The way Alexis had "taken advantage" of me? "I don't think so …"

"Are you charging her the full rate? She has a way of getting discounts out of service people," she said.

"Yes," I said. Why are you lying? How can she help you if you don't tell her the truth? my brain scolded. "That is, I'm charging her the once-weekly rate for twice weekly cleaning."

"So, a fifty percent discount," said Alexis.

"More like forty percent."

"That sounds like Ramona. No wonder she sounded so smug. Well, she always sounds smug, but today was really something. Take it in stride, Damian, but don't fall for that again. Your prices are more than fair. Stick to them."

"I gave Mrs. Casales a twenty-five percent discount, in return for cold drinks every time I'm there."

"That's all right. That's just doing business, as my poor, late husband would say. And Leda needs a discount now and then. Her marriage just broke up."

Was that the reason for the kiss? Another lonely, horny housewife needing to get it on with the pool boy?

Don't be an ass, said my brain.

"Would you like to get together to celebrate?" I asked.

Alexis laughed. "Oh, I would, but not tonight. I have a meeting this evening for a charity I work on. But I'll see you tomorrow, right? To clean the pool?"

That puts you in your place.

Shut up, brain.

I pulled over and put the car in park before I reached Bloor Street. I scrolled through my phone's list until I found Kristen's number and hit Call.

I expected to go to her voice-mail, but Kristen answered on the sixth ring. "It's Damian," I said.

"I do have call display, you know."

"Right, I know … so, remember how I told you that Nick set up this pool-cleaning business and then put it all on me when he took off for England?"

"You know, that internship is very special; they only take really smart people for it."

Sometimes, I wondered if Kristen loved me or Nick.

"Yah, well, remember the business? Cleaning pools?"

"Of course: Pool Geeks."

Why did she remember every detail that Nick told her? "Well, Mr. Genius may have been onto something. I just got three more clients today!"

"Really? So, how many does that make, in total?" Her voice sounded far away, like she was doing something else while talking to me.

"Four," I answered. "A grand total of four. But three in one day!"

"Yes, that's very good, honey. Does that mean you've got any money?"

I had to cough. "Well, I have cheques from all of them, but they're made out to Pool Geeks, and I don't have the Pool Geeks bank account ..."

"Why not?"

"Nick didn't bother giving me *that* before he left."

"Well, I guess you'll have to get in touch with Nick and sort that out. There's no sense in working if you can't get paid."

"You're absolutely right, babe. So anyway, it's been a good business day. Feel like celebrating?"

"Don't call me 'babe.' You know I hate that. And if you want to get together with me, you shouldn't call me at the last minute like this, Damian. Sorry, but I have plans for tonight."

"What kind of plans?"

"It's a youth committee meeting at the church. We're planning some fund-raising. Unless you want to join me there?"

"Uhh, no, not really..."

"What, it's not enough just to spend time with me?"

Think of something, brain! "Well, it's just that I'm kind of tired after working, and in the heat ..."

"But not too tired to go out partying?"

"Well, I just thought we could hang out. You know how it is ..."

"Yes, I know," she said in those clipped tones that told me she was pissed off. She was usually pissed off about something.

"Okay, since you need a bit of notice: how about we hang out tomorrow night?"

"Why don't you just come over on Friday like always?" she said. "I have to go now, Damian, or my baking will burn." There was a click and the phone went dead.

Kristen loved her habits: dates were Fridays or sometimes Saturday nights; getting together during the week was a big deal because we had school or university the next day. Of course, now being summer, neither of us had classes in the morning. And I was the only one with a job — Mr. Petri did not want his princess to do anything as mundane as getting a job before she finished her degree.

I sighed. Two women, two strikes. There was only one more woman in my life. I scrolled through to her number and pressed Call.

Two rings. "Mom? Hi. Is it okay if I came over for supper tonight? Yah, the business is going great — I just got three new customers today! Thanks. Sure, see you then."

Chapter 7

Argument with Kristen

"Well, look who's here. Hello, stranger." Kristen's voice had that clipped sneer in it. She folded her arms across her chest.

I put on my best smile and held out the flowers from the grocery store. "I finally got the bank account straightened out. Wanna have something to eat and hang out?"

It had taken a week of text messages, emails and a fax between me, Nick and the bank before the bank would give me access to the Pool Geeks account. I could deposit the cheques as well as take money out. So, finally, I wasn't paying for the privilege of working. The first thing I did with the access was take out a hundred bucks to take my girlfriend out.

Kristen couldn't suppress her smile when I held the flowers under her nose, although she tried to. Finally, she took the bunch and sniffed. "Well, since you brought flowers ... Where are we going?" She looked up at me, blue eyes shining through the flowers. Her mouth slowly spread into a smile.

"Why not Mama Toni's? And my parents are away for the weekend, so I got a DVD."

Kristen pretended to think about it for about two seconds. "Let me put these in some water."

I stepped inside her house — her parents' house — and waited like I had so many times before. Mrs. Petri came out of the kitchen, wiping her hands on a towel. "Oh, hello Damian," she said. "Why don't you sit down?"

My breath caught whenever I saw Mrs. Petri — even after all these years. She was the neighbourhood beauty: tall and fit with bright blue eyes that she had passed on to her daughter. Her hair was done up high, exposing her long neck, and she wore a sleeveless t-shirt and short pants. I wondered why she always showed more skin than her teenaged daughter.

I followed her to the kitchen and sat at the table; I knew from experience not to sit on the "good furniture" in the living room. Mrs. Petri poured me a cup of tea from the pot that was always filled. "Would you like a cookie?"

I took one from the plate in the middle of the table. Mrs. Petri baked regularly, and I loved her cookies. That's how I first made friends with Kristen. When I was five, I was in a bunch of kids who came over to the Petris' to play. I went back for the cookies. Through school, Kristen and I alternated coming over to each other's houses for homework and other activities. I preferred being at her place, sitting at her mother's kitchen table and munching on cookies. Those cookies were all that got me through long division in Grade 3 and *A Separate Peace* in high school.

I ate three cookies before Kristen returned from upstairs, dressed in her going-out-for-cheap-dinner clothes: khaki pants, a scoop-neck blouse and sensible shoes. She had tied her long, straight brown hair into a pony-tail. Kristen resembled her mother in her blue eyes and symmetrical, delicate features, but she was smaller, shorter. She was like a pretty doll: perfect and fragile. The prettiest girl in my grade, she was more for looking at than holding.

"Thanks for the cookies, Mrs. Petri," I said as Kristen pulled me to the front door.

Mr. Petri came in from the garage at that point. "Where are you going?" he asked.

"I'm taking your daughter out for dinner and a movie," I answered as cheerfully as I could, but I dreaded the response I knew was coming.

"You know you'll never save money for university if you keep eating in restaurants," he said. "A boy your age who lives on his own should know how to cook for himself."

"Oh, Daddy," Kristen said, pulling me out the front door.

"It's alright, Mr. Petri," I said, trying to sound casual and relaxed. Short but with broad shoulders and muscles that rippled in his lower arms, Mr. Petri always made me feel nervous and inadequate. Come to think of it, so did his daughter. "I just got paid by three different customers."

I knew what he was going to say next: "You should save that money in a bank. You never know what you might need tomorrow."

"Oh, Daddy," Kristen repeated and pulled me out the door.

"Be sure to have her home by midnight!" Mr. Petri called after us. And of course, it took three attempts to get my car started as Kristen's father watched us from his front porch. By the time I could pull away from the curb, my face was burning.

Kristen and I could never agree on Mama Toni's restaurant : I thought it was expensive; she thought it was cheap. Of course, she never paid for the food. She thought it was a quaint little place with mementos and pictures from Italy and New York on the walls; I pointed out that it was part of a chain and was owned by a foodservice corporation in Philadelphia. But we both liked the food and I liked to show off just a little by drinking Italian beer — which cost over seven bucks a bottle.

Hell with it: I felt the pool-cleaning cash burning a hole in my pocket.

Kristen ate about a quarter of her plate of pasta; she refused wine on principle and sneered at me every time I took a sip of my Moretti.

"So where are your parents tonight?" she asked while we waited for the bill.

"Up at the cottage for the weekend."

"Why didn't you go with them?"

"I don't live with them anymore, Kristen. I'm a grown-up now. So are you. Besides, this way we have their whole house to ourselves."

She narrowed her eyes at me. "I thought you said you didn't live with them anymore." She sipped her water delicately. Even though she could be judgemental and fucking annoying, she was very pretty in a delicate, little-girl way. A little too thin, maybe. She'd like it if I said that. She worked hard to keep her weight down.

"I *do* have a key to the front door. So we can watch the 50-inch plasma in full theatre-surround sound."

She dabbed her lips with her napkin, then folded it carefully to cover the food left on her plate, as if she couldn't bear to look at it anymore. "What DVD did you get?"

"*Fight Club.*"

"What? Why?"

"Hey, it's the perfect couples movie." I had been waiting all day to say this. "For the ladies, Brad Pitt gets naked. For the men, big, fat, ugly guys beat him up. What more could you ask for?"

I thought it was pretty funny. I still do.

Kristen said "That's disgusting! Watching men beating each other up entertains you?"

I had seen the movie and loved it. "Just kidding," I said. "I got *The Vow*. You know, with that actor you like."

"Channing Tatum." She smiled again. "You had me worried for a second." Did I mention that Kristen is beautiful when she smiles? And that it's easy to make her smile? All it takes is everything she wants, when she wants it.

At my parents' house, Kristen put popcorn into the microwave while I set the home theatre perfectly: dimming lights, setting the balance on the sound system. Kristen stopped me when I started to pour some of my parents' vodka into glasses. "You still have to take me home," she said.

"Kristen, you live next door. We can walk."

"My dad won't like it if he smells alcohol on your breath."

"I hadn't planned on kissing him."

"Why do you think he always kisses you on both cheeks?"

"I thought it was a tradition for your people."

"'My people' have been in Canada for four generations, now. We're not quaint villagers. Daddy's an accountant, for Pete's sake!" She was getting worked up. "No, he always kisses you on the cheek to see whether you've been drinking. I thought you would have figured that out by now!"

"But I've already had a beer."

"Papa understands a beer with dinner."

"You and I both know that he has a drink, himself, occasionally."

"But he doesn't want my boyfriends to be drunks! And neither do I."

Okay, no booze, my brain and I agreed. At least not for now.

We settled onto the couch and I hit Play on the remote. Kristen loved romances, but I thought the movie was painful. The only good thing about Kristen's movie tastes were the way she would cuddle under my arm, taking popcorn from the bowl I held in my lap. Her body was warm against mine. I caressed the skin of her neck and breathed in the smell of her hair. The smell came from her shampoo, but it was still nice.

When the movie got especially boring, I went for a kiss. We smooched long and deep, and when we came up for air, I looked into her big blue eyes, hoping to see desire.

She looked right back at me, lips parted, so I went in for another kiss, then trailed little smooches along her jaw and started on her neck, like I had with Alexis. Kristen sighed and put her arms around me, so I kissed her neck harder and she rewarded me with more sighs.

Kristen's reaction, combined with the thoughts of Alexis I couldn't help but have, gave me an erection that was almost painful. I put the popcorn bowl down on the floor and went back to intense kissing.

"Damian, we're missing the movie," Kristen moaned. I paused it and kissed her neck some more. She was starting to squirm a little, and I thought I saw an opportunity.

I bit her throat gently, then went back up to her lips. Then back to her neck, up to the lips, back and forth. I hoped to really turn her on. When Kristen moaned ever so quietly and ran her fingers through my hair, I thought I had my chance.

I kissed down her neck until my lips touched the neckline of her white blouse. I kissed along it and, very gently, ran my fingertips under the hem. I pulled up as slowly and gently as I could, but Kristen pulled away and put her hands on mine, stopping them. "Naughty, naughty," she warned.

"Yes, I fully intend to be very naughty," I said and tried to kiss that spot between her collarbones.

"Damian, stop," she said, sliding across the couch. "No more than kissing before we're married."

"But why, Kristen? This is the 21st century. And we love each other."

"Damian, we've been through this. I don't think it's moral or proper for unmarried couples to have sex."

I shifted so that my dick wasn't pressing so hard into my jeans. "What's the difference if we're going to get married anyway? Why do we need permission from some church to do something that's only between us?"

"You know how I feel about this, Damian!" Then she tried to give me her consoling tone. "Come on, we've been having a nice time tonight. Don't spoil it by pressuring me into something I don't believe in." She patted my knee and picked up the bowl of popcorn. "Let's just calm down and watch the movie." She cuddled up against me again, put the bowl on my lap and started the movie.

I tried to console myself by surreptitiously pressing the bowl against my penis. It refused to soften. I tried rubbing Kristen's arm lightly, but that didn't do anything for me. My mind bounced between two desires: sex and vodka, both out of reach.

Then my mind settled on another desire and refused to budge for the rest of the night: Alexis. I pictured her body, naked on her wide bed, skin shining in the lamplight.

In the movie, the male lead leaned closer to the female lead, as her lips parted and her eyes closed. Yah, yah, she'll kiss you, dude. This happens in every movie ever made: they're not sure how the other will react, but they both want the same thing. They hesitate, get closer an inch at a time, and finally succumb like mushy pink magnets.

The on-screen couple kissed. I remembered the way Alexis' lips felt on mine. On screen, the action accelerated. The actors tugged each others' clothes off, tumbling onto the bed while keeping their lips locked. I remembered how Alexis' naked skin felt against mine. I reached down and stroked Kristen's bare arm, the only naked female skin within reach. I reached up and caressed Kristen's neck again, thinking of Alexis' throat, the heat of it between my lips. On the screen, the male lead kissed his way down the female lead's body, her presumably naked breasts shadowed and mostly off-camera. The scene faded, replaced by a sunrise shot over a high skyline.

I saw Alexis, standing on her front step, naked buttocks silhouetted in the light from inside her door.

I kissed Kristen on the ear. "Now, now, that's enough of that for one evening," she said and pulled away from me. She folded her hands across her chest and concentrated on the TV.

I ate the popcorn and looked at the TV screen, too, but all I saw was Alexis.

Naked Alexis. Standing beside her bed. Lying across her bed.

Alexis in her pink and white jogging outfit. Her cute little half-socks peeking above her runners.

The movie ended long after the popcorn. I looked at my watch. "Shit, Kristen, we better get you home. It's nearly 12."

"Oh, don't worry. My Papa won't mind if we're a few minutes late."

What did she want? Not kisses. Not a drink. Fuck it, I thought. "No, no, he seemed pretty serious tonight, Kristen." I moved to the door.

Even I could tell Kristen was not happy. Her lips pressed into a single colourless line. She walked with long steps to the front door and whipped it open. She paused on the front step and said "Well? You are going to walk me home, aren't you? Or do I have to walk in the dark, alone?"

I forced a laugh. "It's next door. And this is Toronto, not New York."

"Things happen in Toronto to women all the time. And a *gentleman* wouldn't even think about letting a lady walk home at night by herself." She turned away and stared down the street.

I picked up my keys and stepped out after her, closing and locking the door carefully. "Hey, I was gonna walk you." She stepped ahead of me and I had to practically run to keep up with her, even though my legs are a lot longer. She didn't speak to me, didn't even look at me.

A bluish light came from her parents' bedroom upstairs — they were watching TV. As Kristen unlocked the door, I tried to kiss her. She let me kiss her cheek. "Enough of that," she said in her clipped, pissed-off voice. Then she shut the door.

I took two breaths to make up my mind. I jumped into my crappy car and left rubber on the asphalt. It took me less than ten minutes to reach Mrs. Rosse's — Alexis' — house in Rosedale.

I turned off the headlights before I pulled into her driveway. No matter how hard I tried to be quiet, the driver's door squealed, as usual, when I opened and shut it.

Dim light filtered from the upstairs windows, and the front window hinted at more. I jumped when an outdoor light over the front walk flicked to life. Motion sensor, I realized.

I felt suddenly very stupid at the front door. What if she wasn't home?

No problem. Just go back home. To your parents or your own apartment. Whatever.

What if she is home and gets mad at me for showing up uninvited?

My mouth was dry. I took another breath and stopped myself from knocking on the door. She's a lady, said my brain. Ring her doorbell.

I pressed the button and heard chimes play a tune somewhere inside.

My heart pounded as I waited. Would she come to the door? Would she ignore me? Would she send me away?

Did I hear footsteps? Did the light filtering through the frosted glass in the door change? Did I see her silhouette?

The door opened. "Damian! What are you doing here at this time of night?" Alexis wore a long silk housecoat, black with red flowers in lines down from each shoulder.

"Are you alone?" I managed to say.

"Yes, but ..."

I let instinct take over. I stepped into the house, wrapped my arms around her and pressed my lips against hers. She opened her mouth and I pushed my tongue in. I pushed the door shut with my foot as I kissed her neck.

She pulled away from me. "Well, it's nice to see you, too. Would you like a drink?"

I nodded and kissed her again. When she broke away, she took my hand and led me to a large room lined with built-in bookcases. A huge flat-screen TV hung on the wall, fronted by a sofa. A bottle of wine and a glass, almost empty, stood on the table beside the sofa. I saw speakers over as well as below the TV screen. The manufacturer's logo bounced across it. This was a serious home theatre.

Alexis opened a cabinet that I realized was a wine chiller. "Red wine okay?"

"Sure. Please," I said and wondered why my voice was so hoarse. I felt suddenly thirsty.

She poured me a large glass, then refilled her own. "So, what's the occasion?" she asked.

I sipped my wine, and realized I had no idea whether this was good wine or lousy. It tasted good, though, so I gulped down half of it. "I had to see you," I said. That was as close as I could get to putting the feelings I had into words.

"Well, I'm glad you did." Alexis smiled. "It was a boring night without you."

"What were you doing?"

She sat on the soft sofa and patted it. I sat beside her. "Just watching porn."

Did she really say that? I looked at the screen. Alexis pressed the remote and the screen came to life with a slender, naked woman straddling a pair of male legs, her back to him, giving the camera an unobstructed shot of him penetrating her. She rose and fell, panting. She leaned backward with her hands on his arms; his hands held her hips, raising and lowering her over and over.

"Have you ever done that?" Alexis asked me. I could only shake my head. My mouth was too dry for speaking. "You mean, you've never watched porn by yourself?"

I had thought she meant the sexual position on the screen. But what could I say about watching porn? Should I lie to her and risk her disbelief and contempt? Or tell the truth, risking her judging me as some kind of pervert?

I leaned toward her. "You're so much better than any movie," I said, and kissed her.

The ferocity of her return kiss surprised me. She pushed her tongue into my mouth while pulling my t-shirt up. She pulled away only long enough to pull my shirt over my head and throw it on the floor.

She stood and dropped her housecoat, revealing a sheer nightgown. I stared at her big round nipples poking through the silky material. "Take off your pants," she ordered.

I stood and dropped my drawers while on the big TV screen the slender woman bent over the arm of a sofa to accept her lover from behind. Alexis turned if off and the room was completely dark. "Come upstairs. It's time to take your education to the next level."

She picked up her glass and walked up the stairs. The view from below was fantastic. Naked, I followed her to the bedroom.

"Lie down on the bed with me," she instructed. I did, and sucked on her nipples through her nightgown. "Very nice," she murmured. "Now, you're going to learn how to really go down on a woman. Get down and start licking my pussy."

I slid down the bed and between her legs. I kissed the thick mat of hair where her legs met. I stuck out my tongue and licked her clitoris, then licked it again. "Not bad, but don't press so hard," Alexis instructed. "Make your tongue wetter."

I let a thick drop of spit slide down my tongue and swirled it around gently. She groaned in appreciation, so I repeated the motion, then slid my tongue lower, between her folds. "Oh, yes, Damian, that feels good," she encouraged me. I lapped lightly, then made my tongue pointy and slid it into her, licking upwards as she moaned.

She took my hand in hers and pulled it up to her breast. I toyed with the nipple, rolling it between my finger and thumb. After a few minutes of this, she whispered something.

I lifted my head from her pussy. "What?"

"Put your fingers inside me!"

I pushed my index finger into her slowly. Alexis drew a hissing breath inward. "More," she whispered.

I lowered my head and licked her quickly. I continued to roll her nipple with one hand, and slid two fingers of the other inside her.

She groaned, so I swirled my fingers in one direction and my tongue the other way. She seemed to like that. I did it again, but in the opposite direction.

I kept licking, but switched from up and down to side-to-side. I slid my fingers in and out, then swirled them, then went back to in and out.

"No, do what you were doing before," Alexis hissed. It took me a few minutes to work out what she liked, but I got it: swirling two fingers together at a steady pace while licking her clitoris from side to side. I moved my left hand down from her breast, but Alexis grabbed it and brought it back up.

She began to groan deeply, almost growling. She lifted her hips higher and shrieked as liquid spurted out of her vagina, splashing onto my chin. I drew back, shocked, but Alexis grabbed my head in both hands and pulled me back. "Don't stop!" she screamed.

I licked as hard and fast as I could. "Put your fingers back inside!" I did and swirled, and she spurted again, soaking the sheets below my face. She screamed, louder than I had ever heard anyone scream, and spurted one more time before collapsing onto the bed. Her legs shook and her body twisted.

She looked at me. "Fuck me now!"

I did not understand what was happening, but there was no arguing with Alexis or with my cock. I slid into Alexis in one smooth motion.

Alexis grabbed me close and growled again as she flipped us over. She rode me, sliding up and down. I rubbed her nipples, and sat up to suck them into my mouth as Alexis arched her back and threw her head back. She moaned and ground against me, thrashing and heaving. "Fuck! I'm coming!"

Then I was coming, far faster than I had wanted to, and I was screaming, too. I pushed up into her and she plunged down on me. I felt more wetness flowing out of her, over my hips and around my thighs.

Alexis collapsed on me, her breasts flattening and spreading across my naked chest. Her hair fell over my face, tickling my nose.

I drew a shuddering breath and kissed her neck; all I had to do, really, was pucker a little. I squeezed her ass, her beautiful round ass, and kissed her again.

She lifted her head and smiled dreamily. "Mmm, nice." She got off me and sat up.

"What was that?" I asked, when I could speak again.

"That, dear boy, was a g-spot orgasm. Have you heard of the

g-spot?"

"Yes, of course," I said. I thought I had heard of it, but I had no idea what it meant.

"The g-spot is a particular place inside the vagina, on the front or top wall," she explained. She made a funny scooping motion with her hand against her pubis. "It's slightly different for every woman, in my opinion. But anyway, appropriate stimulation of the g-spot can cause a woman to ejaculate."

"You ejaculated? You mean, like I do?"

She smiled her indulgent smile. "Not the same. A woman's ejaculate is a clear, colourless and odourless liquid. Warm water, really."

"It felt hot."

"And with the right stimulation, the g-spot orgasm is especially intense."

"Was it intense? Did I give you an intense, g-spot orgasm?"

She leaned forward and kissed me. "What do you think?"

"I think you came, really, really hard."

She kissed me again. "You pass. But after a g-spot, I need something to drink." She drained the rest of the wine. "Would you bring me a tumbler of water from the dispenser in the kitchen?"

I padded through her house, naked in the dark. My mind whirled. A g-spot orgasm? Female ejaculation? It was a lot to take in.

When I got back to the bedroom, Alexis had pulled the covers over herself. I gave her the glass and she drained it. "Thank you. Come on, get into bed. Are you going to stay the night?"

"Can I?"

"Of course."

As I pulled back the covers, I saw that she was still nude.

"But I must warn you: your virtue may be in danger," she laughed.

I laughed, too, but then I had to gasp.

"What's wrong?" Alexis said.

"The bed is so wet! It's like a puddle!"

She laughed again. "Is that a problem? It's the puddle that came from both of us." Alexis pressed her naked skin against mine and kissed me deeply, and I needed no more convincing.

I pulled her body tight against me, revelling in the feeling of skin on skin. I breathed her in as long as I could stay awake.

Chapter 8

Cleaning Pools

"Yes, yes, yessss..." Alexis' voice faded into a long hiss. I licked her vagina up to her clit as she arched her back and clutched at my head.

She spasmed and shook and my chin got all wet. I kept licking and reached up to rub her nipple. Her soft hiss changed to a long moan and then a shout. She sat up, hips quaking. She took my face in her hands and leaned down to kiss me. I loved the way she pushed her tongue into my mouth.

She moved down, kissing my neck, my shoulders, my chest. I leaned back against the chaise lounge and stroked her cheek as she sucked on my nipples. Her hands stroked my skin, lower, until she took my penis in one hand and cupped my testicles with the other. She bent down and kissed the tip of my penis.

I looked down at her long curls in my lap, the tan expanse of the skin of her shoulders. She moved her legs back so that she was kneeling on the leg extension of the lounge chair. I enjoyed the sight of her ass sticking up like that almost as much as the feeling of her lips.

Behind the lovely curves of her buttocks, the pool, newly cleaned, glittered in the sunlight. A breeze ruffled its surface, dazzling me, so I closed my eyes and caressed Alexis' hair.

I realized that I could not hold back anymore. I took her chin in my hands and lifted her face to mine. Alexis smiled at me until I kissed her deeply. Our tongues wrestled in her hot mouth.

Alexis shifted forward, climbing into my lap. She moaned

softly into my mouth as she settled onto me.

Alexis wanted to do something new to me every time we met, as if she felt I could handle only one lesson at a time. Today, she didn't lift herself up and down like she had the last time she was on top. Instead, she clenched and relaxed her interior muscles while grinding her hips on mine.

I couldn't help but groan. It felt as if Alexis was pulling me deeper, like my whole body was being drawn into her through my penis. I pushed up as she pushed down, but when I tried to thrust harder, Alexis broke the kiss.

"Sshh." She ground her hips down again. "Just relax this time, Damian. Let me enjoy you." She kissed me deeply again.

I went along with it. I always did. God, it felt so good. I pushed up just a little as Alexis pushed down. I couldn't help it, and Alexis seemed to like it. I started to tremble. I could feel my orgasm building, and I didn't want to come, not yet. This was too good, much too good to rush.

Alexis started moving faster. Her breathing got faster and her skin got hotter against me. She clenched and did not relax this time as she moved up and then slammed down. "Fuck me," she hissed into my ear.

I didn't need any more encouragement. I grabbed her ass in both hands and lifted her high, and then I slammed us together, plunging deeper than I ever had before.

Alexis screamed, but I didn't care if the neighbours heard. I lifted her again, rammed her down again. She screamed again and jerked against me.

I had an idea: I pulled her close and stood. She nearly fell off me for a second, but she got the idea and wrapped her arms around my shoulders and her legs around my hips. Alexis squealed — literally squealed. I slid her up and down like a piston. Her weight was nothing compared to the feeling of her vagina slipping up and down me.

My hands started to slide up her buttocks. I had to get a better grip. One at a time, I shifted my arms so they hooked under her knees. Alexis held tightly around my neck as I moved, and somehow I managed to remain inside her.

I shifted my feet lightly farther apart. I now felt confident in my grip. With my arms under her knees and my hands back on the globes of her ass, I lifted her up, pulling her legs as far apart as I could. She was completely open, and then I pulled her close and thrust my hips up savagely. I slammed into her, lifted her high again and thrust in.

Alexis clenched her eyes shut and threw her head back. Her jaw dropped and her mouth made a perfect O-shape, but no sound other than her breath came out. I lifted and impaled her on my dick again.

This time she let loose a howl that must have rattled the windows.

I lifted her again and again until all I could see was her face. All I could feel was her hot wetness engulfing me. Maybe it was gravity, or maybe something else, but my orgasm was delayed, slowed.

My mind cleared. I concentrated on Alexis' pleasure. She screamed again and I felt hot liquid flow down my thighs.

I lifted her higher and thrust into her harder. She screamed louder, her breasts heaving and glistening with sweat. I lifted her body, loving the feeling as she slid up my length. I slid smoothly and evenly.

I felt my orgasm build, heat climbing like mercury in a thermometer. I thrust faster and faster, lifting her up and down. Alexis bucked against me. And then I came, hard. I clenched my jaw and pistoned Alexis up and down until my knees buckled and I fell onto the chaise lounge behind me.

Alexis rolled to the side. She had to reach out to stop herself from falling onto the pool deck. Her eyes were closed, her mouth open, sucking in the air her body needed. Strands of wet, tangled hair stuck to her forehead, across her nose, over her lips.

"Wow, Damian," she whispered, stretching along me. "No one has ever taken me like that before."

"You're so wet," I said. I wasn't sure how to describe what had happened. "I felt something gushing out of you when I picked you up. Was that a g-spot?"

"Mmm-hmm." I felt proud of myself. "I've had plenty of g-spot orgasms, Damian, but believe it or not, no one has ever picked me up like that before."

"Really? Did you like it?"

"Couldn't you tell?" She smiled lazily. "Well, that was fun, Damian, but we have some business to do. Go and bring your paperwork out here, and your laptop." She took a long drink from the tall glass on the patio table. When I stood up, she lay back on the lounge chair, looking dreamy. "And bring another pitcher of iced tea."

I stepped over our discarded clothing a little unsteadily to fetch my briefcase from the kitchen.

We set up on the patio table: laptop computer, my notes and records, the bank deposit book and chequebook. We were still naked, sipping iced tea under the hot sun. Alexis explained some points about banking, but none of them went into my brain.

"If all you can do is stare at my tits, Damian, I'm not going to bother helping you with business."

"Sorry." I raised my eyes to hers.

Mistake. All I could do then was to look into those brown beauties.

"All right, Damian, that's enough," Alexis said. She pulled on a little beach cover-up, a sort of colorful jacket. But it was see-through, and she didn't bother tying the belt, so while I made sure my eyes were pointed at her face, I could still see her nipples.

Her big, round, brown nipples.

I managed to concentrate on learning how to use the simple accounting software. Under Alexis' supervision, I entered the deposit cheques and recorded my own withdrawals — Alexis called them "drawings." I was getting used to the business jargon.

"Now, then," she said when I was done. She patted my arm and sat back in her chair. The cover-up parted. I tried very hard not to look at her breasts, her nipples, her flat stomach, her soft navel, the thick black hair at the top of her thighs.

"Up here, Damian. We have to discuss our relationship."

"Sorry."

"I'm happy to help you, to give you advice, but when it comes to business, well, Damian, to be kind, it's not your strong suit. Don't get me wrong, I know you're working hard. And you're smart. You can do it all, but you're going to need guidance to handle marketing, promotion and human resources."

"That was all supposed to be Nick's responsibility."

"He was supposed to be the executive and you were supposed to do all the work? Did you not think he was taking advantage of you?" She shook her head. "Damian, you have to learn to take charge. How many clients do you have now?"

"Ten."

"And how long does it take you to clean a pool completely?"

"About an hour."

"Plus transfer time and so on. In other words, right now, you're handling all the work you possibly can. So if you want to make more money, you're going to have to hire some help." She drank some iced tea. I loved watching her throat move as she swallowed. My eyes followed the iced tea down ...

"Damian, I want to get an even tan. Look up here."

I forced myself to say "You wanted to talk about our relationship"?"

Alexis laughed. I loved that laugh. "Our *business* relationship. Now, your friend Nick is the founder and titular head of the company, right?"

"Right."

"But for the summer, until he gets back, you have full rights and retain all the revenues, correct? Good. So, you can pay me to be your business advisor. I've gotten you all of your clients so far, and I'll advise you on more promotion and advertising. You'll have to hire some employees, and I'll help you make sure you bring in the right kind of people. In return, I get five percent of your revenues, plus you keep my pool in tip-top shape. Deal?"

"I guess so."

"It's a great deal for you. I don't usually work that cheap. Even when I'm fucking my business partner. In fact, I've never worked this cheaply."

"Then why are you?"

"Because I like you. And it's as much as you can afford." She looked at her watch, which was lying on the table. "Now, look at the time. Pull on some work clothes. You've got to get to Mr. Feldstein's pool in fifteen minutes. Go on, do a good job, and then you can come back and fuck me some more."

She stood and walked into the house. Her cover-up parted and blew back as she walked, and I got one more look at her naked body before she closed the door.

After I was done on Mr. Feldstein's pool, I was surprised to see him, the shortest, fattest little old man I had ever seen, bring me a glass of water and, believe it or not, a bunch of candies. "You're doing a great job. Much better than the last outfit I had in here," he said as he pushed thick glasses up his nose and then wiped sweat that was soaking his bushy eyebrows. "You take care, now. It's darned hot this summer!"

Next was the LeBlanc house, just down the street from Mr. Feldstein's. He had recommended me to the LeBlanc's. Their pool was small for Rosedale, and didn't take long to clean. They weren't home, so there were no treats. On the other hand, I didn't have to hang around talking to them, losing time. One more pool to clean, I thought, to the end of the day.

I was hot, tired, and completely sweaty. And I did not want to get near another pool for a long time.

But I could not stop thinking about Alexis' promise. It had been a few hours since we had been together ... since we had *fucked*. Trapped under my shorts, my penis stretched out, hot along my thigh.

The sun shone into my eyes as I turned onto Alexis' street. I parked at the curb in front of her house and ran up the steps. "It's me," I growled into the speaker-box at the front door, and pushed the door as soon as I heard the lock click.

Alexis was coming down the curving staircase. She looked surprised: her hair was tied up behind her head, exposing her long neck. She wore a pink t-shirt and very short pants, like gym pants. She was barefoot. "Damian! I didn't expect you so soon! Would you like something to eat?"

I caught her on the third step. I pulled her close, feeling her breasts squish against my chest. The skin on her neck was so soft under my fingers. I kissed her hard, surprised at my own urgency. My fingers found their own way down her back. She was standing one step higher than I, so I stroked the backs of her bare thighs. The skin there was so soft, so smooth.

"Oh, Damian!" she sighed, so I stepped up to the same level

as her and kissed her again. I pressed her against the wall and pushed my tongue into her mouth. She moaned.

I had to have her. Of their own volition, my hands pulled her t-shirt off. They grabbed her breasts and teased her hard, puckered nipples. I kissed down her neck, bent to suck on her nipple. Alexis gasped. I opened wide, trying to get as much tit into my mouth as I could.

My hands went to her waist and pulled on her shorts. Alexis moved one leg up to rub my cock with her thigh. "Do you want to go to the bedroom?" she gasped.

In answer, I took her other breast in my mouth. I could not explain it, but I felt like I wanted to devour her, or at least her breasts. My hands, though, were getting impatient. Finally, they pulled on the cloth and Alexis screamed as the shorts tore.

Her hands undid my pants as I kissed Alexis on the mouth again and pressed my chest against hers. Alexis panted and tore my dirty shirt off as I shrugged my pants lower.

She bit my lip and raised one knee up to my waist. "You're all sweaty," she murmured into my shoulder.

"Sorry," I managed to breathe out between kisses to her neck. I loved the feeling of her warm soft skin rubbing on the bottom of my nose.

"No, it turns me on," she said. She lifted my chin with her hands as she raised her knee higher up my side, and then she kissed me, pushing her tongue into my mouth.

I pressed closer to her. I felt the soft heat of her skin, the roughness of her hair, the wetness at her core.

Alexis gasped. Her eyes clenched shut and she pushed her head against the wall. I pushed my hips up, sliding into her. She cried out as I buried myself in her.

I didn't think then. I was nothing but a rutting animal, slamming into Alexis. She rose up the wall, right off the floor. She screamed as she wrapped her thighs around my waist. Her nails burned into my shoulders, and I slammed her even harder.

Nothing could stop me, not if you put a gun at my back. All that mattered was the feeling of Alexis' bare skin against mine, the feeling of her wetness clenching me.

I pushed one more time and roared as I climaxed. As my

breath left me, I could hear Alexis screaming again. She pressed back against the wall, pushing her hips into mine. She trembled in my hands and then her heaving, sweaty hot body slumped against my bare chest.

The world slowly reassembled around me. I relaxed, letting Alexis down. "I better get down the stairs before I fall down," I said. Alexis kissed my chest.

We sat on the lowest step, panting. I still had my shoes on and my pants were tangled around my ankles. Alexis was nude, her skin flushed and sweaty. I realized that was *my* sweat. "I'm sorry," I said again.

"Where did *that* come from?"

"I've been thinking about you all day," I said.

"Mmm. Well, think about me some more." She stood up. "Come on, let's get some clothes on before we stain the carpet on these stairs." She walked up the stairs, naked and beautiful. Her thighs glistened wet in the low sunlight that reflected off the polished wood.

I felt bad, awkward. "Sorry, I can't stay," I stammered.

She turned and looked down from the top of the staircase. "Oh?"

"My parents are taking me out for dinner this evening. I have to shower and change and ..."

"Oh, too bad. I was hoping for more sex." God, she was beautiful, just standing there, naked. I pulled up my pants, feeling stupid.

"I'm sorry." It sounded so lame.

"Don't worry about it. I'll see you soon. Close the door when you go."

That was it. She went into her bedroom. I went out the door.

The path to my car felt like a hundred miles.

Chapter 9

Mrs. Casales

By the end of the third week, I had Mrs. Casales' pool and deck looking much better. In fact, they looked *great*.

For no reason I could define, I had gone well beyond pool cleaning. I had cleaned the inside of the pool and scraped out all the slime and goop, vacuumed the accumulated dust out of the bottom and cleared the skimmers until they looked new.

Every time I had come, I had scrubbed the concrete pool deck. I even went to far as to bring clippers from my parents' tool shed and hack back the overgrown hedges so that they would not drop so many leaves into the pool. I told myself that I was only making my work easier for myself in the long run, but my brain did not believe me.

Mrs. Casales obliged me by exclaiming how much better her whole back yard looked every time I finished. Occasionally, her two little kids, a boy and girl, both under 10 years old, would scamper in and wait impatiently when I told them they had to wait after I poured in the chlorine. "The water's not good for swimming yet," I said every time. "You'll have to wait at least an hour." They would stand at the side of the pool, bouncing on the balls of their feet, until one would think of something else to do and they'd chase each other across the yard or into the house.

Mrs. Casales always came out with iced tea or lemonade when I was done, and we'd sit at her patio set and chat about the pool-cleaning business, or the upcoming university year, or sometimes about her kids.

She seemed cheerful enough when we talked, but she never

mentioned a husband. I remembered what Alexis had said about her marriage breaking up, but I did not know how to ask her about that without risking spoiling her mood.

At the end of the third week, the sixth time I had cleaned the pool, deck and the back yard in general, I took a deep breath and surveyed my handiwork. Part of my brain demanded to know why I had gone so far beyond pool cleaning, and another part of my brain refused to admit why.

Mrs. Casales came out of the kitchen with two bottles of Heineken. No children were in sight. "The water is perfectly balanced today, Mrs. Casales, so the kids can come swimming right away," I said as I took a bottle from her hand.

"The kids are at their cousin's this afternoon. We're alone today," she said and took a sip of her beer. "And call me Leda."

On that hot afternoon, cold beer went down like salvation. I could feel heat radiating off my skin. I pressed the cold bottle against my hot forehead, relishing the ache it caused.

We sat at her squeaky, unsteady patio table. I stretched my legs in front of me. Mrs. Casales' — Leda's — pool was the last on my itinerary, and the day seemed to be going in an excellent direction.

I looked at her; she was wearing a thin cover-up over a two-piece bathing suit. I watched her neck pulse as she drank more beer. She had tied her crazy hair with one of those scrunchie things that girls like. "Thanks for the beer."

She wasn't bad looking, I thought. A little overweight, but that gave her nice curves. She was no Alexis, but to borrow Patrick's tired joke, I wouldn't kick her out of bed for eating cookies.

"Thank you, Damian, for doing such a great job. I appreciate how you've gone well beyond the pool cleaner's job description. I did notice the way you trimmed the bushes and neatened up the whole yard." She patted my knee and moved a little closer toward me.

"It was just to keep so many leaves and branches from falling into the pool," I said. "So it made my own job a little easier."

"Nonsense. You were trying to make me happier. And I truly appreciate that, Damian. Really, I do. And I should pay you back. One good turn deserves another."

"No, no, the payment is what it is. We agreed. A deal is a deal."

"Then, I should pay you back in some other way." She looked right into my eyes.

My mouth felt dry, and pouring more beer into it did not help.

"Do you always work with your shirt off?" she said, and I suddenly felt conscious of my bare chest.

"Just when it's this hot..."

I could not finish answering her because her mouth pressed against mine. Her tongue pushed into my mouth as her hands went around my shoulders. She pulled herself onto my lap as she ran her hands up and down my back.

From exploring my mouth with her tongue, she went to sucking my tongue into her mouth. Her hands pulled on my belt.

For a minute, I just sat there, feeling her tongue in my mouth and her hands rubbing along my skin. When she undid the top of my pants, I pushed her cover-up off her shoulders and moved my mouth down her neck.

I should have thought of Alexis at that point, or about Kristen, or about how risky it was to be kissing a client, but I wasn't thinking about anything at all. Especially when she slid one hand down my pants.

I pushed her bathing suit bra away from her breast to suck on a nipple and heard Leda's sharp breath.

Leda slid off my lap, shedding her bathing suit top and tugging my cut-off shorts down. I groaned when she took me into her mouth, then gasped when I felt her teeth.

"Sorry," she gurgled. I felt her teeth again but suppressed my gasp. It was good — every blowjob is great — but she was not as good as Alexis.

I pulled Leda off of me and lifted her onto the patio table, my cut-offs falling to my feet. I pushed Leda's legs apart, but the table wobbled and she nearly fell off.

"Come into the bedroom," she said, taking my hand and practically running into the house. I followed, bare-assed.

We tumbled together onto the bed. I sucked a nipple into my mouth again. Her breast was softer than Alexis', but still felt wonderful in my hand. Leda wiggled under me, cooing. I kissed down her body, remembering what I had learned at Alexis' body, between Alexis' thighs.

I kissed Leda's stomach, rounded and soft, unlike Alexis'. I kissed Leda's thigh and slid a finger along her pussy. She was warm and damp, not soaking wet like Alexis would have been.

Stop comparing women, said part of my brain. So instead of my finger, I slid my tongue inside her.

"Ooo," she said and ran her fingers through my hair. I licked her clit lightly and she arched her back, so I licked a little harder. I slid my tongue lower and pushed into her. "Oh, Damian," she whispered.

Now, she's wet, I thought. I looked up, over her tummy. Her eyes were closed and she rubbed her nipples.

She wasn't as responsive as Alexis. Or maybe, she was just responsive in a different way. Or maybe she just liked different things than Alexis.

I didn't think of those things at the time. Instead, I licked her up and down, sliding lower every so often to taste her wetness. But when I pushed a finger into her, the way that Alexis liked so much, Leda sat up and pushed my hand away. "No, no," she moaned. She pulled my arms up higher. "Not your finger." She hesitated. What was there to be embarrassed about at this point? I wondered. "Fuck me," she whispered.

I moved up. Leda shut her eyes tight. She took a deep breath and let it out slowly as I slid into her.

It wasn't as easy as it was with Alexis. I felt a resistance.

Leda sat up, pulling away from me. "Not like that." She rolled us over so that she was on top, then lowered herself onto me. Her eyes closed and her head tilted up as I slid inside until she pressed tight against me.

I pushed up into her, but she said "No. Don't move. Don't fucking move." She shifted her body a little and slid forward and back, rather than up and down. Her eyes were shut tight, her breathing ragged. She drove herself on, faster and faster. I rubbed her little pink nipples but she seemed barely to notice.

On and on she went, thrusting against me, breathing harder and harder, faster and faster. I felt my orgasm start, that white heat climb. She must have sensed it and she paused. "Don't come inside me, okay?"

I nodded. My brain told me that this was very risky sexual behaviour, but my brain wasn't in charge at that point.

I bit the insides of my cheeks, even pinched my own thighs, just so that I could hold back a little longer.

Leda opened her mouth and her eyes wide. She stared into my eyes and bounced on me, panting like a marathoner. "Don't come!" she shrieked. Her breasts moved up and down on her chest in erotic counterpoint. She moaned, eyes bulging. The moan became a scream, a shriek. She pushed back against me one more time and I felt her vagina pulse. She lifted herself off me and rolled onto her back. Her breasts heaved as she tried to find her breath.

I touched her body and she trembled, staring at me. I slid my fingertips down again, but she pushed them away. "No, no, I can't," she panted.

I kissed her. What else should I do? Sex had been an unexpected joy, but I wanted to come. I *needed* to come. "Do you have any condoms?" I asked.

She shook her head. "Something better," she said. She sat up and pushed me down on the bed again, and then took me into her mouth once more. She looked up at me and laughed. Then she closed her lips and sucked deeply, all while looking into my eyes.

She was blowing my mind as well as my cock.

I stroked her hair, pushing it away from her face so I could have an unobstructed view of the blowjob. There were no more teeth, nothing but the soft, insistent pressure of her lips and tongue and the intense tingling in my shaft. One of my knees shook rhythmically.

I tried to hold back, but it was no use. When she winked at me, I lost it. I bucked and she let go of my dick, laughing.

"Did you like that?"

"Yes," I whispered. My voice had gone. She giggled. "Did you like it?"

She giggled again, wiping her chin with the back of her hand. "Oh, that was so *naughty!*"

She stood. She turned and looked into the mirror over her dresser, as if appraising herself. Her long hair was even wilder than normal, sticking out in every direction, despite the scrunchie. Her breasts stood high and her small pink nipples were still swollen and erect. Her stomach was only gently rounded, a reminder when she was naked of the children she had had; her hips swept out just a little too widely. But still, very sexy.

Especially naked. With her skin covered with my sweat.

She turned to look at me. "You're so cute, I could just eat you up. Ooops, I did that already!" She laughed again. "But seriously, Damian. This was wonderful, wicked fun, but you better get going. My kids will be home soon, and I don't know how I could explain a naked pool boy in my bedroom!"

I got out of there. I tried to process the events as I drove home. Mrs. Casales just fucked me. I had to say it out loud: "Mrs. Casales just fucked me."

I still didn't believe it.

I took a very long, hot shower when I got home.

Chapter 10

Dinner Date

"You must be kidding."

"What's wrong?"

"Damian, you're a cute and wonderful guy, but there's no way I'm going to be caught dead in that car."

"Okay, I know it's not new. Or stylish..."

"Stylish! Damian, not only is this car at least 10 years old, there are rust holes on every fender, holes in the quarter-panels and the passenger door is a different colour from the rest of the body. Plus, it sounds like you need a new exhaust manifold as well as a new muffler."

I had to push my jaw shut. I had only a vague idea of what an exhaust manifold was, but I had heard of mufflers before.

"So, what do you want to do? I made reservations, and we're already late."

Alexis laughed her musical laugh. "How far away is this restaurant?"

I estimated long. "Fifteen minutes."

She laughed again. "Oh, Damian." She held out her hand. "Let's take my car." On cue, the garage door behind her rose. She put her key fob into my hand.

I pressed the button, and the lights on the silver Jaguar flashed. She went to the passenger side and waited for me to open the door for her. As she got in, she asked "You do know how to drive stick, don't you?"

I heard my father's voice: "Let the clutch out gently, Damian." I saw him grimacing as the gears ground in our old Sentra standard.

"Of course," I said. "I learned how to drive standard. What else is there?"

Alexis smiled the smile I would learn, eventually, was her kind and indulgent smile. I just hoped that the damage I was about to do to her transmission wouldn't cost too much.

Cost too much for whom? another part of my brain asked. Who do you know who has more money than Alexis? More disposable income?

I pushed those thoughts down, picturing the petulant, jealous me smothered under layers of Alexis' underwear.

Yah. Smothered by her underwear. I had to bend over a little as I walked to the driver's door.

"Relax, Damian. It's just a car," Alexis said as I closed the door.

Just a car! The dashboard looked like the control panel of the space shuttle. Okay, I've never actually seen the space shuttle's control panel, but until that night, I had never seen the dashboard of a Jag before, either. It straddled a very difficult line between overwhelming and disappointing. The speedometer and tachometer were where I expected them to be, but there were instruments that I could not interpret.

"It's a keyless start, so you just have to push that button," Alexis said.

A large button glowed a ghostly white; I pressed it, and lights came on behind the dashboard. The overhead light stayed on for a few seconds, then dimmed.

I drove out of the garage slowly, eyes scanning side to side, along the driveway, anxious for any movement.

Alexis pushed a button on the rear-view mirror, and the garage door came down. I paid close attention to moving onto the street, but this was Rosedale — there was no such thing as traffic. Or if there were, the city council would pass a bylaw against it.

Okay, we're on the street. Please, gears, don't grind.

I shifted out of first, thinking about what my father had said, and eased the clutch out while giving a lot of gas. The engine raced and the transmission engaged, but there was no grinding of gears and no lurching. We moved ahead smoothly.

I exhaled.

"So, where are we going?" Alexis asked.

"It's called Bangkok Garden."

"Sounds great! I love Thai food."

I hoped it would be good. I'd never had Thai food before, but it was trendy.

Google had told me the route from Alexis' house to the restaurant would take 15 minutes. But how well did Google know Toronto and its Saturday night traffic?

Pretty well. The trip took 15 minutes, almost exactly. The best part was accelerating onto Mount Pleasant Avenue: shifting from first to second, then third and fourth within seconds, hearing the engine rev up to a whine, pulling the gear lever down, over and down again, letting out the clutch, hearing the sound drop down to a growl and then race up to a whine, the blur of the headlights of cars driving in the opposite direction...

Oh, my gawd. The Jaguar is so much better than my crappy Suzuki. The gear shift almost moves on its own, it's so smooth.

We flew downtown; I ran a yellow at Bloor Street. Alexis cried out a little at that, and the sound made my heart thump hard.

Traffic crawled along Carlton, and I cursed my decision not to follow Google's suggestion. When I turned onto Yonge, however, I felt vindicated. Traffic here was ten times worse than on Carlton. Fortunately, the restaurant was only a few more blocks away, and I pulled up in front of it only 18 minutes after my reservation.

"I'll let you out here and find parking," I said.

"Is the reservation under your name?" Alexis asked. She had her indulgent smile again.

Now, to find parking. But I got lucky: a Buick pulled away from the curb on Elm Street, and I eased the Jag in, no problem. I swaggered away from the best parking job I had ever done, feeling a deep satisfaction from the beep of the remote lock.

The Thai restaurant was different from any I had ever seen, with elephants and exotic musical instruments on the walls. The menu was heavily laminated in plastic, something I associated with down-market calorie dumpsters rather than finer restaurants, but the prices were closer to the latter. I started calculating: did I have enough cash to cover this?

"I have no idea what to order," I confessed.

"Don't worry," Alexis smiled. "I've had Thai before."

That was obvious: the staff all knew her, smiling and asking how she was, why she had stayed away so long?

"Oh, you know how it is. You get busy with all sorts of things," she answered.

At which point, the waiters and waitresses would look at me, as if to say: yes, we see how you get busy.

Alexis ordered for both of us: big platters with names I had never heard before. I loved the Pad Thai, and surprised myself by how much I loved the red curry chicken. Alexis ordered a Singha beer for me and a glass of white wine for herself. Again, I tried to calculate whether I could cover this.

I made a big show of taking the bill. "I asked you out on a date," I insisted. "I'll pay."

I felt so stupid. I had enough cash for the tab, but not a tip. I would have to convince the waitress to let me put some on debit and pay the rest in cash.

I was rehearsing my explanation in my head when Alexis put her purse on the table. "Don't worry, sweetie. I can cover it."

"No, no, I asked you out! I'll pay the dinner bill."

Alexis leaned closer. "You know, if you don't tip at least 25 percent here, you'll never get a reservation again."

"What! That's ridiculous! Their prices are high enough that a standard tip is already generous! I mean, thirty bucks for a plate of noodles —"

"Not so loud!" Alexis hissed. "Don't embarrass me!"

I shut up, feeling my cheeks burn in a combination of outrage and shame. I mean, really, they expected a twenty-five percent tip?

Life in the big city, said my brain.

I calculated some more. "Alexis, I can cover this, but I won't be able to come back here." Fuck 'em, I thought. No way am I going to give in to their elitist social blackmail. I put cash down on the little plastic tray with the bill and stood up, holding out a hand. "Let's get out of here before the waiters see how I stiffed 'em on the tip."

Alexis smiled her wicked smile. She jumped up, grabbed her purse and stood close by me. I kissed her quickly. "Ready to run?"

I said in my best James Bond voice.

"Ready," she answered, and I thought I detected a slight British twinge.

The waiter came closer, looking concerned. I looked at the door, then at the cash on the table: barely enough to cover the food. No tip.

Hand in hand, we ran for the door. Like a true gentleman, I held it open for Alexis and she skipped through like a schoolgirl. My mouth went dry.

"Hey!" the waiter called from beside our table.

I tried my best to sound like James Bond again "Sorry to eat, not tip and run," I said as I stepped out the door. "But that's how the pad thai crumbles."

Okay, that was bad.

Hand in hand again, Alexis and I ran down the steps and around the corner. I hit the remote's unlock button as soon as I could see the car, and still trying to act like a gentleman, opened the passenger door for Alexis. I looked up the street, but there was no sign of the waiter coming after us.

I slammed the door shut and revved the engine. The car jolted as I shifted into first and cranked the wheel hard to the left to pull out of the parking spot.

"Careful!" Alexis squealed at the same pitch as the tires. "You don't want to attract the police's attention." Her hand was on my thigh already. She rubbed me as I ran a yellow at Wellesley.

Once I shifted into fourth, I put my hand on Alexis' leg. I moved higher, pushing her skirt up. The skin of her thigh got hotter as my fingertips moved higher. I felt hair: damp already. I pressed lightly, not caring that the awkward angle made my wrist ache. I rubbed lightly and Alexis drew a hissing breath.

I slowed the car as Alexis sped up. She opened my belt and pulled down my zipper with practised movements. By the time I reached Bloor Street, she had my pants wide open and was stroking me in her left hand. When she leaned over the centre console to take me into her mouth, I nearly swerved onto the sidewalk. Somehow, I negotiated the left turn onto Mount Pleasant Avenue, and then I had to pull over before I blacked out.

She came up before I climaxed and kissed me deeply, shoving

her tongue into my mouth. Her mouth was hot.

She pulled away to say, "Take me home. I can't wait any longer."

I drove as quickly as I thought was safe through the tree-lined, sedate streets of Rosedale while Alexis continued to stroke me. I held my elbows up high to give her room, which was an awkward way to drive a car.

I left the car at a random angle across her driveway, and felt bereft when Alexis took her hand away from my crotch. Alexis ran to the front door, leaving the passenger door open. I reached over to pull it shut while trying to pull up my zipper with the other hand. I succeeded with the door but continued to struggle with the zipper.

Fuck it, I thought. There's no one else around.

I ran up the stone path to Alexis' wide-open front door, clutching my belt so my pants would not fall down. As soon as I shut the door, she pounced on me. Her lips were all over my face, my jaw, my neck. She tore at my shirt. I pulled off her top as she steered me into the living room.

My leg banged against the coffee table, but with Alexis sucking on my nipple I did not care about the pain. I fell onto the sofa with Alexis trailing kisses down my chest. My pants spilled open and Alexis pulled them the rest of the way off. She stripped so fast it was as if her clothes just evaporated. She straddled me as she pushed her tongue into my mouth and then she was pushing her hips down onto me. I felt wetness on her thighs and then I slid into her.

She rode me, raising her ass until I was barely touching her and then pushing down. Her body shook and she clutched at my upper arms.

All I had to do was lean forward a little to lick her nipples. Alexis moaned louder and slammed her hips harder onto me.

I pushed her breasts together, squeezing and mashing. Alexis ground her pelvis against me, spreading wetness over my lap. Her hands roved over my head, through my hair. I managed to get both nipples into my mouth for about two seconds, long enough to flick them twice with my tongue, but then the pressure of those big beauties popped them out.

Faster and faster Alexis rode me, until she pushed down hard one last time, screaming out and pulling on my hair. She collapsed against me, panting.

I needed to come. I rolled over, pressing Alexis onto the sofa. I pushed her thighs up and out and looked down; in the last of the daylight from the big windows, I looked at her magnificent naked body, splayed before me. I watched myself slide in and out of her. Her breasts shook every time I pushed in. Alexis stared back at me, panting. I slammed in and out, hard, faster and faster. Her whole body shook and she screamed out another orgasm.

I didn't care anymore. I slammed as hard into her as I could, reaching for my own orgasm like a runner going for the finish line. I hit it and felt my strength stream out of me. I kept pumping, kept sliding and realized that I was screaming, too. My strength gone, I slowed, pushed into her one last time and slumped forward, panting.

"You're hurting my legs," Alexis panted. I realized that I was clenching her thighs and relaxed my grip. Alexis pushed herself up, and I yelled again as I slid out of her. I collapsed onto the sofa.

Alexis kissed me. "Mmm, that was exciting," she said. "I'm going to have to get that sofa cleaned. Again." She went to the liquor cabinet. I enjoyed watching her walk around naked.

"Would you like a drink?" she asked as she poured two vodkas and went into the kitchen for ice.

"Sure," I panted. My breathing was starting to come under control.

"Then come on upstairs. I still have plans for you." Naked, with a glass in each hand, she walked out of the living room and up the stairs. Her twitching ass pulled my dick up the stairs, and the rest of me followed.

In the bedroom, she put one glass in my hand. I swallowed nearly half of it. The vodka burned all the way down. She took the glass from my hand and set it on the night table. She threw all the bed covers onto the floor and knelt on the mattress. I thought about how that beautiful ass would settle onto her heels.

"Come closer," she said. I stepped up and felt a tingle.

She put her hands around me and kissed my chest. She kissed

lower and took my equipment in both hands again, one hand cupping underneath and the other fluttering along its length. I jumped as her fingers touched that sensitive spot on the underside. "I don't know, Alexis; I'm pretty sensitive still."

"Oohh, can't take it, yet?" she laughed, looking up at me with those big brown eyes. "Well, then, there's something you can do for me." She lay back on the bed, pulling me toward her. I kissed her hard on the mouth, loving the taste of her.

"It's time for a new lesson," she breathed as I bit her throat. I kissed down. I could not get enough of those breasts, those big luscious tits. As I swirled my tongue around her nipples again, she said "Go down on me again."

I must have hesitated, paused momentarily in flicking the very tips of her nipples. "I know you just came in me," she said between pants as I sucked her nipple in. I wanted to get as much tit into my mouth as I could. I stretched my jaw wide and sucked in, rewarded as more of her breast flowed into my mouth. She arched her back, pressing more into me. "Oohh, yessss. Now lick my pussy. Go down and make me come again."

I reached down between her legs and rubbed three fingers up and down. She was wetter than I had ever felt her before. How much of that is her, and how much is me? I wondered. I spread the liquid around, rubbing her clit and loving the way she pushed more of her tit into my mouth when I did.

"Lick my cunt," she whispered.

I still hesitated. Did I want to lick up my own semen? I kissed lower, along her flat stomach. I licked inside her navel, then made my tongue flat and swept it lower and lower.

"Lick my cunt!" she ordered. Then she raised her voice louder, so loud I was sure the neighbours could hear her. "LICK MY CUNT!"

Oh, yeah? That perverse part of my brain said. Not perverse in a good way — perverse in the way it liked to piss off people who were doing what I wanted them to. So I kissed her, lower and lower, and slid two fingers into her. I kissed her pubic hair and stuck my tongue out. It found wetness, so I pressed harder and felt her clit. I licked it and slid my fingers in and out of her. God, she was so wet!

How much of that is me, and how much is her? I wondered again.

I kissed along her leg, lower and lower, dragging my tongue on her perfect skin. I slid lower and lower until I had to take my hands out of her, and she groaned when I did that. "What the fuck are you doing?" she growled.

I kissed her ankle, then her instep and finally sucked her toe into my mouth. It didn't seem to have any effect on her, though.

I moved to the other side and kissed her left foot, then started kissing higher. She twisted her fingers in my hair and pulled me up. "Stop fucking around!" she hissed.

I kissed the inside of her left thigh, working my way higher. As she moaned, I slid back down to her right knee and kissed her hard. I moved up, biting the inside of her thigh until I was breathing in her musk.

I kissed her pubic hair, gently, then harder. I kissed her vulva and sucked in our combined wetness. Alexis squirmed and moaned, so I stuck out my tongue and gently licked up the length of her vagina, pushing between her wet lips until I found her clit again.

Alexis grabbed my head in both hands and called out my name. I flicked my tongue back and forth, slowly and softly at first. But then I couldn't wait anymore and I flicked as fast as I could. Alexis arched her back. I moved my tongue down, between her labia and as deep inside her pussy as I could, until the skin under my tongue burned from the stretching.

Delicious. Her pussy tasted different from the way it had before. Our combined taste, I thought. I pressed up and slid my tongue up, pressing hard, until I reached her clit again. This time, I flicked it up and down. I felt good when I heard her deep moans.

I was hard; I moved my hips, rubbing against her sheets and thinking of thrusting into Alexis while I sucked her clit between my lips.

"Oh, Damian, are you thinking of sliding your cock into my pussy?" Alexis moaned.

How does she keep reading my mind? I wondered. "Soon, baby, soon," I said. I sucked her clit into my mouth as gently as I could, then lightly flicked my tongue across it.

She sucked in her breath sharply and arched her back even higher. I repeated my action, over and over. Her thigh shook. Is she close? I wondered.

I slid a finger into her, then a second. She screamed again as my fingers ground against the edge of her pubic bone and I licked her clit upward, bottom to top, at the same time.

I licked her clit and curled my fingers upward, the way I knew she liked, and rubbed. Alexis arched her back and screamed. "Don't stop! Don't fucking stop!" I pressed down with my tongue and licked as fast as I could. "Don't you dare fucking stop!" Alexis screamed. I licked as fast as I could and churned my fingers in a circular pattern inside her, pressing upward.

Fluid squirted out of her pussy, hitting my chin with hot force. I licked harder and pressed up. I curled my fingers and stroked toward me, and she squirted more with every stroke, screaming out every time.

My cock pressed into the mattress. I couldn't take anymore. I licked her harder, pushing my fingers into her and pressing upward. Alexis lifted her hips off the bed and screamed, and gushed what felt like a gallon of hot water against my face. I held on, licking her pussy as hard as I could as Alexis let loose a banshee howl. When she collapsed onto the bed, chest heaving, I could take no more. I rose to my knees and flipped Alexis over. I grabbed her hips, raised them off the bed and spread her thighs.

She looked over her shoulder at me. "Damian—" was all she managed to say before I slammed into her.

"You are so wet," I groaned through my clenched jaw.

Those were all the words my mind was able to form. I grunted and babbled like a caveman as I slammed forward, smashing into her as hard as I could. Alexis screamed. I felt her spasm around me, but my next orgasm was still some distance away, and I kept thrusting, fucking deeply. Alexis wailed and trembled. Her knees gave way and she would have collapsed to the bed, but I lifted her up, smashing my hips forward to get as deep into her as I could. She howled again, her thighs shaking, and I kept going.

I could feel my orgasm building, trying to escape. I held it back. No, Alexis, this is going to last. I thrust into her. I felt liquid pour out of her and down my legs. I didn't care. No — I loved it. I loved the feeling of sex liquids running out of her and all over me. "More, Alexis, more," I groaned, barely aware that I was saying anything.

I could not hold back another second and my orgasm rocketed out of me. "No!" someone yelled, and I realized it was me. I thrust again, and again, over and over. Heat, wet and sticky, poured down my legs. Alexis screamed again.

I kept thrusting, kept pushing, kept fucking Alexis until I could not move my hips anymore. I collapsed, falling sideways and down onto my back. Alexis fell forward, panting. I looked at her face in the dim evening light. Her eyes were closed. Stray hairs hanging in front of her face moved back and forth in her panting breath.

Alexis rolled onto her back and opened her eyes. "Oohh, Damian, you really outdid yourself," she panted. One hand slid down between her legs, then came back up to her face. I could see our juices, reflecting the little light there was off her fingers. "Oh, I'm definitely bringing you back here again."

I don't remember any more of that night.

Chapter 11

Dom and Sub

Time to look at the books. That's what the text message had said. That, and a time: 5:00 SHARP.

I swung into Alexis' driveway at 4:58 just as the garage door closed the last few centimetres. Proud of myself for not being late for once, I gathered the chequebook and other business statements from the passenger seat and knocked on the front door.

"It's open," Alexis said through the squawk box. I headed for the study.

Alexis wore what I had trouble reconciling as a business suit: a severe jacket with no lapels or pockets and a narrow skirt, but in purple. How could any Bay Street executive take her seriously when she's wearing purple? She had on a single strand of bright white pearls and her wrist sparkled: a single band of diamonds that went all the way around.

She had the day's *Globe and Mail* spread out on the cubist desk, so I put the PoolGeeks books on the side table. "I got your text message," I said.

"Change of plan. I've had enough of business for the day. Go get some wine from the cooler, and two big glasses from the kitchen cabinet," she ordered.

I hesitated, then shrugged. She was doing so much to help me, I couldn't begrudge fetching her some wine. Especially since she told me to bring two glasses.

"Make it the Chablis, on the right side," she called after me as I headed down the hall.

It took me a few minutes of searching wine labels to identify

Chablis, especially since I didn't expect it to be spelled "Chablis."
By the time I got back to the study, Alexis had taken off her shoes
and was lounging on the sofa.

"What's the occasion?" I asked as I struggled with the
corkscrew. Why do the French still insist on corks?

"Don't you read the newspaper?" she asked, sounding a little
annoyed.

"Not much," I admitted and handed her a glass. I started to
pour another, for myself, but Alexis said: "Wait. That was a hint,
dummy. Take a look at the newspaper."

I craned my head to read the pages splayed out on the desk.
Report on Business. I scanned down to a big, full-colour picture on
the front of the section. "Hey! That's you!"

Alexis nodded and drank her wine. I read the headline: Red
Capital Completes Blaine Takeover. "What, you took over a
company?"

"I did that a month ago. It just cleared regulatory approval."

"Wow. I had no idea ..."

"That I had a brain in my head?"

"No, I mean, yes. I mean, I know you're smart and great at
business, Alexis. You've done wonders for me! But, wow, front
page of the *Report on Business*! Wow."

Damian, you really sound like an idiot, said my brain.

"I'm not just a pretty face, Damian." She reached behind her
head and took out her hair clips. Her curls spilled out over her
shoulders and she looked so much more relaxed.

"You've been working on this a long time? What's 'Red
Capital'?"

"It was my late husband's company. I own it now. I've
transformed it from a passive hedge fund into a pretty aggressive
capital acquisitions firm."

I skimmed the article in the paper: there seemed to have been
some controversy in the acquisition; the Blaine managers had
resisted the takeover. "Impressive," I said.

"They had no idea how to handle me," Alexis said, rubbing
one foot up and down the opposite calf. "Everyone thought I
married Charles for his money and social status. And I admit, that
was part of the attraction.

"But I really did love him. And I would have been a force on the Street with or without him. Having access to his money just brought me there a little sooner. This coup proves it. I've made a mark on the Street and the old boys aren't going to forget it for a long time." She drank the rest of the wine and held out the glass for a refill.

"Now, it's time for me to reward myself. I've just made a hundred million dollars for my company, and several million in personal commissions for myself. And I'm going to spend it. But first, a different kind of treat for the Queen." She stood and put her glass down on the table. "Undress me."

"Sorry?"

"I want to feel free, and I don't want to be bothered taking my own clothes off. So are you going to undress me, or do I have to order up a gigolo from CraigsList?"

I didn't wait any longer. I stepped behind her and slid her jacket off her shoulders, pulling the sleeves down her arms so smoothly it almost didn't even touch her.

Her sleeveless blouse had buttons in the back. I didn't bother puzzling over that (is there anything stupider than buttons in the back of a shirt?) and pulled down the skirt zipper at her hip.

"Fold them nicely," Alexis admonished. "I love my clothes."

I folded everything and placed them in a neat stack on the sofa. Alexis held up her arms. "Bra," she said.

I unhooked the lacy purple bra and gently pulled the straps off her arms, careful not to touch her skin. I wasn't sure what she really wanted, but that seemed like a safe decision. I hooked my forefingers under the elastic strap of her lacy purple underwear and pulled it down her legs. It took a lot of willpower not to kiss the perfect roundness of her buttocks when it was right at face level.

Alexis stepped out of her underwear and I folded them and put them on top of the rest of her clothes. She stretched her arms up over her head and breathed deeply. "God, that feels better. It was all I could do to stay in my clothes in that boardroom. Those fucking assholes were so stupid and so mad, I just wanted to tear off my clothes and then scratch out their eyes! No, yank out their tongues. Assholes." She drank down the rest of her wine. "Fill that up, then bring another bottle to the bedroom." I watched her hips and ass sway out of the study.

I ran back to the kitchen and found another bottle of Chablis. I shoved the corkscrew into my pocket and carrying wine glasses in one hand, the open, one-third-full bottle in the other and the full bottle under my arm, I ran up the stairs to her bedroom.

"Not there; the other bedroom," she called from across the hall. "The Play Room."

The "Play Room" was all red and black: red walls, black cabinets. A thick carpet in deep colours cushioned the floor. In what I thought was a strange place, the very middle of the room, was the biggest bed I had ever seen. It had a headboard and a footboard of dark metallic bars, like fences, and shiny red sheets.

A mirror covered half of one wall beside the bed; dark red curtains covered a window on the opposite.

Lying on the middle of the bed, leaning on several pillows, was the naked Alexis. She held out her empty wine glass. I put the wine bottles, glasses and corkscrew on a long, low black bureau beside the bed and then poured the remainder of the first bottle into Alexis' glass, careful not to look at her breasts in order not to spill the wine.

"Pour a glass for yourself, too. But first, take off your clothes," she ordered.

I ripped my clothes off and shoved them under the bed. I didn't want to take away from the impact of the "play room." My hands shook when I poured some of the second bottle into my glass. I spilled a few drops when Alexis reached over and stroked my butt.

I choked on the wine when Alexis ran her hands up my sides. I leaned down and kissed her. She lay back on the bed, pulling me toward her. I kissed the little hollow at the base of her throat where her collarbones came together. But before I could kiss any lower, Alexis rolled over onto her stomach. "I want a back-rub," she said.

I did not know how to give anyone a back-rub, but I straddled her. The insides of my knees touched her buttocks and my penis lengthened and stiffened. I put my palms just below her shoulders and started massaging in little circles. Her skin was so smooth, so soft.

"Lower, the small of my back." I slid lower and my penis slid along her round ass. I pushed the heels of my hands against the narrow part of her back and looked at the sides of her breasts where they bulged out under her. "Yes, like that. Don't press quite so hard, though. That's it."

I rubbed her for a long time, wondering what would happen next. Isn't this good enough? asked my brain. You're kneeling, naked, with your dick pressing against the naked skin of a beautiful woman. You've got a glass of wine better than anything your friends have ever had.

Yes, that's enough, I told my brain. But it would be very nice if … my cock twitched as I thought about where the evening could lead.

I don't know how long I massaged Alexis. Every so often she would stir, moan, stretch or shift a little. Every time, her ass would just touch my penis. It was fantastic and maddening as hell.

Finally, she rolled over and sat up. "That was very nice." She twisted to arrange the pillows, then sat back against them and spread her legs apart. "Give me my wine," she instructed, and when I put the glass in her hand, she said "Now, make me come."

She sipped her wine and ran her fingers through my hair as I kissed one nipple, then sucked the other one. I massaged the insides of her thighs for a few seconds and then gently rubbed her vulva.

"No," she said. "Lick my pussy."

I slid down the slippery bed and planted a big, wet kiss right on her clit. I looked up at Alexis. She smiled and sipped her wine.

I licked from the bottom of her vagina to the top, flicking at the clit at the end. Alexis moaned quietly, so I did it again. And again.

She got wet, and not just from my tongue. I got the idea to swirl my tongue in circles. That made Alexis groan louder. I did that until my tongue started to get tired, and then I went lower and pushed my tongue as deep inside her as I could. She gasped, so I licked upward again and looked up at her face. Her eyes were closed and she was rubbing her nipple with one finger. Her other hand held the wine glass, now almost empty.

I had another inspiration. I took the wine glass from her. As she looked down in mild surprise, I carefully poured just a few drops onto her clitoris. "Mmm, getting creative down there?" She laughed as I slurped the wine off her.

I poured a little more wine, watching it trickle between her pussy lips. I licked it up; the taste of wine and Alexis was a surprising combination of cold and hot.

Alexis took the wine glass from me and poured the last of it onto herself so that it flowed through her pubic hair, over her clitoris and my tongue. "Be sure you get it all!"

I dove into her, licking deep, slurping and sucking. Alexis slumped back against the pillows. She put her hands under her knees and pulled her thighs farther apart.

You're supposed to be the one servicing *her,* dumbass, said part of my brain. So I put my hands where hers were and pushed her legs even farther apart. When I licked her clit again, Alexis arched her back and screamed "FUCK!" Her thighs clamped my head, her legs trembled and her whole body convulsed, and then she collapsed onto the slippery pink sheets.

I looked at her heaving breasts, the glistening skin on her wet thighs. What does she want me to do now? My brain had no help for me, so I followed my dick's advice and moved it to her pussy.

"No." She put her hand on my chest. "Not just yet. Today is *my* day to celebrate." She got off the bed and from a drawer in the long dresser took out something pink. When I saw what it was, my heart nearly stopped.

Thick pink rope. It seemed to be covered with velvet, and it felt very soft.

"Lie down on your back in the middle of the bed," Alexis said.

I hesitated for just a second. I had *heard* of bondage. Curiosity won, so I lay back. Alexis tied my hands to the rails of the headboard (so that's what they're for!) and used another rope to tie my feet to the foot board. I was spread-eagled, helpless.

"Now, this is how I like my men." She reached for the bottle and poured it slowly on my body, starting near my neck and moving slowly lower. "You had a good idea. I'm going to try it, myself."

She licked the wine off me, slurping when she reached the pool in my navel. She looked up at me and laughed before she licked the underside of my penis. She flattened her tongue and licked from top to bottom, then licked the rest of the wine off my body.

"You know, these things cause more problems …" she said, taking my penis in her hands and looking at it as if she were some kind of perverted quality control expert. "So many men use them to think instead of to fuck." She moved it back and forth, enjoying the look of hope and frustration that must have been on my face. What is she planning to do — just tease me all night? I pulled on the ropes. They stretched a little, but held my hands and feet secure.

"Oh, some wine dripped here," she said. She slurped wine off my belly, making it convulse.

Alexis then got serious, taking me deep into her mouth. One hand started tickling my stomach. I bucked against the ropes. "Don't do that!"

"Why not?" Alexis laughed. "You're not ticklish, are you?"

I looked down at her, lying on the bed between my legs. I knew I should not admit it, that she would just tickle me more, but lying there, unable to move, seeing her pink nails waving a millimetre over my stomach — I couldn't lie. "Very ticklish!" Just couldn't. "Especially there."

I knew what would happen. Alexis laughed and traced her long nails along my skin, feather-light. I laughed and squirmed but I wasn't going anywhere.

See? I was right.

Alexis kept tickling me, moving her fingers randomly, unpredictably across my torso. Her other hand tickled my side, pressing a little harder.

"No fair!" I yelled between laughs. I twisted, trying to trap her hand under my side, but that just left her other hand freer to find new sensitive spots.

When she sucked just the tip of my penis while continuing to tickle, I thought I would lose my mind. The world disappeared. I saw only gray, but felt a riot of sensations from my head to my toes: Alexis' fingers dancing all around me, the tickling sensations shooting through my body; the velvet rope pulling my hands and feet apart; strains on my elbows, shoulders, hips and ankles; and the unbelievable pleasure of Alexis' lips.

I yelled, gasped, writhed. It was too much, but I could not form words anymore.

Finally, she relented. I didn't even have time to catch my breath when I felt warmth and pressure on my face. I opened my eyes to look up at all of Alexis' naked glory.

She straddled my head and lowered her vagina to my mouth. "Eat me, Damian. Lick my pussy again." She pressed herself forward and I stuck out my tongue. I tasted her, musky and salty and sweet, and a hint of the wine. I stretched my tongue to reach her clit.

Her breath hissed through her teeth. "That's it, pool boy. That's right. Mmm." I curled my tongue and licked some more. "Ooh, what are you doing now?" I kept it up and she pushed her pelvis forward, nearly smothering me.

"Sorry," said Alexis, rising a little so I could breathe. I raised my head as much as I could and slid my tongue into her. I found the right rhythm, swiping back and forth, then up and down. Her breathing got shallower, more ragged. She moaned and shuddered. I felt her thighs twitch and buck.

I wanted to reach up and fill my hands with her breasts, squeeze them and pull on her nipples, but my hands were tied.

I arched my back, straining my hips toward her, but my feet were tied.

I looked up, straining my eyes to get a glimpse of Alexis' body, but her body pushed down on my face.

I kept licking. It was the only thing I could do. I licked, pushing with my tongue, going as fast as I could.

And then Alexis came. She screamed and her thighs squeezed my head and I kept licking. She shuddered and cried out again.

I kept licking.

She screamed once more and pulled herself off of me. I could see her face: skin flushed, eyes closed, mouth open to pull in as much air as she could. After a while, she regained control over her breathing. She opened her eyes and looked at me and smiled.

And then, she went crazy. In one smooth move, she slid down the bed, reached between her legs and guided me into her. She looked me in the eyes and thrust back, whooping like a cowgirl as she rode. Her breasts bounced. Her skin flushed, red spreading from her cheeks, down her neck and over her body.

She had amazing stamina, bouncing and riding, sliding up and down, whooping and screaming. She threw her head back and screamed especially loud. I felt her vagina clench.

Alexis' whole body shuddered. She opened her eyes and laughed, and then made the most awesome move I had ever seen a woman make. She pivoted over me, straddled me again and plunged down on me — but now, she was facing backwards, her hands on my knees.

I had a fantastic view of her beautiful round ass bouncing over my hips. God, I wanted to grab that ass.

She looked at me over her shoulder and said "Don't you dare come yet." All of her skin shone with sweat. Her hair hung in a tangled mess down her back and still she rode me.

I strained at the ropes. I could move my hands a little, but the knots were secure. I thrust my hips up against her as Alexis crashed down, making her scream louder. She shuddered and slammed herself back and down. When she came up again, I slipped out of her. She howled, a long wailing scream and spurted hot water all over me.

She had to pause then. She sat back against me, her beautiful, hot, soaking wet ass pressed onto my chest. I could only lie there, looking at her back, her sweat-soaked hair, hoping like hell that she'd take me inside her again. I needed to come, needed it like I needed water on a hot day, needed it like a starving man. All I could think of — no, *think* was too strong a word — my whole being just wanted to sink into her and explode.

Alexis caught her breath and turned around again. Once more, she guided me inside her and started riding. She didn't bounce this time: she moved her hips so that she glided smoothly. At the bottom, she ground her hips into me and made a little circular swirl. She looked me in the eyes as she rode up and down, then leaned forward and shoved her tongue into my mouth. When she came up for air, she laughed.

I erupted deep inside her as she swirled her hips against me. I pushed my pelvis up and roared, straining at those god-damned ropes. I didn't know anything then except the focus of release and pleasure, the flow of something unnameable out of me.

Gradually, I became aware of weight on my chest and an uneven noise, a wet harsh sound. It was my own breath. I opened my eyes to blurry greyness that resolved into Alexis' forehead. She was lying on me, limp and wet, her face pressed onto mine. She took a deep breath and rolled off. I don't know how long we lay there, panting. A long time passed before I could form any coherent thoughts. Eventually, Alexis rose onto one arm and looked at me. "Did you like that?"

I could only nod. I did not have control over my tongue yet.

"Hey, are you hungry? I'm famished."

I nodded and managed to croak out "Untie me."

Alexis untied the ropes. I watched her slide across the bed and step to the dresser. She took a tablet computer from a drawer and flopped back onto the mattress beside me. She propped the computer on her chest, its bottom edge pressing into her breasts.

With a few taps, she ordered up a pizza. "They say half an hour, but for me, they always bring it in 20 minutes." She tossed the computer back into the drawer and took my hand to pull me off the bed. "I can't wait that long. Bring the wine back down to the kitchen. Oh, and you'll find a robe in the closet." She stepped, graceful as a deer, naked and still glistening with sweat, into the hall.

I found a man's robe, one-size-fits-all, along with a few other pieces of clothing for men in the closet. I gathered the wine and glasses and went to the kitchen, trying not to wonder how many different men had been in that bed, in that vagina, and how often it would have to be to justify keeping spare clothes in the "play room" closet.

Alexis took things from the refrigerator. The cool air made goose pimples on her naked skin. She sliced up cheese and placed the slices onto those expensive crackers. "Pour us both some wine. Or would you prefer beer?"

"Beer, please."

"Help yourself. There's some on the left side." Two rows of assorted bottles lined the side of one shelf. I chose a Stella Artois — I had heard once that it's the most expensive beer in the world.

I asked the question I had taken time to figure out the best way to phrase: "Why do I have to wear a robe when you get to be naked?" I loved looking at her naked.

"I don't think the pizza deliverer would appreciate you answering the door in your birthday suit."

"Good point." I washed down a cheese-and-cracker combo with beer. Not just beer: Stella.

Weird, random thoughts shoot through my brain after sex. Like, maybe I should marry Alexis. I could get used to luxury.

Alexis drank wine and I watched her throat as she swallowed. She had such a sexy throat. My eyes trailed down her throat, over her chest, tickled her nipples. Such big, dark nipples. I wanted to kiss them. Again.

She caught my eye and laughed. "Did you enjoy that?"

"I came, didn't I?"

"You sure did! But did you like my little dom-sub scene?"

"Dom-sub?"

"Dominant-submissive. Being tied up, silly!"

"I'm not sure. I liked the sex. I liked how you went down on me. I loved it! And I loved going down on you, too. But being tied up, restrained ... I don't know. I wanted to touch you, too."

I watched Alexis eat another cracker, watched her tongue poke out slightly from behind her teeth for a split second. "Do you like to be tied up?" I asked.

"God, no!" She laughed. "No, I like a lot of freedom in sex. In every way."

Just hearing her say the word "sex" sent a little thrill to my crotch.

That, and looking at her standing naked in her kitchen. She sipped her wine and a drop escaped between her lip and the glass and dripped onto her chest. I watched it run down onto her breast. Did she know? Yes. She enjoyed watching me watch wine drip onto her breast.

The doorbell rang. "That'll be the pizza."

"I don't have any money with me." I felt embarrassed for the first time that night, as if not having any money made me less of a man than being tied by a woman did.

"All taken care of when I ordered online."

The pizza guy was older than I expected, older than me, and he looked like he was used to this door being opened by a man in a robe. He even winked at me.

Alexis set up little tables in her TV room, and we watched some silly old comedy while we ate pizza, naked. But we lost interest in the movie quickly.

"You sent me a text that you wanted to look at the PoolGeeks books," I said.

"Yes, but after the meeting I had this morning, I was in no mood for bookkeeping."

"What happened?"

Alexis finished her pizza and leaned back on the sofa. She licked grease off her fingers and drank more wine. "You saw the article in the ROB? The merger — the takeover, actually — closed yesterday after regulatory approval. Today was the first board meeting with the new people in charge."

"You?"

"As CEO and COO. The old Blaine board didn't like it, and they're too stupid to know when they're beat."

"So, you're going to run the whole thing?"

"It's time that someone did something with that company. Billions of dollars collecting a miserable little return. Enough to justify the boards' stipends and management bonuses. No imagination. No balls." She sat up, back erect, eyes on fire. "Even in this day and age, there are still men on Bay Street who refuse to take a woman seriously in the boardroom!"

"That's hard to believe. There are lots of women executives," I tried.

"Not that many. It's a tough road for us girls. Old, obsolete attitudes are hard to overcome. And stupid comments don't help!"

"What kind of stupid comments?" I was getting angry, too, as if anger were contagious. Maybe it is.

"Oh, you know. One asshole had the temerity to suggest that the company would suffer when its CEO and COO took maternity leave! And to top it off, he actually told me, to my face, that my 'biological clock is ticking,' and it's only a matter of a couple of years before I'm pregnant!"

I didn't know how to respond to that, but my brain didn't keep my mouth from opening. "Um, well, do you plan on having children? Most women do." I was sounding apologetic for both me and the unnamed asshole from the boardroom.

"That's not the issue! Not today, not ever! The issue today is that the old board was doing nothing but sucking what they could from the company, and they resent when anyone else, particularly a *woman,* shows the whole fucking world what incompetent assholes they are!" she shouted. "If and when I have a baby, it's not going to hurt the company I've worked this hard to take over!"

"I'm sure of that," I said. She was leaning toward me, hair wild around her head, eyes bright. Her mouth was open and she was even panting a little. "I take you seriously, Alexis."

"You fucking better!" She launched herself at me, pushing her tongue into my mouth and raking her nails over my shoulders. Her thighs straddled me and only when she engulfed me did I realize I was hard.

She rode me again, sliding up and down, fast and hard. Her hard nipples poked my chest and she alternated between kissing and biting my throat, and tossing her head back in ecstasy.

This time, my hands were free. Free to squeeze those beautiful breasts, to rub those big, sensitive nipples. I kissed and sucked her neck, too, and wrestled her tongue with my own. Finally, I grabbed her ass and lifted her up. I took control, sliding her up and down. My orgasm surprised me, and her too: a stream of energy shot from the base of my spine straight out my penis. I rammed my hips up and slammed her down onto me. Alexis' eyes and mouth opened wide. She wailed and gushed over me again. I pulled her close and kissed her as hard as I could. Our mouths slid over each other, but I pushed my tongue into hers, taking her hard and deep, spasming into her, feeling her body quake in my arms.

We held each other like that for a long time. I think I even fell asleep for a while. I came to when Alexis rolled off me.

"Oh, I did *not* see that coming." She laughed at the pun. "Well, I was going to toss you out tonight, but I want more of *that* in the morning. So you can stay in the guest bedroom."

That gave me way more to think about than I could handle in my state. "Okay. You mean where we were?"

Alexis laughed. "No, that's the Play Room! That's reserved for special games. Do you really think you could sleep on those wet sheets? Don't worry, Van will wash them in the morning. No, tonight you can sleep in the Blue Bedroom."

"How many bedrooms does this house have?"

"Seven. Oh, now I'm hungry again. I think there's some chocolate cake in the fridge. Want some?"

I watched her ass jiggle with every step she took to the kitchen. My mouth watered when she bent into the fridge, but I was so tired, I just plopped my bare ass onto the high chair.

Alexis took out a cake obviously from a Rosedale bakery. She cut two big slices and pushed one to me.

"Why can't I sleep with you?" I asked with my mouth full of cake. Was it ever good!

I enjoyed watching her throat as Alexis swallowed a bite. "Because I like to sleep alone when I sleep. Really sleep. I've had a tough work day today, and tomorrow looks tougher, so I'll need my sleep. And knowing a man like you is next to me ... neither of us would sleep.

"But be ready to get up early. I'll want a sexual workout in the morning. I'm firing the rest of the Blaine board." She finished her cake and put the dishes in the dishwasher. "I'm going to have a shower and then to bed. If you're still hungry, help yourself to anything you like. More cake, more beer if you want. There's some ice cream, too."

I watched her ass jiggle again as she went up the stairs. I thought about fucking, but my penis stayed limp.

Exhausted.

I decided against beer or ice cream. I cleared up Alexis' kitchen. I heard the shower, and started poking around. A picture on the wall: a younger Alexis with a man who looked in his forties. The late Mr. Rosse? A relative? No, it must have been her husband. He had that look of old money.

The shower stopped. I went upstairs and found the "Blue Bedroom": simple, tasteful and expensive furniture. Blue walls, blue bedclothes, blue curtains.

I collapsed onto the bed and fell asleep immediately.

Chapter 12

Hell and Heaven and Hell Again

A woman, an angel, a demon runs its hands down my naked skin. I'm cold; a chill wind rakes my naked skin.

The demon laughs. I can't make it out clearly. Everything is foggy. Its claws reach for my helpless genitals.

I cannot move. I cannot cry out. I struggle, I push against invisible bonds across my chest.

No, it's my hands. My hands are tied up, over my head. No, wait, they're here by my side, but they're still tied to the bed and I cannot move them.

My legs are tied, too. I'm spread-eagled, lying on ... what am I lying on?

I have no strength. The demon's claw closes around my testicles, squeezing them ... gently? My penis stiffens.

It's a dream, my brain tells me.

A dream?

The demon rubs my testicles again, lifting them up like it's weighing them. It laughs, deeply, horribly, musically.

I strain against the invisible bonds. They evaporate. The grey mist clears, replaced by blue.

The blue blur resolved into sheets and Alexis' face. As usual, she was nude, pressing her naked skin against mine. One hand held my balls.

"Boy, you sleep hard," she said, and kissed me on the cheek.

Her hands stroked me, so softly.

I lifted my free hands. They're not tied, I realized.

That was last night, dumbass, said my brain.

My arms wrapped around Alexis and I rolled on top of her. I inhaled her nipple into my mouth. Her thighs moved up alongside mine and over my hips, and her feet wrapped behind my calves. My penis slipped inside her. "Oohh, yes, Damian. That's what I need this morning."

I clenched her body to mine. I realized for the first time just how much smaller she was than me. I pressed my hips forward, trying to push deeper into her.

Alexis bit my shoulder lightly and moaned. I picked up the pace, swivelling my hips so that my entire length slid out, then in.

Her thighs slid higher up along mine and I felt myself get even closer, even deeper. I lifted my head so I could watch her face as she climaxed.

If anything, she looked even more beautiful first thing in the morning, with her eyes shut and her mouth open, head writhing side to side as well as up and down from the motion of our hips.

She shrieked and I felt her contract around me. It was no use trying to hold back my orgasm. Instead, I kept pumping as I spurted, making Alexis wetter and slipperier with every thrust. Alexis arched her back and screamed again.

Am I still dreaming? I wondered. I shuddered one last time, and then could not move my hips any more.

Alexis' smile was dreamy. "Yes, exactly the pick-me-up I need." She got out of bed, chipper and bright and beautifully naked. "Go make coffee while I have another shower. You do know how to make coffee?"

"Sure."

"Good. Just regular coffee today, not espresso. The percolator's above the stove and the coffee is in the tin beside it." She just about skipped out of the guest room.

I heard the shower again as I spooned coffee into the percolator. It was the same one my parents had at home, the kind that bubbled water up a tube in the middle of the pot so it would splash through the coffee grounds in a basket at the top. "The only way to make real coffee," my Dad would always say.

By the time Alexis came downstairs in a blue suit, the last few drops of coffee splashed into the bottom of the pot. "Perfect timing," she said, fastening a big hoop earring. She flounced her hair and filled a travel mug. "Have a croissant," she said, pulling a bag of them out of a breadbox on the counter. "Then put on some clothes. You have pools to clean. Don't be late for your customers!"

She looped a briefcase over one shoulder, put her other arm through the strap of a purse, grabbed her coffee and croissant and was gone. From the garage door, I heard her call "Don't forget to pull the doors shut! They'll lock automatically, and the security system is set to go on after you leave, so don't forget anything."

And she left me, standing naked in her kitchen with half a croissant in my mouth.

The air conditioning came on. I shivered.

I looked at the clock on the stove: no time for a shower. What the hell: I'll be working outside, and it's already bloody hot. I'll be sweaty in no time. I told myself I could always take a dip in one of the pools, as long as the owner wasn't home.

I retrieved my clothes from the Play Room, picked up my bookkeeping stuff from the study, found another travel mug in a cupboard and filled it with coffee, and took another croissant. I piled all that stuff by the front door, then went back to make sure I had everything and turn off the percolator. Out the door, into my crappy Swift, and I was at my first client only 10 minutes late.

"Money is both simple and complex," Alexis said at the end of the day in her study. "The simple part is that, to be successful, you have to take in more than you're spending. I'm happy to see that PoolGeeks is starting to do that."

"What's the complex part?" I asked. No matter how hard I hoped, her clothes stubbornly stayed on her body.

Her text message today had said the same as yesterday: *Time to do the books, 5:00 pm.* But today refused to turn into a replay of yesterday. I shifted in my seat so that my penis didn't press so much against my shorts and tried to concentrate on money.

"The complex part is what I do. It takes a lot of education and experience, but basically, you can invest money into complex financial instruments and multiply it."

"You can multiply money?"

"*I* can. It's a talent I discovered I had in university. Of course, back then it was all theoretical. But since then, I've found how to make my theories work in reality."

"Is that how you make money?"

She smiled at me. "Complex financial instruments give me control of larger sums of capital, which in turn give me control of some companies — like my late husband's Red Capital."

"Why is it called 'Red Capital'?"

"Rosse means red. I thought everyone knew that."

"Oh, right. I knew that," my mouth managed to say. "So, you like manipulating money?"

"I have a talent for it. An ability to see opportunities that most others miss. What I like, though, is what it gives me: control over companies, leverage. That in turn leads to more money, more control. And that gives me the freedom I need to live my own life.

"But right now, Damian, we need to concentrate on the books in front of us."

And that's what we did. Alexis checked my entries in the ledger and had me copy them into another ledger in separate categories: payments, expenses, fixed costs, drawings.

"Growth is very good, Damian. Congratulations."

"Thanks. Most of it due to you."

"I recommended you to a few friends —"

"Rich and influential friends."

"Yes, but all that did was get you in the door. You did all the rest. You've gained a substantial number of clients."

"Thirty, already."

"Not all of them are my friends and neighbours. Some are referrals from my referrals."

"The online ads have brought a couple, too."

"Good. So there is something to free advertising. But word of mouth is the best promotion."

"To tell you the truth, Alexis, I don't think that I can handle many more clients. I'm working 10 to 12 hours a day as it is."

"Then, you need to hire some help."

Alexis' words sparked a burgeoning pride and a mind-freezing fear at the same time. Me? A boss? An employer? I remembered my father's words about having employees: "It's nearly impossible to find someone you can trust." And "Making the payroll is a huge responsibility. Week in and week out. It doesn't matter how good sales are, or whether your customers are paying you. When you have employees, they're depending on you to pay them on time."

Could I make payroll?

"Do you think I could really handle an employee?" I asked Alexis.

"The important thing is to hire the *right* employee. It's probably the most important thing in any business, and the most difficult. Make it easier on yourself by starting with a part-timer. Pay them as an hourly contractor, not an employee. No benefits, no tax or EI deductions."

"Yah, that sounds good."

"Do you know any good workers among your friends?"

I thought of Patrick. He had always been reliable and smart at school. But he already had a job — he'd been working at the same place for three summers in a row, as well as for a few hours per week during the school months. There was no way that PoolGeeks could compete with that.

And Tyler? Big, joking, bullying Tyler? Tyler was not what anyone would ever call "reliable."

"I'll think about it. Maybe I could put a Help Wanted ad on Craigslist?"

"Do you want to spend days going through crap resumés from every goofball in the city? No, use word of mouth. Ask around. You'll get a friend of a friend. It's much better to talk to potential employees face-to-face first.

"And you need a better computer program for tracking expenses and income. Once you start growing like this, you'll never manage to keep up with little envelopes for receipts and a ledger book." She jotted down some recommendations on a notepad, tore off the paper and handed it to me. Even her fingertips were sexy.

"You good to go?" She was looking at me, her eyes wide and innocent, her lips parted as if she were about to ask me something.

"Well …" How to say this? She'd always initiated everything till now.

Just ask, dumbass, my brain said.

I walked around the desk, trying to look manly and commanding. I touched her face, grateful that my hand was not shaking. She just looked up at me with those big brown eyes. "Want to fool around?" Was that the right way to say it? Did people still say "fool around"?

Alexis tilted her head and smiled a little. "Hmm. Well, it will have to be a quickie. I have a charity event this evening."

My heart stopped beating for ... well, how can you tell the passage of time when your heart's not beating?

Alexis kicked off her shoes and placed her little jacket carefully on the back of her chair. She wiggled her hips to slide her matching skirt off, leaving her in lacy black underwear. She folded her blue blouse and put it carefully on top of her skirt on the chair and went to the sofa.

She wasn't wearing a bra, and her breasts looked at me as she said "When I said 'quickie,' I meant you can't stand there, wasting time. Get your clothes off!"

I tore my t-shirt as I pulled it over my head. Too bad — I had gotten it at a concert the previous fall. Alexis slid her panties off gracefully and sat on the sofa.

I pounced on her boobs. She laughed as her hand wrapped around my hard penis. With her other hand, she lifted my face to hers and kissed me.

She pushed me onto the sofa and sat straddling me. Then she pushed herself onto me. I couldn't believe how wet she was already. Did she get this aroused, this quickly? Or had she been sitting there, horny, all this time? Did looking at accounting ledgers and talking about money turn her on? Or was it talking about herself, her talent for managing money that made her so hot and wet?

I could not ask her any questions because she was sucking on my lips and tongue. Her scent, not perfume but the intoxicating smell of Alexis' body and the taste of her tongue invaded my mind. Her hands roved over my shoulders and the back of my head. The wet sounds of sex filled the room.

I pushed my hips up. Alexis' movements got faster, urgent, her breathing ragged. She bit my neck, wrapped her arms around me and clasped me tight as she rammed her pelvis forward. I felt her vagina pulse, felt her fluids flow down my thighs.

I would never get used to that. My own orgasm shot out of me, surprising us both. Alexis' eyes opened wide and she gasped as I thrust up. My shoulders shook.

Alexis closed her eyes and moaned as my dick slid out of her — wet, sticky and cooling fast. "Ooh, that felt good." She smiled and kissed my cheek. "Very nice, Damian. Now, I have to get ready for my charity event. And you have some work to do, too: you have to catch up on your book-keeping and get a good accounting package for your computer."

Naked, she walked to the hallway. "Get dressed. You can take another t-shirt from the guest room."

On the drive home, I promised myself that I would figure out whether it was money or me that turned Alexis on.

I heard a knock on the door as I was taking my third beer from the fridge. I opened the door to see Kristen and popped the cap off.

"How many is that?" were the first words out of her mouth.

"First one tonight." I took a big swig so that she wouldn't smell beer on my breath and know I was a liar.

"Liar," she said. "Honestly, I don't know why you guys drink that stuff. Do you have any milk?"

I opened the fridge. "Sorry, right out. I have some Red Bull."

"Ugh! Even worse than beer! Give me a water. Not from the tap!"

"Sorry, I only drink water from the tap. And beer, when I can."

She scowled. "Tap water will have to do."

"So, what brings you over tonight?" I asked as I handed her my cleanest, least-chipped glass.

She looked at it suspiciously before taking a tiny sip. "I just wanted to see you. It's been a long time since we spent any time together."

"We hung out on Friday night."

"That doesn't count. We hang out every Friday. But we used to spend a lot more time together. Doing homework, reading, walking ..."

"Well, you know I've been busy with this pool-cleaning business."

We sat down on the couch and I clicked the TV on.

"Damian, what happened to your neck?"

I touched my neck. "What's wrong?"

"There's a mark on it!"

I flinched when she touched the side of my throat: there was a tender spot there. I went to the bathroom and looked in the mirror: yes, a definite hickey.

"Oh, that," I said. Think fast, said my brain.

That's what you're for, brain.

"I, uh, I had a very slight accident today."

"Cleaning pools," asked Kristen, standing in the bathroom doorway. She did not look convinced.

"Yah. You know, I was leaning way over the edge of the pool with the long-handled net, the sweeper. You know?"

"I know," said Kristen. She crossed her arms. That's never a good sign.

"Well, I reached too far and overbalanced. I tried to stop from falling into the pool by jamming the pole to the bottom, and I fell on it. On my neck. The end of the pole hit my neck. It just hurt a little. I forgot about it until you mentioned it, just now." Did that sound lame, or what?

Kristen looked at me for a few seconds. She shouldn't have believed me. Anyone could see that it was a hickey. The only thing that made sense for Kristen to say was, "Who's been sucking on your neck?"

Her face softened. She opened her arms and reached for me. "My poor baby," she said. She brushed her lips over the hickey. "You've always been clumsy, Damian. What would you do without me to take care of you?"

I kissed her, softly, just on the lips, the way she liked. My dick tingled, but I knew she would not like me to bring that up.

It's time to push this relationship somewhere, something in me said. Not my brain. I led Kristen back to the living room. "Sure you don't want a beer?"

"No! And I think you've had enough, too."

I sat beside her on the couch. "I've missed you," I lied.

"Well, you've been ignoring me."

"I've been working hard." That was true. "At least 10 hours a day." I did not tell her about the time for sex with Alexis.

I couldn't help but smile at that thought: it sounded like a TV show. "Time for Sex with Alexis."

"What's so funny?" Kristen asked.

"I'm just happy to be with you," I said.

"Liar." But she let me put my arms around her and kiss her.

I held the kiss for a long time. Take it slow, said something in my head. Okay, maybe that *was* my brain. So I kissed Kristen's lips and stroked her hair until I felt her body relax in my arms.

I kidded myself that I knew what I was doing. I pulled her closer, molding her body against mine. I kissed her some more, then turned the kisses into little nips on her lips. I moved to her chin and kissed along her jaw.

She didn't seem to mind. I kissed up her jaw and breathed softly into her ear. One hand roved lower on her back.

I kissed her throat, just below her jaw. Her warm skin gave under my lips. "Mmm," she moaned, so softly I wondered if I had imagined it.

I kissed lower along her neck and felt her skin get warmer. I stroked her hair and kissed her neck repeatedly. I opened my mouth wide and dragged my lips closer, pulling just a tiny bit of skin between them, but not hard enough to leave a mark like Alexis had on me.

Alexis had marked me, I realized. She had claimed me.

Take it slow, my brain reminded me. I went back up to kissing Kristen's mouth. She parted her lips a tiny bit. I gently sucked the lower one between my lips and felt her sigh.

I licked across her lips; I didn't push my tongue into her mouth like I wanted to, but just gave her the slightest touch. The dampness on her lip excited me.

Kristen sighed again, and I kissed her a little harder. My hand moved from her back to her side and I leaned forward, pressing her against the sofa.

Her breathing quickened. Yes, I thought (I did, not my brain). She's responding to this. My hand roved to her leg. My fingertips traced random patterns on her skin. I sucked her lip into my mouth a little harder this time, then trailed kisses under her chin, down her throat.

I went back up to her mouth. I repeated that pattern twice more: sucking on the lip, kissing down her neck, tickling the bare skin on her thigh.

She was breathing hard, moaning quietly. We must have been making out for half an hour. Now, I thought. Now, she's ready.

My lips attacked hers. I pressed down, moaning. My tongue crept forward, touched her lips, started to slide inside.

My fingers moved upward. They found the hem of her t-shirt. They slid higher. I touched the skin on her side. Kristen squirmed a little. I gave her a little more tongue, just touching hers. She moaned a little louder.

I pushed my tongue into her mouth, and she responded with her own. Yes! She had never been willing to tongue-wrestle before.

I pushed her over further until I was almost lying on top of her while sliding my fingers up her belly. I touched her bra …

Kristen shoved me away. "Stop it!"

Her face clenched, eyes flashing. She actually bared her teeth like a dog.

"Why? Why stop, baby?" I said in my softest, smoothest voice. "Don't you feel good?"

"Don't you dare!" She pulled away and sat up on the sofa. She looked at my crotch, where my erection strained against my shorts. "You have only one thing on your mind, don't you?"

"What else is important?" I tried to smile.

My dick started an argument with my brain.

Dick: Rip her clothes off and fuck her! She'll love it!

Brain: Throw her out and go see Alexis!

Dick: Kristen's right here, right now! Take her!

Brain: She's got thighs like a steel trap — you'll never get them apart without a diamond.

Dick: She's hot! Angry can turn into horny in a second! You want it, she wants it! Fuck her!

Brain: She'll tell her father you raped her. Even if she does enjoy it. And you know she'll never admit that she enjoyed it, least of all to herself.

Dick: Just fuck her! Just fuck her! Just fuck her!

Brain: Damian, really, don't listen to Dick. Think this through.
I listened to Dick.

"Kristen, we're in love. Why can't we make love?" That
sounded reasonable.

Not to Kristen. "No sex until we're married! How many times
do I have to say it?"

At that, Dick went over to Brain's side.

"Well, Kristen, I'm not going to wait until I'm married to you
to have sex." I stood up, guzzled the rest of my third beer and
went for another one.

Kristen followed me to the kitchen. "What are you saying?"

"I'm not waiting for some celibate priest to tell me I'm
allowed to have sex! If you don't want to make love to me, your
boyfriend for — Christ, we've been together almost our whole
lives, Kristen — if you can't fuck me after we've been making out
for six fucking years, then I'm saying, I've had enough!"

She just looked at me, mouth hanging open. We stared at each
other for a long moment.

Then Dick spoke up again. I grabbed her, pulled her close and
smashed my mouth against hers. I pushed my tongue inside her
mouth and pulled her t-shirt up. She froze, tense, long enough for
me to get my hands under her bra-strap. Then she squirmed away
from me and slapped my face with the full force of her arm.

"You pervert! I know that's a hickey on your neck, and I
didn't give it to you! If you want to screw your floozy, you go right
ahead! I never want to see you again!" She pulled her t-shirt
down, picked up her old-lady purse and slammed the door on her
way out.

Good, said Dick and Brain together. It's over. You're free.
I drove to Alexis' place.

Chapter 13

Testing the Theory

"Tonight, I'm picking the restaurant," said the attenuated version of Alexis' voice in my crappy phone.

"Okay, then you're paying this time." Did that come across as funny and brash, or snarky and cheap?

"At least I have enough money to leave a tip." She hung up.

I decided tonight would be a good opportunity to figure out whether it was talking about money or herself that made Alexis horny. My brain agreed.

Alexis took us in her Jaguar to a small place in a decidedly unfashionable part of the city. My parents would wonder why anyone would go there.

"The food here is unbelievably good," she said as I slid into the booth beside her. "Very genuine, regional cuisine, but at the same time, they're starting to incorporate North American styles, too. The chef is very talented."

I slid over until I was close enough to Alexis that we could share the same menu. Alexis ordered a bottle of wine that sounded expensive. She sipped it and declared it acceptable. We toasted and ordered our food.

I began the experiment. Procedure, step one: Alexis, herself.

"So, you studied finance in university? Why — I mean, what made you decide to go into that field?"

"Money is important. I've always found it interesting."

"You're fascinated by money?"

"No, not fascinated. But interested enough to learn how it works, how it behaves, how it affects people in different ways."

"Doesn't it affect everyone the same way? Everyone wants more money."

"No, not at all. Money motivates some people more than others. *You* are motivated partly by money, and also by the need to please your parents. That's why you haven't told them about me."

"I've told them about you!"

"You've told them that your first client, a widow, is helping you with your bookkeeping and marketing, in return for pool cleaning services. You haven't told them you're fucking me."

"I haven't told them I'm fucking anyone!"

"That's because you aren't fucking anyone else."

Bring the conversation back to the experiment, dumbass, my brain warned. "I told them you're a financial expert, one of the best in the city."

"*The* best in the city. This city, anyway."

I toasted her on that. "Okay, the best. That really impressed them. But I want to know what makes you so good at it."

"I had some insights into the way money works. The way that a person with the right knowledge and the right connections can make it grow, multiply; conversely, a person without that knowledge or those connections, or who makes the wrong decisions, can destroy wealth — make money disappear."

"Like in the '08 financial crisis."

"Yes, exactly. People with poor or no information made bad decisions, inflated the prices of a lot of bad financial instruments well beyond their intrinsic value, and then made more poor decisions when the whole mess started to fall apart."

Bring it back to her, said my brain. "When did you have those insights? Into how to make money grow or disappear?"

"In my third year of university. I had a sort of a breakthrough when studying derivatives. I explored it in my fourth-year project, and wrote a paper about it in graduate school."

"Really? Was that your master's thesis?"

"No. It was a first-year master's paper. I wanted to develop it into a thesis paper for my master's degree, but my advisor would not let me."

"Why not?"

"The idea was too new. Too contrary to the accepted

wisdom." Her lips thinned. She took a big swig of her wine. That thesis advisor still bothered her.

"A lot of people don't like new ideas," I ventured.

"That's for sure!" She drank more wine and tore apart a piece of bread. I copied her, breaking my little loaf into pieces and dipping them into a little puddle of olive oil mixed with vinegar that looked black in the restaurant's dim light.

Time to move decisively into Phase Two: money. "What was your idea?" I asked.

"It was very technical. You need a lot of background in financial instruments to understand it."

"Give me the high-level view."

She gave me her indulgent smile. "It was an analysis to quantify risk parameters across groups of portfolios in an enterprise, and showed an exponential effect in cumulative derivatives."

"Wow! Sounds fascinating!" my mouth said for me while my brain looked for something I could understand.

Alexis smiled again. "Essentially, I showed that, when derivatives became further removed from actual wealth creation, risk rises exponentially. Also, agglomerations of derivatives were inherently and exponentially more risky. The more you invested in collections of financial derivatives, the faster and higher your risk increased, approaching infinity much sooner than the prevailing wisdom of the day predicted."

I impressed myself by saying "Wasn't that exactly what the banks did in 2008? Invested in agglomerations of risky derivatives?"

Apparently, I also impressed Alexis. "Exactly. The brokers selling the asset-backed paper and certificates based on asset-based paper, and derivatives and agglomerations of that, said that every step, every derivation or accumulation diffused risk. They were wrong, and the multiple-trillion-dollar loss that summer proved that. Fuckers should all have jumped out of windows, but the governments bailed them all out. That means taxpayers — people like you and me."

Bring the focus back to Alexis. "And you predicted that?"

"Years ahead." She smiled. "But this must be above your

head."

"Not really," I lied. "I have to learn about finance, after all. I am in business school."

"Ah yes, my alma mater. But that's the problem: they're still stuck in outmoded thinking."

"They don't accept your theory?"

"They won't agree with the arithmetic they invented," Alexis snorted. The waiter brought our dinner. "Fifteen years ago, Ellen Fromme—"

"Professor Fromme? I'll have her this fall! I mean, I'll be taking a course from her."

Alexis smiled at my inadvertent innuendo. "Well, watch out. She shook up the financial academy when she was in graduate school with some very innovative thinking, but she sure doesn't seem to want to hear new ideas, these days."

"Was she your thesis advisor?"

"Back in the day."

"Strange that a woman wouldn't support another woman's new ideas."

Alexis took a dainty bite of her pasta and shrugged. "It's not about being a man or a woman. It's about which side she thinks her bread is buttered on. Now, she sees a better chance for advancement in the university ranks by supporting the accepted thinking, not by shaking it up."

I poured the rest of the bottle of wine into her glass, and topped up my own. I was determined not to drink too much; I had to remain in control of this experiment. "So it's politics, not economics?"

"Yes. Very astute, Damian." She raised her hand, and when the waiter came closer, said "Another bottle, please."

"So, how did you arrive at your conclusion? About the derivative risk, I mean."

Alexis was rolling. She told me about anomalies she had noted, failures and write-downs written up in academic papers about high finance. "These economists and analysts would hold out this data they said supported their theories. The thing I noticed is how often the data pointed in the opposite direction. But no one else would see it."

"Sounds like a case of the emperor's new clothes," I said around a mouthful of noodles.

"Yes! That's it exactly!" She launched into a detailed description of a mathematical model famous among economists. She found holes in it. I lost the thread almost immediately, and concentrated on her mouth: the way a dim sheen from the candlelight moved across her lips as she spoke and ate, the way her throat moved when she swallowed her wine or her food, the rise and fall of the upper curve of her breasts above her pale blue summer dress as she breathed and spoke.

"You were the only person to notice this?" I asked.

"I showed my roommate; she didn't believe me at first — she was as hoodwinked by the conventional thinking as everyone else. Eventually, I could show her the huge gaps in the theory. But she couldn't follow my reasoning to the wall."

"The wall?"

"The point in extending derivation to where risk begins to rise exponentially!" Her face was flushed.

"I guess your roommate just wasn't as smart as you," I said. I pushed my plate away.

"Fuckin' right, she's not." Alexis drained her wine and I refilled her glass. I moved closer to her as I did so that my clothed leg was pressed against her bare one.

What happened to her roommate, I wondered. Never mind: focus on Alexis.

"Don't be so hard on her, Alexis," I said, tilting my head very close to hers. "You must be the smartest person I have ever met. Including everyone at university. All my professors." I touched the tip of her nose with one finger, and put my right hand on her thigh.

"Flattery will get you everywhere," she smiled. I kissed her lips and put her glass into her hand again. My right hand moved down her leg until I hooked the tips of two fingers under the hem of her silk dress.

"So, you couldn't use your theory in your master's thesis. What did you write about?"

Alexis drank half the glass of wine in one shot. "A new accelerated calculation tool for swap aggregation," she answered, rolling her eyes. I had no idea what that meant.

"And what about your original thesis? Your idea? Were you ever able to use it?"

She smiled, narrowing her eyes. She leaned so close her lips were almost touching mine. I looked into her dark eyes, wondering about the flecks of gold, yellow and brown radiating from the pupil. "Every day, once I got out of school. I used it at Red Capital and earned half a billion dollars for the fund in my first quarter." I could taste her breath on my tongue.

"What about the financial crisis?"

"Hah! Saw that coming, dodged it completely!"

Now. I slid my hand up the inside of her thigh, pushing her dress up under the table. Her eyes widened and she gasped, but not before my fingers touched her lacy panties. "Damian, beha—" she began.

My fingers slipped under the lace. My theory was right: her pussy was wet. Soaking wet. And hot. She made a little cry.

I pushed the tip of my finger between her pussy lips and rubbed her clit. She moaned and bit her lip. "Damian," she whispered.

"Everything all right, Mrs. Rosse?" the waiter asked. I jumped, but managed to keep my fingers on Alexis' clit.

"Yes, yes, everything is fine," Alexis stammered.

"I thought I heard you cry out," the waiter said.

"A little wine went down the wrong way, that's all."

I kept swirling in little circles.

"Would you like some coffee?" the waiter asked as he picked up our plates.

"Yes, please," I said. Idiot! said my brain. That will just bring him back!

He'll come back with the bill, anyway, I told my brain. Now concentrate on the experiment.

Once the waiter walked away, Alexis let out a long, ragged breath. She closed her eyes and bit her lip again as I kept swirling my finger. After a minute, she whispered "What do you think you're doing, young man?"

I leaned into her, brought my lips to her ear. "Making you come," I whispered.

I kissed her ear, ran my tongue down the outer edge, kissed her neck. I had to push her hair out of the way with my nose, and I smelled her arousal.

She tried not to show how hard she was breathing. I bit her neck lightly while pushing my fingers lower and deeper. Alexis ground her teeth together. But she parted her thighs more.

I saw the waiter coming closer with coffee, so I slid my fingers out of Alexis, leaving my middle finger grazing her clit. She held her breath, smiling strangely at the waiter as he placed two cups and two dessert menus on the table. Neither of us heard him recite the dessert specials.

"Give us a minute to think about it," I said. He smiled and left us, and Alexis let out another long, ragged breath as I slipped my fingers into her again. Then I tasted my fingers. Alexis's eyes widened as she saw my middle finger pop into my mouth, so I wiped my finger on her lip.

She closed her eyes and whispered a moan. I returned to rubbing her clit.

I slipped my fingers up and down until her legs began to shake. She closed her eyes and arched her back against the booth.

But just as I could see she was about to come, the fucking waiter was back. "Any decisions on dessert?"

"No thanks, we're not hungry," I snarled.

Alexis shot me a look. "No, thank you, Gerald," she said sweetly. How could she do that when I just slid two fingers up her? I wondered. I flexed my fingertips, searching for her G-spot. She still managed to say "Just bring the cheque, please" sweetly.

When he was gone, I doubled my effort in her pussy, flexing my finger rapidly. I tried to bring my thumb to her clit, but that was a very difficult position when we were trying not to make it look like we were doing anything but sitting close together.

Alexis gasped. Her thigh twitched. I slid my fingers inside her again, then wiped upward over her clitoris. She bit her lip and clenched her eyes shut. Her hand gripped my thigh, squeezing hard.

Alexis squeezed my leg harder. Her leg trembled. She tried not to let anyone else in the restaurant see that she was panting. Then she bucked and spasmed against me. She grabbed me around the neck and kissed me, hard, mouth wide open like she wanted to swallow me whole. Her body shook once and then she pulled away from me, sliding back in the booth. Her head slumped forward.

I lifted her chin and smiled into her eyes.

"You're very bad," she said.

"Sorry."

The waiter coughed and put the little plastic tray on the table. I smiled at him.

I felt happy. My experiment was a success.

Alexis reached for her purse and put a credit card on the tray. "When we leave, walk very close behind me."

I liked the sound of that. "Why?" I hoped it was so that I could rub my hard dick against her ass.

Nope. "Because you made me get my dress soaking wet! It's silk, and it's ruined. I should make you buy me a new one."

"We both know that would be everything I've earned all summer," I laughed.

The waiter brought the mobile payment machine. Alexis stabbed buttons like she was mad at it, and when the waiter left us for the last time, she said, "Hurry, take me home and fuck me hard."

Chapter 14

Human Resources

Tyler slumped in his chair, thumbing his iPhone. He hadn't even touched his beer.

I sat beside him. "What's wrong?"

"Tyler lost his job," Patrick said, mouth full of chicken wings. The waitress brought him another mug of beer.

I ordered one for myself. "Which job was that?"

"At the grocery store," Patrick said. He chugged half the beer and slammed the mug down. Drops splashed my arm.

"What happened?"

"I was late," Tyler mumbled.

"They fired you for being late?"

"Every day for two weeks," he said. It was as if his eyes were glued to that damned iPhone.

"Two weeks! Why were you late so often?"

Tyler shrugged. I looked at Patrick, but he had no better answer.

"So, what are you going to do?" I asked.

"That was the third job he's lost so far this year," Patrick said.

"Shut up," said Tyler, looking up from his phone at last.

"Well, it's true," said Patrick. He sucked the meat off another chicken wing and tossed the bone into the basket. It bounced out and fell onto the floor.

"I fuckin' needed that job," Tyler said. "I need to make some money this summer!"

You should talk to Alexis about this first, my brain said, but it was too late, because my mouth blurted, "You want to come work for me?"

Tyler stared at me. Different expressions seemed to be fighting for control of his face. I could see surprise, disbelief … maybe hope? "Work for you?" he said.

"Yah, you know, cleaning pools." The waitress slammed down my beer. I took a drink.

"Oh, man, no, you need the work more than I do …"

"No, man, for real. I need some help — I have more customers than I can handle by myself. I can pay you …" Shut up now! my brain screamed silently. He's a terrible employee! Alexis will be pissed! "… eleven bucks an hour. It's not huge, but …"

You asshole. You're trying to make a profit on this? You can afford thirteen, said another part of my brain.

No, you can't! You cannot afford this guy at all, said the smart side of my brain — the part I never listened to.

"For real?" Tyler asked, and hope was winning on his face.

"For real." Idiot! You had an out there! "I have the equipment you need. I have the addresses. All you have to do is go over to the house, clean the pool, leave a card to tell the customer you've been there — they're usually not home when I go — and go to the next appointment."

"When can I start?"

This is your chance to back out of this! Put him off a couple of weeks! Tell him you've got to line up some clients, first, and then find some other excuse!

"How about Monday?"

Tyler just looked at me with wide eyes and an open mouth. "Monday? So, what, I come by your place?"

"Yah. Eight o'clock."

Is that look respect? Does Tyler respect me?

I felt something different then: a slight tension across my forehead. It felt like the times when I was a little kid, trying to act grown-up — like when my mother put a little suit on me and I determined to look serious and comforting at my grandfather's funeral.

Respectable.

"One thing, Tyler," I said, giving in to the smart part of my brain at last. "Don't be late. Right?"

"Oh! Okay. No sweat. Don't worry, man. And thanks!" Tyler chugged his beer and laughed.

Alexis was pissed.

"You should have talked to me about this first," she said the next day. "We're supposed to be partners, remember?"

I had gone to her house after cleaning my last pool of the day. She had PoolGeeks' account books spread out on her cubical desk and the spreadsheet open on her gigantic monitor.

I was disappointed to find her dressed in tan slacks and matching jacket over a white blouse. She wore big bangly gold earrings and three fine gold chains around her neck.

"I've known Tyler all my life," I said. "He's a good guy."

"And yet, he was fired for being late? How reliable is he going to be for you? You can't afford to disappoint customers, Damian."

"He's a hard worker."

"When he shows up."

"I trust him."

She looked at me, pursing her plump lips a little. "Well, I hope he works out. If he is not reliable, it can really hurt you. Do you think you'll be able to fire him?"

The word "fire" went through me like a knife. "If I have to, sure," I lied.

You really did it, said the smart part of my brain.

Don't be an I-told-you-so, brain.

Alexis accepted the lie. We moved on to other subjects: deposits, profits. "Has Mr. Feldstein paid you?" I pulled a cheque out of my pocket. "Good. Make sure you deposit that on the way home."

She stood and took off her jacket, hanging it on a special rack she had beside her desk. Then she pulled off her jewelry, arranging it carefully on the credenza. "Well, we're done working for the day." She took off the blouse and folded it beside the earrings, and then unzipped her pants. She slipped off her red lacy panties and sat down on the sofa facing her desk. "Now take off your clothes and lick my pussy for a while." She spread her legs and rubbed her pussy.

I dropped my cut-offs to the floor, struggled out of my

sneakers and tore my shirt off. I got on my knees between her thighs and kissed her pubic hair, looking up to watch Alexis pull off her bra and pinch her nipples.

I licked her pussy from bottom to top, savouring her. I put my hands under her legs and pushed her feet up on my shoulders. "Ooh, Damian," she whispered as I dove into her. She arched up and forward and ran her fingers through my hair as I flicked it back.

I pushed her thighs further apart and licked down. I felt wetness running down my chin. She clutched at my head and pressed her pelvis forward. "Shit, I should have covered the sofa," she said, but then could not speak anymore as I attacked her clit with rapid, wet, back-and-forth licks. I reached up with one hand and rolled her nipple between thumb and finger, enjoying her moans.

Alexis trembled. I took one more lick deep inside her, pinched both nipples a little harder and moved my tongue up to lick her clit fast and hard.

Her moan rose into a shriek. Her hips spasmed and her thighs squeezed my head. I couldn't breathe, but I kept licking until she spasmed again, shaking her legs once, twice, again.

She fell back onto the couch, sliding forward. She pushed my face away from her crotch. "Okay, now fuck me."

She turned over and lifted that beautiful ass high in the air. I climbed between her legs, grabbed her hips and moved deep in one smooth motion.

I pushed against her, grinding my pelvis, enjoying the feeling of her skin against mine, the heat and wetness of her. She groaned when I pulled back, gasped as I pressed in again. Alexis rocked back as I pushed forward. We established a good rhythm, sawing in and out. I reached around her to play with her breasts, squeeze and roll the nipples.

Alexis spasmed again, legs shaking. I grabbed both hips firmly and slammed forward. I came suddenly, surprisingly, like my entire body just opened up, life spurting out of every pore. Somehow, I held onto Alexis' hips and kept thrusting, loving every scream, yelling until Alexis collapsed below me and I fell onto her back.

Nothing existed in the world then but the feeling and the smell of her neck against my nose and the soft, beautiful press of her round ass against my stomach. I took a long time just to learn how to breathe again.

"Get off of me," Alexis moaned. Reluctantly, I got up. I leaned down again to kiss that round, beautiful ass.

Alexis turned over and smiled at me. "Very nice. You're getting better and better. Come on, we need to shower. I have a meeting tonight."

Tyler surprised me by arriving five minutes early on Monday in the six-year-old Corolla his father had bought for him. I was actually jealous of it — it was half the age of my Suzuki Swift.

"Wow, eight ay-em and it's already getting hot," he said as he helped me load supplies into my mini-truck.

"It's only going to get hotter. Careful you don't bend that pole."

"Do you work in the rain?"

"I don't know — it hasn't come, yet."

As we drove to the first customer of the day, Tyler said "Look, man, I just wanna say 'thanks' for giving me a chance like this. I need to save up some money for college and make my car insurance payments, too. My old man says if I can't keep up the insurance, he's going to sell my car."

"About that," I said. I had prepared a little speech. "I kind of went out on a limb offering you a job like that. My business partner wasn't too happy about not being consulted, first."

"Nick wasn't happy about hiring me?"

I realized that I had never mentioned Alexis to any of my friends. "No, not Nick; he's not even in the picture. I haven't heard from him in a month. My business partner is Alexis Rosse."

"Who?"

"She was my first customer. She's giving me a lot of good advice, and she actually lined up a bunch of customers."

"So, is she now gettin' her pool cleaned for free?"

"Yes, and five percent of profits." Did I really need to tell him that? the smart part of my brain wondered. He's an employee, not a partner.

Tyler nodded.

The first house was not in Rosedale; this one had come through the ad on LinkedIn. It had a big yard for Toronto, but the pool itself was not that big. I thought it was a good place to start training Tyler.

Training — what a joke. No one had trained me; I had my pool maintenance book and online research. Tyler surprised me again by making a few suggestions that actually made sense. We got through the work in a little more than half the time that I usually took by myself. The last step: leaving behind a printed card to show the customer that PoolGeeks had been there. "Your pool is clean as a whistle, thanks to PoolGeeks!" it said. I had designed it myself and Alexis had told me which printer to take it to.

"Nice," Tyler said as he looked at the card. He put it in the mailbox and we went to the next house. This time, I let Tyler do most of the work. I had to admit, he had learned the procedures.

We broke for an early lunch as the temperature climbed into the stupid range — where it's so hot, you cannot think anymore. We looked over the list of houses and pools to clean for the next day and decided which he would do. I tried to give him a mixture: some more difficult, some easier — all with what I thought were easy-going customers.

Mistake number one.

At the end of the next day, I was cleaning Mrs. Casales' pool when my cell phone went off. By the time I put down my tools and pulled the phone out of my pocket, it had gone to voice mail. I looked at the caller ID: Mrs. Ostap in Don Mills.

Shit. That's the first place that Tyler was supposed to go to. I looked at my watch: he should have been long gone. I had saved Mrs. Casales' pool for last.

"Mrs. Ostap? This is Damian Serr from PoolGeeks. You called?"

She sounded breathless, panicky. "Did you send someone else to clean my pool today?"

"Yes. That was Tyler." I hesitated before I added. "He's our best employee." It was true — PoolGeeks' only employee.

"Oh, I see. Well, my neighbour told me, when I got home this afternoon, that there was a strange man in my back yard. I had told him about you ..."

I remembered meeting Mrs. Ostap through Mr. Demetrios, pool-cleaning customer and a friend of my parents. I thought of Mrs. Ostap as my first second-generation customer — a referral from a referral. She had two separate locks on her back-yard gate, and I needed to memorize the code to temporarily disable the outdoor security system. I also had to be introduced to her neighbour. "Mr. Babchuk keeps an eye on my house when I'm away from the house." Mrs. Ostap worked from her house in an upper middle-class neighbourhood in Don Mills. Not Rosedale — I didn't trust Tyler in Rosedale yet — but not poor. Houses in Don Mills were probably double the cost of my parents' house.

"... but he did not recognize your employee. He was ready to call the police before the man left."

"I'm sorry, Mrs. Ostap. I should have told you ahead of time that I was sending someone else to clean your pool, today."

"Well, I should think so! It certainly wasn't what I expect, and it wasn't in our agreement, either. I signed a contract with you, not with some other ... person."

My heart was pounding. Was I going to lose this customer? "I'm sorry. It won't happen again. I'll clean your pool personally from now on."

"Well ... all right."

"Did Tyler — my employee — did he do a good job?" I had to sit down at Mrs. Casales' patio table. My back tingled as if someone were holding a knife-point to it.

"I suppose ... not as good as the job you did last week."

"I apologize. I'll come tomorrow and fix it, just the way you like."

"Good. I'll be home tomorrow to check on that."

"See you tomorrow morning, then."

I snapped my cheap phone shut. I realized that I had better send messages to all the customers that Tyler was scheduled to visit today. Kind of late, said my brain. It's the end of the day. Tyler should be finished.

I sent text messages to all Tyler's customers: "Dear valued client," I thumbed into the phone. "Today, a new PoolGeek, Tyler

Cherny, will be cleaning your pool. He is our best employee. Please let me, Damian Serr, COO, know if you have any issues."

I hoped that would be okay. I told my brain that most of Tyler's customers would be out of their homes during the day, so that they would probably not even notice that anyone different was there. And since they'd get my message at — I glanced at the phone's clock — 4:37, most of them would just be coming out of work, wouldn't be home yet. So, it was just as if they had gotten notification in advance.

Not really, said my brain. In fact, not at all.

Mrs. Casales came out of her kitchen with two glasses of iced tea and sat at the patio table beside me. "Everything okay?"

I drank half the iced tea in one gulp. "I hired an employee to help with some of the new customers," I said. "One customer didn't know who he was."

"Maybe you should go around with him the first time to introduce him to new customers," she suggested.

She had changed from her work clothes into short shorts that strained against her thighs and a thin, sleeveless blouse. I could not keep my eyes from following the neckline down to where it met the curve of her breast. Then my eyes moved up to watch her throat pulse as she swallowed iced tea.

I realized it tasted unusual. What was in the iced tea? "I think you're right. I had better get going."

She put a hand on my shoulder to stop me as I stood up. "Damian, it will be all right. You're doing a great job as a pool cleaner, but also as a business person. I've spoken with Alexis. She tells me that she's giving you —"

I stopped breathing at that point.

"— business advice, and I think you're doing just fine. Don't worry about the occasional upset customer. I mean, yes, take it seriously. But don't fret about it." She stood and kissed me on the cheek. "Take care of yourself."

I left as quickly as I could without looking like I was running.

In the car, I thought about my reaction. Would she be insulted that I had left quickly? Did she expect sex every time I came to her house?

I felt a little dizzy. What had she put in that iced tea? Booze?

If so, I hadn't tasted it.

No, some part of my brain rationalized. You've been to her house since you had sex. She has to understand that you're feeling pressure from business.

I pushed Mrs. Casales out of my mind and called Tyler. "Where are you?"

"I just pulled up in front of the Dojc house."

"Dude, you should have been finished that place an hour ago!"

"Sorry, man. I'm still learning this stuff!"

"Okay, but wait before you go in." There was one good thing about Tyler being slow. "I'll call the customer and tell them that you're going to be there, instead of me. I'll call you back when it's time for you to go in."

"Umm ... look, Dam, it's okay. I'll knock on the door, introduce myself and explain ..."

"No! No, they don't know who you are. And besides, you're really late. It's after five p.m. They know me, they signed the contract with me, so I have to be the one to tell them what's going on." I was the boss. Right?

"Well, how long am I gonna hafta wait out here?"

"Are you in the driveway?"

"No, man, there's two cars in the driveway already. I'm parked across the street."

"Okay, just hang there for a coupla minutes. I'll call you right back." I dialled Mr. Dojc's work number and fretted through four rings. "Mr. Dojc? It's Damian from PoolGeeks calling. Don't worry, there is no problem. I just wanted to tell you that, instead of me," I hesitated: what should I say about Tyler? I couldn't tell them I was passing them to the new guy. "Instead of me, due to, um, circumstances, *another* employee, named Tyler, uh, he will be cleaning your pool."

"All right," said Mr. Dojc in his heavy European accent. "Will Tyler be cleaning my pool from now on?"

"Yes, that's the plan, Mr. Dojc. Unless you're unhappy with that."

"We will see." His voice sounded distant all of a sudden, and I wondered if he was doing something else that moved his mouth away from the phone. I pictured him, hand over the mouth-piece, giving an assistant instructions. "If his work is acceptable, I see no problem. I will check this evening when I get home."

"Thank you, Mr. Dojc."

"Good-bye." The line clicked.

Well, that went better than I had feared. I called Tyler back. "It's okay; go ahead. Is this your last pool today?"

"Second-last. One more after this ... um, Patel."

"Okay. Try to hurry up, but do a good, thorough job."

"Yassah, boss," Tyler said in his aggravating slave impression.

"Look, if you do see the customer, the home-owner, introduce yourself, tell them you'll be doing their pool from now on."

"Okay, I'll say I'm the new guy."

"No! Don't tell them that! If they ask if you're new, sure, tell them. Don't lie. But don't go out of your way to tell them you're new. Okay?"

"Shit, stop being so paranoid, dude. Everybody's new sometime."

"Yes, but when did *you* ever ask for the new guy for anything you were paying for?"

"I ask for the new waitress when she has big tits!" Tyler laughed.

"Very funny. Just do it, okay?"

"Yessir!" he said in his phoney military voice. He hung up.

I had a bad feeling.

Chapter 15

Mom's Advice

My mother finally voiced the words I had been dreading for over a week.

"Why haven't you brought Kristen over in such a long time?" She still rolled the *r* slightly, even after all these years in Canada.

I took a deep breath and looked at the tree Mom sat beneath. Another hot, dry summer day in Toronto. I sat down on the patio chair and poured myself a glass of iced tea from the pitcher. It was my Mom's special Sunday afternoon iced tea recipe: I didn't know the exact proportions, but it involved a generous dollop of tea and lemon with the vodka.

She lay on the hammock, reading a book. She looked like what I thought of as a typical European intellectual: small, thin with lots of thick black hair. She had wide but thin lips and a long, straight nose that I had inherited.

I realized that my entire concept of intellectual European women was based on my own mother.

A little aluminum table at her elbow bore a tall glass. "Watcha readin?" I asked to change the subject.

She showed me the cover: *Fifty Shades of Grey*.

"Oh, no, not you too, Mom!"

"Everyone is reading it, so I thought I'd see what the fuss is about."

"I heard it was all about bondage and kinky sex."

"Hmp. Not so much. There is some sex, yes, but not a lot of bondage. Mostly, it's contractual language and copies of emails."

"Sounds like a lot of filler."

"That's it! Exactly right, Damian. And the characters are completely unbelievable. The hero, this Christian Grey, is oh-so-handsome, and incredibly rich, too."

"I thought that all heroes in women's romances were rich and handsome."

"Oh, sure, but this author just goes on and on about it ... and we're supposed to believe that not only is he so rich and has forty thousand employees or something ridiculous like that, but he's accomplished all this by twenty-seven years of age!

"And the heroine — such a ridiculous, soap-opera name: Anastasia Steele. I mean, really! Who could believe that! Grey, Steele — you see? And she's a virgin at 22 years of age? What world is this author living in?" She tossed the book onto the hammock. "Now answer the question: how's Kristen? Why don't you invite her over?"

"Mom, Kristen and I broke up."

I couldn't believe how saying those words made my throat constrict. My eyes burned.

Broke up? With Kristen?

"Broke up? With Kristen?" my mother echoed. "Oh, shweetie, what happen?" Her accent always became more pronounced when she felt stressed.

What had happened? "I just think ... well, we both realized that we had some ... fundamental differences of opinion on some important matters."

"What are you talking about? You had a fight, I understand that. What about? Usually, these things seem silly after a while, when you both calm down and can look at it rationally."

"I don't think so. Kristen's mind is made up and she is not willing to budge her opinion an inch."

"Did you try talking about it?"

I thought about Kristen and me, "talking" about sex. Or the lack of it. "Kristen talks, but she doesn't listen. She won't even think that there is a point of view, other than hers, that could be right!"

Mom got off the hammock gracefully, leaving it swinging. It barely missed the aluminum table. I knew how carefully Dad had measured the table and experimented with hanging the hammock to get it at exactly the right height.

Mom refilled both our iced teas and sat at the patio table. Our knees nearly touched. "This seems like an issue that's been building for a long time. It requires a serious talk." She pushed a glass to me and took a gulp from hers.

"Yah. It's been between us for a couple of years, I guess."

"You've spoken about it more than once, I hope?"

"Oh, yah. Well, tried. It doesn't go very far."

"What's the argument about?"

What could I say? I figured that Mom being a woman would take Kristen's side. I drank half the iced tea. It was strong. "Sex."

My mother's face showed shock. "Sex? What are you trying to do to the poor girl?"

This was going even worse than I had feared. "Nothing! That's it! That's the disagreement!"

My mother then did the worst thing possible: she laughed. Loud and long. "What! I don't believe it!"

"What do you mean?"

"Damian, you're both twenty years old, and you've been dating since you were fourteen! I just assumed that at some point, the two of you had sex!" She gulped more iced tea. "But I see the problem. What's with that girl?"

"She wants to wait until we're married to have sex."

"What does she think this is, the nineteenth century?"

"She's become very religious," I explained.

"Pah!" Mom waved her hand. "Back home, the religious girls were the biggest sluts."

"Well, this isn't Europe, Mom. This is Toronto the Good."

"Oh, sure, all the unmarried girls here are virgins." I loved it when my mother was sarcastic. "Well, I can tell you, Kristen doesn't get these ideas from her mother."

I had to agree: Mrs. Petri was the "hot mom" of the neighbourhood. Tyler and Patrick used to make jokes about how lucky I was to go to Kristen's house when I was 13 and 14. She didn't dress like her daughter: she was attractive, even beautiful, and she knew it. She always had her fair hair done fashionably. She liked to wear tight blouses and tight pants, high heels and jewelry.

"I've seen your father looking at Mrs. Petri, you know," my mother said. She refilled our glasses again, emptying the pitcher. "Have you tried being romantic?"

Was it strange to talk to your mother for seduction tips? "Sure," I answered.

I told her about last Valentine's Day. I had gone all-out: reservations at an expensive restaurant, a dozen red roses, a box of chocolates. Kristen enjoyed all of it, and we went back to my apartment. I had contrived to make sure that Nick was gone. We settled in to watch what I had heard was a sexy, romantic movie: *I am Love*.

I thought the movie was boring and illogical. Tilda Swinton fucks around. What man — or what straight man, anyway — is interested in seeing that flat-chested wonder naked? Kristen professed disgust at the love scenes.

When Kristen went to the bathroom, I brought out my secret weapon: a bottle of red wine. It was from France and cost over fifteen bucks. That should have made it a sure thing.

I should demand my money back. From France, itself.

I poured two glasses and put them on the coffee table, then sat back in the sofa as if I hadn't moved since Kristen went to the bathroom.

"What is that?" she said when she saw the two glasses.

"Bordeaux," I said with my best French accent. "Perfect for lovers."

"You know I don't drink alcohol! Damian Serr, are you trying to get me drunk?"

I stood up to put an arm around her shoulders and kissed her neck. With the other hand, I brought a glass to her mouth. "You know it. All part of my nefarious plan to take advantage of you."

Ain't I smooth?

Kristen twisted out of my arms. "Put that away! We don't need to be drunk to have a good time."

She said "good time." I thought, That's a good sign. "I didn't say anything about getting drunk. Try this. It's expensive, and it's from France. It's got to be really good!"

She scowled. "No. Alcohol just clouds your mind. It's not

necessary! Now put it down and let's watch the rest of this movie."

"Why? You're disgusted by it."

"Just fast-forward past the sex parts."

"Those are the only parts worth watching!"

"Don't be disgusting."

I slugged back my wine in one shot.

"Damian Serr, if you get drunk, how are you going to drive me home?"

"I planned on you staying the night."

"Just what kind of girl do you think I am?"

I looked at her over my wine glass. "My girl." I sank another glass. "My Valentine. My love." I leaned forward and kissed her neck.

I put my glass down and took her in my arms. I squeezed her, held her close, pressed her whole body against mine. I kissed her mouth, her neck.

She responded. She kissed me. I swiped my tongue along her lips. I kissed her jaw, her ear, her neck, stroking her hair.

Her breathing accelerated. I felt a flush of heat. I leaned forward, pushing her along the hallway toward the bedroom.

She squirmed out of my arms. "Stop it! Stop before we do something we'll regret."

"I'll never regret making love to you," I said. See how cheesy I can be?

Cheesy doesn't work.

"No. No. What part of 'no' don't you understand?"

I continued fighting Kristen's clichés with cheesy lines. "I don't understand anything but the feeling of your lips."

Kristen put a hand flat against my chest. "This has been such a nice Valentine's Day. Don't ruin it."

I slumped into the sofa and watched the rest of *I Am Love*. Kristen drove herself home.

"Don't put pressure on Kristen to have sex. It won't work," my mother said. "You have to give her time to come around on her own. You see, Kristen is afraid of sex." She was really rolling her *r*s now.

"Do you know what your father did to get me into bed the first time?" she asked, and my heart stopped.

Actually stopped.

"Mom!"

"He bit my bottom lip, not hard, of course, more like he sucked it into his mouth while he was kissing me, and he stroked the back of my neck — "

"You can stop now, Mom," I said, but her eyes were closed. One hand moved in the air, showing me how my Dad had stroked her neck.

"And then he started kissing my throat, so softly ..."

"Tried that, Mom. Didn't work. You can stop now." Hearing about my parents making out caused me to reconsider Kristen's opinion.

"And then, he slowly kissed down — "

"Stop, Mom!" I drank the rest of my iced tea.

Mom laughed again, delighted at my discomfort. She patted my knee. "Oh, shweetie, where do you think you and your sister came from?"

"I just don't want to hear a graphic description of it, okay?"

"All right, prude." She laughed again. "Of course, it also helped that we were naked. And when I saw your father's — "

"Mom!" I went into the house to watch sports with my dad.

I could hear Mom's laughter all the way into the kitchen.

Chapter 16

Complaining Customers

Mrs. Casales' contract said PoolGeeks would come twice a week. I reorganized my schedule. She expected me on Friday, right after noon. I went to her house first thing in the morning. I moved as quickly as I could, sweeping and skimming, cleaning the filters. I added chemicals and when the testers showed I was close, I ran back to the car and threw my tools in the back.

As I pulled away from the curb in front of the house, I saw Mrs. Casales' Toyota in my rear-view mirror.

Shit.

I pressed on the accelerator, but the block was long. I saw Mrs. Casales pull into her driveway, get out of her car and look after me, her hands on her hips.

I turned at the first corner.

Mrs. Casales — Leda — texted me soon after. "Expctg U 2day."

"Already done!" I texted back.

"U come bk 2day?"

"Sorry. Full sched."

She texted me three times a day over the weekend, but I couldn't face her again. I gave her to Tyler. That is, I told Tyler that I was adding Mrs. Casales to his list.

"Man, how am I going to fit that in?"

"Don't worry. I'll take the Youngmans' place instead."

"Why are you doing this? I just worked out the route. Now, I have to drive all the way to Etobicoke."

"Go to Mrs. Patel's before Mrs. Casales. It's a natural

progression."

Tyler didn't like it, but I was the boss, after all.

Complaints about Tyler started coming in the second week he was working for me. Soon, half the emails and voice-mails PoolGeeks got were from his customers. "Pool not clean."

"He left without cleaning the skimmers out," said one very pissed-off homeowner.

"Your new man left behind his tools and came back to pick them up when we had dinner guests!!" Mr. Richardson in York emailed.

The worst were the texts from Mrs. Casales. "New man prmnt?"

"Wen U rtrn?"

"U do bttr jb than new guy."

She stopped sending texts by the end of the week, which would have been after the second time that Tyler serviced her. But the other customers kept complaining.

Something like an alarm went off deep in my head.

When sweet Mrs. Patel left a voice-mail to complain that her pool "just isn't clean," I knew I could not put it off any longer. I texted Tyler and met him at the end of the day at a coffee shop near Mrs. Patel's. I bought him a big, sweet, gooey drink.

"How's it going?"

Tyler slurped his melting, coffee-flavoured ice cream. "Okay, I guess."

I sipped on my drink, thinking about how to say this. "No issues?"

"Nope." He kept looking at one of the servers, a girl with a purple streak in her black hair.

"Well, I've heard from a number of your customers."

"Really? They're that happy?"

"Not exactly." Why are you hesitating, my brain asked. You're the boss, dumbass! "Actually, every message has been a complaint."

"Complaint? About what?"

"Basically, quality. Mr. Richardson said you left your tools behind ..."

"That was okay — I got them back!"

"Well, Mr. Richardson wasn't happy that you interrupted his barbeque party to do it!" I felt like I was squirming. I wanted just to tell him that it was okay, that he should just try a little harder, make sure he completed his job.

But my brain kept insisting I tell him the whole story.

"I heard from another customer that you didn't clean the skimmers."

"Sorry. I'll make sure I do that from now on."

"Good to hear it." Carry on, said part of my brain. No, there's more! Give him a warning! said another. "And then there's Mrs. Patel."

"What about her?"

"She says you just didn't clean the pool."

"Oh, come on! I did the whole deal! What does a dirty Paki know about clean, anyway."

The wimpy side of my brain came over to the smart side then. "Shut your fucking mouth, Tyler."

He was shocked. His mouth actually hung open.

"This is Toronto, asshole. The most multicultural city in the world." Where had I heard that? Well, it sounded true. "So put your fucking racist ideas away while you're working for me."

Well said, my brain told me.

"Sorry."

"You're going to her house today, right now, and you're going to do the best fucking job you've ever done in your life."

"Okay, okay!"

I took a deep breath. "Now, tell me about Mrs. Casales."

Tyler shook his head. "What do you want to know? She's not bad looking. Seems lonely. I think her husband left her."

"Any problems?"

"None that I know of. Is she complaining, too?"

"Yes," I said, to maintain the upper hand in this conversation. "Not so much about the work, but about ... your attitude."

"Dude, that's fucked up!"

"Why is that fucked up?"

"Cause she's always nice when I get there! Well, I've only been there twice, but ... well, she seemed happy."

"Has she said anything? Anything about her ... different from the other customers?" How could I ask if he fucked her?

Just ask him, "Did you fuck her," said my brain. Dumbass.

"She has a hot bikini. She's a bit overweight for it, but still, not bad to look at."

"And that's it?"

"That's it."

Was he lying? His face was blank. In books, people can always tell when someone is lying by looking in their eyes. I looked into Tyler's eyes. What's the difference between the eyes of a liar and someone who's telling the truth, I wondered.

"Was Mrs. Casales happy with you when you left?" I asked.

"I guess so."

"You guess so? She didn't say anything? Do anything unusual?"

Tyler looked at me, then looked over each shoulder. He thought about his answer for a few seconds. Then: "Okay, I fucked her."

Oh, no.

"Dude, it wasn't my fault! The first time I went there, last week, she was all 'Where is Damian? Why didn't he come? Is he going to come back?'" He spoke in a high-pitched voice, flapping his hands around, doing a lousy job of imitating Leda. "Dude, she's fuckin' crazy about you!" He went back to the imitation. "Damian, oh Damian!"

"She's a little ... intense," I said.

"Intense! Dude, she's fuckin' insane!" He leaned closer and lowered his voice, although there was no one else around. "You totally coulda had her, dude. She's hot for you. Or, she was," he leered. "The first time I was there, she was a real bitch to me. Telling me what to do, criticizing every spot I missed on the deck, every leaf, every fuckin' crumb of dust in the water. She made me clean the skimmer twice!

"But the second time, she only asked once about you. I told her all I knew is, I'm s'posed to clean her pool. She looked really pissed, but she didn't tell me what to do. And when I was done, she's like, 'Get in the house.' I thought she was going to lecture me or fire me or somethin', I dunno. But when she closed the door, she went fuckin' nuts! She tore off her bathing suit like it was on fire and told me to take off my clothes. As soon as my pants were down, dude, she was on my cock! She sucked me so hard I thought I'd pass out.

"And then she fucked me. She climbed on top and fucked me like she was mad. Dude, I think she *was* mad. Really angry at you, or maybe at me, I dunno." He leered again. "I made her come."

I didn't know what to say, but my brain brought up those high school lectures. "I hope you at least used protection."

"Don't worry. The second thing she did after she pulled her clothes off was slap a condom on me." I really didn't want to hear any more details, but Tyler was enjoying himself. "She didn't let me come in her, though. She finished me off in her mouth. Well, sort of."

Part of me wanted to tell Tyler to shut up, but something else just kept listening. "She didn't like the taste of the condom, I guess. She sucked me for a coupla minutes, then jerked me off in the condom. So it wasn't the best sex I ever had, but it wasn't bad. Hey, I got it in and I got it off. And I got her off, too. So, thanks for the job, dude!"

Leda Casales, I thought. Pool-boy fucker.

"I should fire you right now, Tyler," I said.

He looked shocked, again. "What? Why?"

"For fucking the customer, for one thing. I think it's like one of the basic rules of business: don't fuck your customers. Unless you're a whore."

You hypocrite. You fucked her, first.

I swear, if you don't stop giving me a hard time, brain, I'll lobotomize myself.

"But mostly, you're fucking up all the other customers." I tried to skewer him with a severe look. I have no idea to this day whether it worked. "We're friends, so I'm giving you one more chance. Stop fucking up. Do a good job, the way I showed you. Don't forget your tools. And I'm taking Mrs. Casales away from you. Don't go near her place again."

"So, you're going to do Casales? Good. She wanted you, anyway."

I punched him in the nose. "One more complaint, and you're fired." I left him bleeding in the coffee shop.

It's too bad I can never go back there. I liked their coffee.

Chapter 17

Mrs. Rosse, Mrs. McQuaig and Whipped Cream

The heat was never going to break. Sweat dripped off of me into the pool as I swept the vacuum pole back and forth.

Did July mean "brutal" in some dead language?

Done. The pool was clean, the deck swept. Alexis' whole back yard, in fact, looked great. The gardener was gone for the day — probably sitting somewhere air-conditioned, enjoying a beer, I thought.

It was the last pool of the day. I always made sure that Alexis' pool was the last of the day. I could not help but think "Save the best for last."

I looked to the gate, the door: all quiet. I moved my tools away from the edge of the pool, checked the walk-out again (dark) and jumped into the pool.

Alexis wouldn't mind if she were here, I told my brain.

Oh, bliss. Cool water closed over my head. I stayed under, swimming back and forth, two whole lengths. I was determined to stay underwater as long as I could, just like when I was 10.

I came up at the edge of the deep end and looked at the house: still quiet, so I swam back and forth a few times more.

Stop pushing your luck, said my brain.

I ducked underwater again, determined to do three lengths without breathing this time.

When I came up in the shallow end, I saw that my luck had run out.

"Julia, this is my pool boy," Alexis said. "Damian, Mrs. McQuaig."

Alexis and another woman stood at the corner of the house, dressed in jogging clothes. Alexis wore her pink runners, pink-and-white short shorts and her matching jogging top stretched across her chest. A matching headband pulled her curls away from her neck. Her companion wore blue and yellow, similarly coordinated. They could have been Power Rangers in exercise clothes.

The other woman was taller, thinner and older than Alexis, with straight blonde hair and a horsey face: long jaw, big lips, narrow nose. She had long arms and legs and prominent knees. She stood with one hand on her hip. Her smile did not look friendly. "Is this what your pool company calls full service, Alexis? They not only clean the pool, they swim in it for you, too?"

I pulled myself out, conscious of the water streaming off my body onto the spotless deck. "I'm sorry, Alexis — Mrs. Rosse. It's just that it's such a hot day ..."

"Well, I have to say I am surprised at you, Damian," Alexis snipped. I looked at her: her face wore an annoyed expression, but there was a strange light in her eyes. Was she playing a joke on me?

Her voice sounded genuinely pissed. "I certainly did not expect this from you."

Are you kidding me? I've been in your pool before. I've swum in it. I *fucked* you in it!

Of course, I did not say those things. Not in front of Alexis' new friend. McQuaig, was it? Yes: Julia McQuaig.

I started gathering my pool cleaning tools. "Leave that for now, Damian," Alexis snapped as she unlocked the sliding walk-out door. "We're going to have to talk about this. Right, Julia?"

"Oh, you can't let something like this go," her friend answered. "You have to let the help know their place."

I could feel my face get hot at that statement. But I complied with Alexis. I put down the tools and stepped to the walk-out.

Alexis stopped me just outside the threshold. "Oh, no. I don't want your cut-offs dripping all over my floors."

"Umm ... maybe we could talk out here?"

"Take them off," said Mrs. McQuaig.

I laughed, but both women's faces were stoney. "You heard her. Drop 'em."

I opened the button and let my shorts fall to the patio.

"Britches, too," McQuaig said.

I swallowed, but Alexis did not look like she was joking. Down went my soaking wet underwear. I straightened, unsure whether to be embarrassed or not.

"All right, come in," Alexis said, and I wondered about dripping water onto her floors when I was naked.

"You were right, Alexis. He *is* cute. Kind of skinny, though."

"Slim, yes," said Alexis. "His long reach can come in handy."

They both looked at me as if I were some curious creature. I was conscious of my penis' shrunken state after swimming. The air conditioning felt uncomfortably cool on my wet skin.

"He has to be taught a lesson," said Alexis.

Mrs. McQuaig took my hand in hers. "What shall we do with him?"

Alexis led us down the hall. "To the games room," she said.

The games room? But it was just her big, comfortable family room or rec room or whatever rich people call it, the one with the big sofas and the huge flat-screen TV.

Alexis touched a remote and music started playing jazz. I hate jazz. "What did you have in mind?" McQuaig asked.

"Look, Alexis, I really didn't think you'd mind..." I started.

"You never asked me." She sat and pulled off a running shoe.

"But I've ... been in your pool before!"

"When I have invited you." She pulled off the other shoe and placed both carefully in a corner. "You know, I shouldn't have to put up with this kind of impropriety."

"Look, I'm sorry. Really." Why is she acting like this? Why am I standing here naked?

"Don't let him get away with it," McQuaig said. I wanted to ask what the hell it was to her, but I did not want to upset Alexis any more than she already was.

"No, I won't. You're going to have to make up for this, Damian." She held out her arm, and McQuaig stood beside her.

Alexis carefully removed her friend's top and folded it on a side table, then unhooked her sports bra. McQuaig had small, almost flat breasts and small, dark red nipples — not like Alexis' luxurious beauties.

Stop comparing them, said my brain.

"You're going to have to make Mrs. McQuaig come," Alexis said.

Am I dreaming?

You're not dreaming, my brain told me. First useful thing my brain has ever said.

McQuaig smiled, revealing what seemed to be far too many large teeth, completing the horsey look. She put her arms around me and kissed me. Alexis pulled down her shorts and McQuaig pressed her skinny body against mine. Her skin was covered in a thin film of sweat. It smelled slightly, but not bad.

I kissed her and she opened her mouth. Our tongues met. She squeezed my ass.

She broke the kiss but kept kneading my buttocks. "I don't think there's an ounce of excess body fat on this boy, Alexis."

Alexis took her clothes off. She was also covered in sweat.

I had never before imagined that a woman's sweat could be sexy, but it turned me on. I kissed McQuaig on her big jaw, then licked down the side of her neck. She tasted musky and salty.

"Oh, he's a live one, Alexis. No wonder you're so happy with him!"

Did they talk about me? I wondered. About sex, or just cleaning pools?

Who cares. Just concentrate on the naked woman in front of you.

McQuaig took my stiff penis in her hand and used it to lead me to the big sofa. Alexis took a bottle of wine out of the cooler, poured two big glasses, and sat in the easy chair. Her eyes never left her friend and me.

McQuaig lay back on the sofa, pulling on her little nipples. I sucked one, then the other into my mouth. She seemed to like it, so I sucked harder until she groaned.

Different women like different things, I realized. I gave each nipple a little bite. McQuaig yelped and laughed.

"Very nice, pool boy. Now get down there and get to work!"
she said. "Don't worry. You've already got whatever I have since
you've been fucking Alexis!"

So much for safe sex, I thought. I licked down her stomach as
she stroked my erection. She spread her thighs wide and I
flattened my tongue to give her a good licking. I could taste her
sweat and her musk.

"Oh, no, lover boy. Turn around and do it properly!" she
ordered.

I stepped between her knees, which took my penis out of her
reach. Ah well, I'm here to please her, not the other way around, I
thought. I licked her vulva from bottom to top. McQuaig groaned.
I looked up to see her toying with her nipples again. She pinched
them and pulled them so that the whole breast stretched toward
the ceiling.

My tongue found her clit; it seemed larger, longer than
Alexis'. She gasped a little and even giggled as I licked it lightly
and fast, the way that Alexis liked. But she wasn't moaning
anymore, so I gave her a little more pressure.

That got a moan.

She likes it rough, I thought. How rough? What should I do?
What are the rules here, anyway?

I licked hard, flicking her clit mercilessly. I reached up with
one hand to pull on her nipple the way I saw her doing it and
heard her moan louder.

"Oh, Alexis, he's good at this. I think he has talent!" she
gasped.

I slid my tongue inside McQuaig again. I wished I could see
Alexis; I twisted a little, but I did not dare to take my mouth from
McQuaig's pussy.

I pushed a finger into her and sucked her clit hard. She arched
her back and clutched at my head, scratching my neck. I licked for
what felt like ten solid minutes. I started to feel a little sore where
my tongue joined my mouth, but I kept licking. I curled my finger
up and McQuaig screamed.

"Fuck, Alexis, he found my spot!" I rubbed and licked and
sucked and pulled on her nipple all at the same time. McQuaig
thrashed under me and profanity streamed out of her mouth.

Then she wasn't saying words anymore. She yelled over and over. Her vagina pulsed and she made one last, loud yell before pulling away. She lay on her side, panting, eyes closed.

"My turn," said Alexis. I turned around: she was sitting on the big overstuffed easy chair, legs splayed over its arms. One hand moved up and down along her pussy, while the other gently pinched her big nipple. "Come on, Damian. Lick my cunt."

I dove in, pushing her thighs higher and farther apart and lapped like a kitten at a saucer of milk. "Oh, Damian!" she laughed and stroked my hair. She tossed her head back and closed her eyes as I sucked her.

I knew how she liked it: gentler than McQuaig did, lighter, more finesse.

She was dripping wet when I started. I could feel a film of sweat on her thighs. Her smell drove me crazy. I almost felt like I could come, just from tasting her.

Something touched my thigh. I looked down to see McQuaig take my penis in her hand and smile. She kissed Alexis' thigh, then my side. She lay down on her back on the floor and scooted up between my legs. I rose up a little to give her room and then nearly fell down again when she started sucking my cock.

I pressed harder on Alexis' clit and rolled her nipple between my fingers. I'm in a three-way! kept echoing through my mind.

I looked up at Alexis. She was still pressing her head into the back of the chair, still clenching her eyes. I knew her orgasm was far away, and my position, straddling McQuaig while leaning forward into Alexis' thighs, was worse than awkward. I moved forward and slid my penis inside Alexis.

She looked at me, shocked, mouth open for a loud moan. But she started bucking against me. Her pussy made sexy squishing sounds.

Alexis came, yelling and shuddering. She closed her eyes and arched her back right off the chair and I obliged by thrusting as deep as I could go.

"Don't you dare come in her!" McQuaig ordered as Alexis collapsed, shaking. "Not until you fuck me first!"

McQuaig pushed me onto the sofa, climbed up and impaled herself on me.

How different two women feel, I thought. She wasn't as wet as Alexis, not as tight, but somehow warmer. She rode me, hard, sliding up and down, faster and faster until she rose off of me and rubbed her clit furiously until she squirted my body with hot, clear liquid. She screamed and convulsed and collapsed beside me on the sofa.

"Christ, Julia, you're going to ruin my upholstery," Alexis said.

"If you and I haven't wrecked this sofa by now, we never will," McQuaig answered.

Alexis bent over McQuaig and they kissed, simultaneously intense and gentle.

McQuaig broke the kiss to look at me. "Well, he's done a good job, but his balls will be blue if we don't take care of him."

"Which of us shall do the honours?"

"Why don't we share?" McQuaig slid to her knees on the floor and sucked my penis again. She seemed to enjoy it.

Alexis got on the floor beside her, cupped my testicles in one hand and licked the side of my penis as McQuaig licked the tip. She let Alexis take my penis into her mouth and they passed me back and forth, laughing.

I felt like I was sitting on the edge of a knife, wanting to come, needing to come. If they would just put a little more pressure in the right place, I could.

McQuaig laughed. "Oh, the poor boy! Look at how red his face is, Alexis!"

"Let's put him out of his misery," Alexis said. She started stroking while McQuaig sucked the tip.

I could not help yelling as I climaxed. Alexis kept stroking, applying exactly the pressure that I needed, and I spurted again and again.

When I was done, both women laughed. "Okay, Alexis, I think you've got a keeper, here. What he lacks in brains and obedience, he more than makes up for in oral technique and volume!"

"Julia, I don't think any woman likes semen as much as you do," Alexis said. The women stood up and drank their wine. I still didn't know whether to believe what was happening. Were there really two naked women standing in front of me, drinking wine casually?

McQuaig looked at the clock built into the stereo and said "Oh, look at the time!" She drained her glass of wine and kissed Alexis on the cheek. "Gotta go! Got a hot date, tonight!"

As McQuaig pulled on her jogging clothes, Alexis asked "Do you want to shower here?"

McQuaig pulled her top over her head. "Nah. Don't think I'll bother. I should've let Damian come inside my cunt — that would have made tonight more interesting!" She laughed, gave Alexis another kiss on the cheek, gave me a pat on the head and ran out the door.

Alexis looked after her with a thoughtful look on her face. Still nude, she sipped her wine. I wondered what to do. What's the accepted post-three-way etiquette?

"I guess I should get going, too?" I asked.

Alexis turned as if she had forgotten I was there. "Hmm? Aren't you hungry?"

"I guess so." I was starved.

"Come. Let's take a shower and then we'll eat."

I followed Alexis to the bathroom on the main floor, which had a glass shower stall. It was a close fit inside; Alexis lathered me completely, efficiently and somehow innocently soaping my genitals. I felt a little tingle, as if my erection wanted to come back to life. Alexis smiled and handed me the soap. "Now, you do me."

I wiped the soap all over her smooth, beautiful skin. She smiled and closed her eyes in pleasure as I soaped her breasts and nipples. But when I tried to rub slippery lather over her clit, she gently pushed my hand away. "Later. I thought you were hungry."

"I'm starving."

"All right, let's eat."

We dried off with thick, soft towels and padded, still nude, to the kitchen. I enjoyed watching naked Alexis taking dishes from the immense refrigerator, whipping ingredients in bowls and heating them on the stove. I opened another bottle of wine from the fridge and we sat naked, side-by-side on the high chairs at the kitchen counter to eat.

"Did you enjoy your first three-way?"

"How do you know it's my first?"

"Oh, come on, Damian! I took your virginity a month ago! What have you been up to in the meantime?"

"Okay, yah, it was great. Mrs. McQuaig seems …" I didn't know what to say. She had just blown and fucked me, but I didn't think I liked her.

"I think you can call her "Julia" now that you've had your cock inside her, Damian!" Alexis laughed. "But it's true: she can be abrupt. Even rude, I agree."

I wondered how to ask the next question. "Do you and her …"

"We're fuck buddies," Alexis shrugged. I was fascinated by the bounce in her breasts as her shoulders rose and fell. No matter how many times I saw Alexis nude, I would never get used to it. "We usually run in the mornings, but schedule conflicts today delayed our run until this afternoon."

"Do you often …"

"She's not married, I'm not married, so when we feel like it, we fool around. She prefers fucking men, but she's very good at cunnilingus." Alexis took a big bite. "She could teach you a thing or two. Oh, don't blush! You're fine. I'm just saying a woman's touch is … different. Something everyone needs."

I hesitated to ask the next question. But I had to know. "If Julia is a fuck buddy, what am I?"

Alexis touched my face. "You're my new lover. And my favourite one. Don't worry, Damian. Julia is no threat to you. Now, would you like some dessert?"

"Um, sure."

Alexis took out a basket of bright red strawberries. "This is what I love best about summer: fresh local fruit. Clean these, will you?"

While I cut off the greens and rinsed the berries, Alexis whipped heavy cream in a bowl. "Let's go sit on the pool deck."

We sat, still naked, at the patio table, eating strawberries with fresh whipped cream. I wondered whether Alexis' back yard was really well screened, or if she liked showing off to the neighbours. I don't think I would have complained if I lived next to her. On an impulse, I wiped a fingerful of whipped cream onto Alexis' nipple and then licked it off.

She smiled, so I smeared more whipped cream all over her breasts and licked it all off. My penis tingled and began to stiffen.

No more cream! I ran back to the kitchen to fetch the bowl. I led Alexis to one of the chaise lounges and made her lie back, then smeared all the whipped cream over her body, from her neck, over her breasts, across her stomach and into her pubic hair. "Don't get any inside me," she warned. "That can lead to a wicked yeast infection."

I wasn't sure what that meant; I had only ever heard of yeast infections in TV commercials, and all the women in those looked happy.

I kissed Alexis, then started licking off the whipped cream from her neckline down. I took the opportunity to suck her nipples for a long time, until she was groaning and rubbing my head.

She gasped as I licked the cream off her stomach. I licked her navel, getting little gasps. I worked my way down and made sure that I licked and sucked all the dairy out of her pubic patch.

I found the taste of her pussy made a strange mix with the cream in my mouth, so I washed down the combination with wine.

Alexis sat up. The bowl was in her hands. "Come closer," she said, and I stepped beside the chaise lounge. She plopped big dollops of whipped cream onto my half-hard penis. It stiffened fully as she smeared the cream all over the shaft and around my testicles. She leaned forward, stuck out her pink tongue and licked just a tiny bit of whipped cream from the tip, without ever touching me at all. She smiled at me.

"Get down," she said, patting the lounge chair. She licked the cream from one side of my cock, then the other before opening wide and taking me into her mouth like a long ice cream cone.

I thought I was going to lose my mind when she started licking the whipped cream off my testicles. "I'm not going to last long like this," I warned her.

Still stroking my cock steadily, she said, "Really? You just came, not long ago. You really don't think you can last?"

"I don't know. It's so good … I never even thought that was

possible."

"You mean, coming twice in one day? Surely, Damian, a healthy young man like you must have masturbated more than once a day? Even when you were a teenager?"

I must have flushed in embarrassment, because Alexis laughed. "No, not that … I mean, yes, I did masturbate more than once a day … once or twice."

She laughed again and ran her tongue from the tip to the base of my penis. "Oops, there's some whipped cream I missed." She lapped at a stray blob on my thigh. Then she licked the tip of my cock. "Yummy."

"I meant, I didn't know you could suck on my balls." It was getting close to impossible to form words as she kept stroking my cock. I lay back and enjoyed it as she took my balls into her mouth, one at a time. When she sucked them both in, I endured the intense pleasure as long as I could. It felt like the best torture imaginable, and I couldn't stand it for more than a few minutes. Good as it felt, it wasn't going to make me come. I took her face between my hands and kissed her.

The second best thing about a woman sucking on your dick is the way it heats up her mouth for kissing.

Alexis straddled me on the lounge chair. My cock found its way into her and once again I heard those wonderful squishy sounds as we moved together.

The sun was getting lower, shining into my eyes, but the air was still hot. Alexis's skin was hotter as she pressed against my body. I kneaded her buttocks and lifted her up a little so that I could thrust smoothly in and out of her.

Alexis' mouth went crazy on mine, sucking on my tongue, then kissing and sucking down my neck. I knew I was getting hickeys as she sucked the skin on my throat, but I didn't care.

She must have been right about coming already, because I was lasting a lot longer than I thought I would have. She shifted against me, and instead of me thrusting up and into her, she was bouncing her hips so that she slid up and down my length.

She groaned as she moved her hips faster and her pussy clenched my dick. She pressed her breasts into my chest, tilted her head back and yelled.

She collapsed, her back heaving as she panted against my shoulder. I shifted, moving my arms under her legs, and stood. Alexis cried out as I penetrated even farther. I lifted her off of me, then let her slide back down again, loving the look on her face: eyes screwed shut, mouth stretching open. I lifted her up and this time thrust my hips up as I let her come down.

Alexis screamed. I wanted to come. I could feel my orgasm again at the base of my penis like a cat, crouching before it sprang on its prey. I lifted Alexis a little higher and thrust my hips harder. Alexis clutched me, her mouth found mine and she sucked my tongue as we moved together.

Urgency built. I lifted her higher, thrust harder, let her drop. Alexis wailed and I yelled and my semen flowed up and out of me, filling her. I felt as if I were expanding outward in all directions, but somehow I kept lifting and lowering Alexis. I felt her spasm again but my own flow felt steady and strong …

… not strong. My knees buckled and I fell on my ass onto the chaise. Alexis squealed in shock and surprise as she fell off me.

I collapsed onto my back. We panted while the clouds moved across the red and yellow sky.

"Damian, you bad boy, we're going to need another shower, now," she said once we had caught our breath. She sat up, and I did too, just so that I could continue to feel her skin against mine. "Separate showers. No sense tempting ourselves yet again. I have things to do tonight."

I drove home wondering whether I was really dreaming, and if so, when the dream had begun. When Nick had left the apartment for London?

I let my tattered cut-offs and ratty t-shirt fall onto the floor and collapsed naked onto my own bed. I fell asleep wondering if I would wake up on my sofa reading Mad magazine.

Chapter 18

Rosedale Park

"Sometimes, I wonder why I ever wear clothes." Alexis untied her halter and let it fall to the grass. She wore no bra, as usual. And as usual, I stared at her breasts for a full minute. Alexis laughed and said "Close your mouth, Damian." She pulled her short-shorts down, and her lacy panties, and put everything into her colourful tote bag.

So that's why she brought that, I thought. I struggled out of my clothes and let them fall into the grass, then stretched out on the blanket alongside Alexis. I leaned on one elbow and drank in her splendour.

Little shadows from the trees dappled her skin and rippled as they moved in the breeze. I scanned her, from her full lips, flawless skin, big dark nipples, the curves of her hips and thighs, down to her heels resting in the sweet smelling grass. "Pass me my wine," she said with her eyes closed.

I watched her breasts shift as Alexis sat up to drink her wine, watched her throat pulse as she swallowed. I kissed it.

I had shown up just before noon on a Saturday and asked Alexis if she would like to come on a picnic. "Oh, how sweet! I would love one!"

When she saw the plastic Thermos cooler I had brought, though, she suggested her own wicker picnic basket. It looked like the ones in the old Yogi Bear cartoons, the kind with a high handle and two flaps on top. But while it was wicker on the outside, it was lined with high-tech insulation and divided into compartments. Velcro ties nested two wine glasses in one corner.

I transferred the food I had bought at Alexis' favourite Rosedale deli into her basket: French bread, Italian ham, German cheese, California grapes, Swiss chocolate. I felt very cosmopolitan.

Alexis picked up the bottle of wine I had chosen, the same as a bottle I had seen on her rack — her wine-rack. "Not bad, but a little too sweet for the food you've chosen." She swapped my bottle with one from her wine cooler. "This will be better." She smiled at me, so I could not argue or even feel resentful. "I'll go change," said Alexis.

She came back down wearing short shorts and a halter top. She had taken off her jewelry and tied her hair behind her head with a simple elastic clip. "Ready to go?"

"We're taking my car this time," I insisted.

"Okay," she shrugged. "Where are we going?"

"I thought Rosedale Park. It's closest."

"Okay, it's nice."

I knew it was nice; I had scoped out a nice, secluded part of the park, well off the trails and walking paths. It looked like no one had ever been there.

I parked the car on the side of the road and led Alexis along a shady path. It was a long way, taking us far from the playgrounds and the backyards of Toronto's wealthiest.

When we reached the place I had chosen, Alexis said "Oh, beautiful! Damian, I've been in this park probably a hundred times, and I've never even imagined this spot!"

We were on a grassy, shallow slope that ended at a sharp drop-off. The Don Valley stretched out ahead of us, its multi-arched viaducts in the distance.

I spread out a blanket and started taking out the food. I opened the wine and Alexis sliced cheese and spread out the meats. "Good food," I said.

"Did you get it at the Rosedale Deli?"

We continued with small talk. We ate until we were full, then put the food away and sipped the wine. Alexis looked dismayed when I poured the last of the bottle into her glass. "Don't worry, I have a backup." I took the bottle I had chosen out of the basket. "A little sweet, I know ..."

"That's okay. We won't really notice now that we've drunk a whole bottle."

"Hot day," I said when I couldn't think of anything else to say.

"Why don't you take off your shirt?"

"I didn't take any sunscreen. And I'm not as dark as you."

"You've got a good tan. We won't be out here that much longer. Go ahead."

"Only if you do," I said. I really didn't expect her to take off her top. That was when she had stood up and dropped her halter top.

I kissed her throat again, and moved my lips up to her mouth. Her lips parted and her tongue met mine. I leaned closer until I pressed against her. Her sun-heated skin, a little sweaty like mine, slid against me.

Alexis rose and turned on her side. Her hand went behind my head and her leg went over mine. She kissed me and then lay back down on the ground, her hands behind her head. She arched her back. "God, it feels so good to be nude outdoors, under the sun."

I could not resist any longer and kissed her nipple. She sighed and arched her back further, pushing her nipple into my mouth and mashing her breast against my face. One hand went behind my head again and the other wrapped around my penis, stroking gently. I couldn't help but moan.

She lifted her leg over mine again, so I slid my hand up her thigh. She was already wet. I sucked her nipple harder as I slid a finger inside her. I rubbed her clit in a circle as I bit ever so slightly on her nipple.

She groaned. I wondered briefly if I had really made a good choice in this spot in the park, whether someone might stumble across us. What if it was a cop?

Who cares, I thought, as Alexis cupped my balls in her palm.

She swivelled around and knelt astraddle my face. I looked up briefly at her perfect round ass as her pussy settled onto my face. Then I felt her mouth surround my cock. I tilted my head to taste her pussy.

Alexis erased every thought from my mind as she nearly swallowed me. There was nothing in the world but the sensations of Alexis's mouth, and her pussy in my mouth.

I drank her in. I reached around her thighs and slid a finger inside her, then a second and a third.

And then I came hard. She gagged, choked and sat up. Somehow, I kept licking and pushing my fingers into Alexis, groaning against her vagina.

I felt her mouth around my penis again. My whole body jerked at the feeling of her mouth on my cock immediately after an orgasm. I wiggled my fingers inside her, sucked her clit and flicked it with my tongue. She rewarded me with a flood of her juices. She sat up, calling out, and then collapsed on me.

"A very nice performance," said a voice.

We both bolted upright. Standing under the trees were two cops, a man and a woman, in summer uniforms: bicycle shorts, short-sleeve shirts, flack jackets with reflective tape, yellow helmets and big mirrored sunglasses. Two bicycles leaned against the trees. The male cop was scribbling in a notebook.

"Indecent exposure, lewd behaviour, conduct unbecoming ..." said the woman.

I stood and tried to cover my genitals with my hands. "Officers," I said, but what was there to say?

"I'll call dispatch for a truck," said the woman cop to her partner.

"Well, I'm glad you enjoyed it, officers," said Alexis. She looked completely unconcerned about being caught naked, no, caught fucking in a public park.

"Oh, the judge will enjoy it, too. Put your clothes on," said the woman cop.

Alexis picked up her shorts, but instead of pulling them on, she reached into the pocket. "Please stop writing for a moment, officer, until you hear what I have to say." She walked toward them, hips swaying, confident in her nudity. She leaned close and whispered something that I could not catch, and gave each of them a hundred-dollar bill. "That's just a sweetener. The real bribe is in getting to see this." She laced her fingers behind her head in mock surrender and arched her back, showing off her breasts.

The cops just goggled: eyes wide, mouths open. Alexis calmly reached for the male cop's notepad and tore off the top sheet, then ripped it into shreds.

Then she did something that no one else in the world could ever get away with: she kissed the woman cop on the mouth, long, deep and hard.

The cop just stood there, hands sticking out slightly from her side; her partner stared, open-mouthed. When Alexis broke the kiss, she looked up at the man — he was almost a foot taller than her — and smiled. She kissed her fingertips and touched them to his mouth. Then she turned and sashayed back to me, wrapped her arms around me and kissed me deeply, raising one knee up along my side.

Without turning, Alexis said, "Thank you, officers. Have a good day."

The male cop looked at his partner, who stared at us. Finally, she shook her head, picked up her bike and walked back to the path. The male cop looked at her, looked at us again, shrugged and followed his partner.

"I'm really sorry about that," I said.

"You owe me a hundred bucks," said Alexis.

"Huh?"

"We both got caught. You picked this spot out, and I trusted your judgement. We're both at fault, so we split on the bribe."

"Okay."

She smiled at me. "Don't let it get you down. This isn't the first time I've been caught naked outdoors. First time in a few years, though."

"What did you whisper to them?" I asked.

"It's kind of a code, something shared by friends of … someone very well-placed in the city government. Kind of a 'get out of jail free' card. Come on, let's go home. I feel like a swim. And you owe me a really big g-spot orgasm now."

We dressed, packed and walked back to the car. I kept expecting the cops to jump out from behind a tree and charge us for bribery on top of public nudity, but nothing happened until we got back to my car.

The cops had not let us off completely: there was a big yellow parking ticket on the windshield.

Chapter 19

Correcting Mistakes

The complaints about Tyler didn't stop. They did not even slow down. They got more frequent and more intense.

"You didn't show up today. I had a pool party planned!"

"I'm not paying you for half a job!"

"We will no longer require your services. We have selected a pool cleaning service that provides service."

Tyler, in professional parlance, was a fucking disaster. There was only one person to turn to for help.

On Sunday, I went to my parents' backyard. I found my Mom lying in the hammock, holding a tablet computer.

"Damian! You're early!"

"Did you finish *Fifty Shades of Grey*?" I asked.

"Pfft. Piece of crap. I'm reading something much more exciting."

"*You* bought a Kindle?"

"Better: I bought an iPad." She showed me.

"Cool. So, what are you doing? Surfing the web? Facebook?"

"Nah, I don't bother with those things. I use it to read books."

"Whatcha readin'?"

She swiped a finger across the screen a number of times until an image appeared.

"*Gray Justice*? You're reading a thriller?"

"It's by an independent writer named McDermott. It's like that TV show with that short man, what was his name... Donald Sutherland and Shirley Douglas's boy."

"Kiefer Sutherland? 24?"

"That's it." She put the tablet down. "Now tell me: what's wrong?"

"Why do you think something's wrong?"

"In 20 years, you've never been early for anything. You were even born after your due date." She always says that. "Well, dinner won't be earlier than we planned. You can help your father barbeque."

"What, you *don't* want burned steaks?"

"Why didn't you get yourself a beer?" She held out a plastic wine glass: "And bring me some more of that white wine in the fridge."

My heart stopped for a second: her gesture, her posture, something as she held out that wine glass: my mother for a second looked exactly like Alexis.

Sunday dinner with my parents followed a routine that varied only with the seasons. I'd usually show up after 6, when my Dad would have almost finished barbequing the steaks to black shoe-sole consistency. But since I had come early this time, I had to help out like I had when I was 14.

I entered the kitchen from the back yard at the same moment that Dad came in from the hallway. "Hey, big guy!" he boomed, as usual, while opening the fridge and taking out a big, flat dish. Four big, red steaks marinated in a thick, red sauce. "Came early to help out?"

"Helping" Dad meant starting the barbeque — no propane for him. He insisted on charcoal, and that meant starting an hour before you wanted to eat, pouring briquettes into the ball-shaped bottom of the barbeque, dousing it with some liquid that smelled suspiciously like gasoline and trying to touch a lit match to the fluid while standing as far back as you could. After that, "helping" would involve fetching barbeque utensils, barbeque sauce, another bottle of beer and anything else that came to his mind.

"Sure," I said, reaching for the tray. That brought me close to him, and I realized for the first time that day how reluctant I was to stand next to him, now that I was taller than him. I had outgrown Dad in height a couple of years ago, but being able to look down on him did not make me feel any stronger than him, not with his wide shoulders and forearms like wrestling anacondas. But for how long had I been so loathe to stand close enough that my height superiority was obvious?

"It's too soon to take the steaks out, son. You can start the briquets burning."

My heart sank.

While we waited for the briquettes to turn gray, I sat on a patio chair and chatted with my Mom. I was guiltily aware that I didn't do this much, and she loved it. "So, how's the book?"

"Exciting. Lots of action, and I can really see eye-to-eye with the character. Sometimes, I'd like to do the things he does."

"It doesn't seem like your usual reading material."

"I've read everything by Bulgakov and Nabokov and Gabriel Garcia Marquez. I thought I would try some of these new writers for a change."

At supper, my little sister and I dutifully chewed through the steaks and kidded Dad about his complete lack of barbequing ability, as usual.

"What are you talking about? They're perfect!" he argued, as usual.

At least I could wash it down with beer. Diana, my sister, wasn't old enough, yet, but Dad let her drink some of Mom's wine.

Supper over, Dad said he had to work on a contract and went upstairs to my old bedroom, which he had converted into an office. After Diana and I cleaned up the kitchen, I went up to my old room, too.

"Dad, I need some advice."

I have never seen anyone simultaneously look so surprised, gratified and thoughtful. He put down his mechanical pencil and took off his bifocals. "About?" Without glasses, his hazel eyes squinted a little.

I sat down in the "guest" chair in his office — an antique foreman's chair, made of solid oak or something. It weighed a ton and was as comfortable as sitting on stone. I had always wondered where he had found it. It was as far removed from his desk chair as a feather bed from a Catholic altar.

"You know I hired Tyler to help with cleaning pools. And I set him up with a bunch of clients."

"I've never found it wise to hire your friends. It never works out," Dad said.

"What? But you're friends with John Andrienos, and he's your foreman on half the jobs!"

"I hired him and *then* made friends with him," Dad answered. "That's okay. That works: you work alongside someone, come to respect them, become friends. It's natural. But when you hire a friend to work for you, they seem to think your friendship is a free pass or something."

"You're right. Tyler isn't working out."

"What do you mean, specifically?"

"He's always late. Half the time, he doesn't show up at customers' places. When he does, he never does a full job. The customers are getting pissed off."

"Have you spoken to him about this?" Dad leaned back in his comfortable, ergonomic chair and swung his glasses between his fingers.

Dad loved being asked for advice.

"Yah, I told him the issues. I even gave him a warning."

Dad looked out the window, where the setting sun made the sky pink and orange. He pushed his thick grey hair back from his forehead before answering. "I've heard he's had some employment problems, already."

"He's been fired three times already this year."

"Hmm. Sounds like Tyler has a problem. Three employers already have had enough of him, and now, you."

"Yah."

"So, what do you want advice with?"

This was hard. Dad had this annoying habit of making you voice exactly what you mean. Using real words.

"What should I do?"

Dad looked at me with his unnerving look. "What do you want?" he asked finally.

"Huh?" God, you can be lame, said my brain.

"What do you want for your pool-cleaning business?"

"Geez, Dad, why do you always have to make these talks a

lesson? I want it to succeed."

"Good. And what does that mean?"

I knew this answer from years of business lessons from the city's most philosophical contractor. "Profits."

"Let's cut to the chase, son," Dad said. "You have a problem: your employee is causing customers to complain. What is the outcome you want from this?"

"I want my customers to like me again."

"So, what do you need for that to happen?"

Dad: always making me confront reality. "I need … to get rid of Tyler."

"Not necessarily. Do you think that Tyler can change? Can he behave differently, so that he doesn't make your customers leave?

"I don't know. Anyway, I've decided I don't need to worry about that anymore. I need someone to replace Tyler. I just can't take back all his clients — there aren't enough hours in the day."

"So, you've decided to let Tyler go?"

I took a deep breath. This was still hard to say. "Yes. But who can I get to take his place?"

"You want a recommendation?"

I nodded. "You know a lot of people."

Dad looked at the sunset again. "You know, the construction business has slowed down a lot, lately. I haven't had enough work to give out to my usual crew."

"I'm sorry."

"It's not your fault, son. You know, I'm glad you've found a new way to make money this summer. It's taken a lot of pressure off my shoulders."

"So, do you know anyone that could help me?"

He looked out the window again. "You know Philip Lamontaigne? Bob and Maureen's son? He's a bit older than you, but he's a good worker. I have not had enough work this year to be able to hire him, and he's been looking for work."

I remembered Philip. One of those skinny guys with a skanky beard. He always had weed on him, always had a new girlfriend and a next girlfriend. "Phil is a good worker?"

"I had him on-call last summer. He never failed to show up on time, always did more than asked of him."

Wow. Phil Lamontaigne, professional dirtbag, was a good worker. "So, you think he'd be a good pool cleaner?"

"Can you show him the ropes?"

"No problem."

Dad flipped through screens on his laptop and wrote a phone number on a post-it note. Dad has always loved post-it notes.

Phil arrived fifteen minutes early the next morning, dressed ready for work under the hot sun. He had shaved off his skanky beard, but his hair was still long.

"Hey, Damian. Long time, no see. How's your old man?" His voice was raspy, probably from too many cigarettes.

"Business is slow this summer for him. So, have you ever cleaned an in-ground pool before?"

"Nah," he shrugged. "Is it complicated?"

"Not at all. The key to this business is giving the customers what they expect."

"So, it's no different from every other kind of business."

"Whaddaya mean?"

Phil shrugged. "Customers want stuff. We do it to make sure they stay happy. Or as happy as they think they're entitled to be. And don't fuck it up."

Clean up the language, and it was exactly what Dad, and every business guru who charged for a lame-o conference, always said: give the customers what they think they want, and don't fuck it up.

Phil and I spent the day going to my customers. By the third one, Phil was doing half the work. By the end of the day, I just sent him in and sat back in the car, flipping through emails on my phone. I had paid for an upgrade to a minimal data plan. But I was damned if I was going to pay twenty-five bucks every month for a fancy phone like Tyler.

Working with Phil, unlike with Tyler, made the work go faster. We were done a full day's worth of pools before 3 p.m. I dropped him at his house, thanking him profusely.

"Be at my house tomorrow at 7:30," I said.

"Sure thing, boss. And thanks."

I texted Alexis. "Need to tlk biz. U home?"

The reply came in two minutes: "Yes. Come to back yard."

I found Alexis on her knees, pulling weeds from her herb-and-vegetable garden. She was wearing that big floppy white hat she had worn that first time I had seen her, and those big dark glasses, and a pink halter top and the bottoms of her bikini. Pink canvass gloves covered her hands.

"What's up, Damian?" she asked, tilting her head high so she could look at me over the tops of her glasses.

My eyes would not listen to my brain: they traveled from the curve of her cheek, down the side of her neck and along her collarbone. They stuck to the curve of the top of her breasts and followed that into the halter top. Then they jumped to the curve of her hips, the bare skin coming out from under the bikini bottom. My disobedient eyes swept along her leg and back up the insides of her thighs.

"Damian, what is it?" Alexis stood and brushed dirt from her knees. She wore cute little canvas shoes, pink of course. "Is something wrong?"

Something was wrong, all right. My pants were hurting me.

I took her head between my hands and mashed my mouth onto hers. She let out a muffled cry and I heard something thump into the soil — whatever gardening tool she had been holding, I guess.

Alexis pulled away. "Is this what you came to talk about?"

"No," I said as I pulled her close to me again and kissed her throat. I started nibbling downward, nipping at her collarbone.

"Damian, wait a minute, I'm in the middle of my gardening!"

"No," I repeated. I untied her halter and dropped it onto grass.

"Damian! You're so bad!" she squealed. But she made no attempt to cover her naked breasts.

My answer was to suck her nipple. In fact, I tried to cram her whole tit into my mouth. I rolled her other nipple between my fingers. "Damian," Alexis groaned. "Oh, I have so much gardening to do ..."

I slid my hand down, over her belly and under the top of her bikini. I pushed through the thick hair. Alexis gasped as my finger pressed her clit. "Damian, you're so bad ..." she repeated. "Bad,

bad," she whispered as my finger slipped between her lips. She was already moist. I rubbed up and down, and was rewarded with more moisture.

I spread the dampness over her clit, eliciting another gasp. I rubbed lightly, making Alexis' breathing fast and shallow.

I dipped my finger lower. "Damian, I have to do something," she whispered, but she moved her legs farther apart. Two of my fingers made a squishing noise as they pushed up inside her.

Her hands went down my sides and opened my belt. She pushed my pants down and stroked my cock with both hands.

I could not wait any longer. I manoeuvred her to her solid patio table, pushed her face-down on it and stepped between her legs. Before should could say "Damian—" I buried my length in her.

I saw her hands grip the edge of the table. I saw her profile. I saw her clench her jaw to keep from crying out. I saw her ass shake as I smashed into her.

I grabbed her hips and thrust as hard as I could. I wanted to be deep inside her, to own her.

I wanted to fuck her.

Alexis was biting on her finger and breathing hard. I reached around her leg and found her clit again. I pressed on it. Alexis cried out and I felt hot liquid spray my hand and thighs. She pushed against me, finding the perfect rhythm with my thrusts.

Alexis screamed around her fist. I growled, pulling her hips and smashing my pelvis forward as my own orgasm shot out of me.

I staggered back and fell into a chair. It took a long time for my heart to slow down.

Finally, Alexis asked: "What was that all about?"

"I'm going to fire Tyler."

"Firing your friends gets you randy?" She stood up, a little shaky.

"No. I came to tell you this, as my business partner, before I did it. But when I saw you in that halter ..."

She smiled and stood up. "I need something to drink. Want some red wine?" She led me into the kitchen, gloriously naked.

I could never get enough of looking at that.

"Could I have a beer, instead?"

She handed me a bottle and poured herself a big glass of wine. "So, you're firing Tyler, finally? Good. I've heard complaints."

"*You* have?"

"Mr. Hedges called me. You really shouldn't have given that client to Tyler. He lives a block away from me!"

"What was his complaint?"

"He just said the pool wasn't clean and that your worker had come very late. Mr. Hedges likes punctuality."

"Well, he's not the only one to complain," I said.

"There's never just one complaint. And don't forget that for every complaint you get, there are probably 10 unhappy customers."

"That means that *all* Tyler's customers are miserable."

"So, what are you going to do for his clients?"

"Already taken care of." I gulped down some beer. "I got a recommendation for another employee, and he's ready to start tomorrow."

"Really? Can you be sure he'll be better than Tyler?"

"I told you, he comes recommended."

"By whom?"

I felt embarrassed to admit: "Well, by my father."

Alexis nodded, sipping her wine. "Your father's been in business for some time, hasn't he?"

"Yah, but things are slow this year, so he hasn't been able to give Phil much work. So this worked out for everyone."

"But you haven't told Tyler, yet."

"No. I thought I should let you know beforehand."

She smiled and kissed my cheek. "Absolutely. Well done: you've recognized the problem, found a solution and cleared it with me, first. Go tell him. I warn you: it won't be easy for either of you. But it's an important lesson for you both, as well.

"Meet him somewhere neutral. Then hurry back: I'll order in some food, and then I'm going to fuck you like you've never been fucked before." She smiled, kissed my cheek again and went upstairs.

I sent Tyler a text message: Meet me at Starbucks, Danforth and

Gough.

When? Tyler texted back.

6 pm.

Can't make it still at Fongs

Whn cn U B thr?

6:30

Not a minute later!

I bought myself a black coffee and one of those gooey, sugary things that Tyler liked. Tyler, of course, was late.

Twenty minutes.

He lumbered in, saw me and smiled. He fell into the chair on the other side of the little table from me.

"Wassup?"

"How's it going with the customers?"

"Great! No complaints." He sat back and grabbed the gooey sugary drink without asking whether it was for him or not.

"None from you, but plenty from the customers."

"From who?"

"All of them."

"Fuckers! I busted my ass for them!"

"Tyler, I gave you a chance. I put my business in your hands. All you had to do—" I had to take a deep breath. "All you had to do was the job that I showed you how to do. It's not hard."

"Fuck, Damian, I've been working my ass off!"

"You already said that." I paused. Get this over with. It wasn't that hard to say once I made up my mind: "I have to let you go."

"Fuck you, Damian!" Tyler yelled. Everyone in the coffee shop looked at us. He stood up, and his chair made a loud noise scraping against the floor. At least it didn't tip over. "Great fuckin' friend you are!"

And he was gone.

I slumped back and looked at my watch as I sipped my coffee. The text message from Patrick took less than a minute: "Dam, WTF? Tyler!"

A minute later, I got a text that surprised me: "Why did U fre Tyler?" It was from Kristen.

My friends sure didn't waste time spreading bad news, at least about me. And they all seemed to think that I owed them explanations.

Fuck that, I thought as I snapped my phone closed. I started my car: Alexis had promised to fuck me like never before.

As I eased out of the parking spot, I wondered if I would survive the experience. I was smiling.

Chapter 20

Goodbye, Mrs. Casales

I make mistakes all the time. I try to tell myself that everyone does, I'm only human, but I feel so stupid when I repeat the same mistake.

Like not checking the call display before I answer.

"Damian! It's actually you!"

Shit. "Hello, Mrs. Casales. Is everything all right?"

"No, it's not. Not at all. You sent that one worker over to me, Tyler, and he was okay. But now, there's another stranger in my back yard!"

I knew I had not repeated the mistake I made when I hired Tyler. "Didn't you get my message about a new worker?"

"You never answer my texts, so why should I answer yours?"

I couldn't think of an argument against that. "Well, Philip is very good, much more reliable than Tyler ..."

"I had no problems with Tyler."

Yah, I know, bitch.

"But I don't know this man at all. I'm sorry, but I don't think that this is very good customer service, to keep changing the worker like this ..."

Why don't you just fuck him, too, and then you'll know him as well as you know Tyler, I did not say. "As I said, I have complete confidence in Philip. Is his work good or—"

"I wouldn't know. I sent him away. I don't need any more strangers in my life."

I felt empty just below my navel. I knew what she was about to say next.

187

"Damian, I want you to come over."

"Okay, I can come over around 10 tomorrow morning."

"No. I want you to come over here *now*."

"Geez, Mrs. Casales, it's getting late ..."

"My name is Leda!" Her voice got lower. "I need to see you. *You*. Now. Or not only am I firing you, I'm calling as many of your customers as I know."

I was there in fifteen minutes. She led me to the back yard. After a month of Tyler's care, it was a mess: overgrown bushes, whole branches floating in the pool. The skimmers were full of junk, and the water itself looked slimy. "I knew that Tyler wasn't doing a good job, but what was he doing when he came here?" I knew what he had been doing.

"Damian," Leda said, behind me. I turned to see the naked Leda. Her wild hair spilled around her shoulders, reaching almost to the dark nipples that pointed at me. Her round stomach looked like a smile, and there were little dimples at the sides of the tops of her thighs that I had never noticed before. She reached for me, and I stepped back.

She burst into tears, covering her face with her hands. That brought me closer again. "Mrs. Casales, Leda, I'm sorry. What's wrong?"

"I'm all wrong," she sobbed. "Why would I think you would want an old woman like me?"

Old woman? She was at most a year older than Alexis. I hoped like hell her two little kids weren't at home to see their naked mother pawing the pool boy.

I put my arms around her. "Leda, you're young, you're beautiful. Why are you doing this to yourself?"

She shook her head, sobbing, turned and ran into the house, leaving the sliding walk-out door open. I couldn't leave her like that; I picked up her swimming cover-up from the pool deck and followed her sobs to the family room.

I found her, sitting on the edge of a sofa, head in her hands, shoulders shaking. "I'm old, I'm fat, I'm ugly!"

I sat beside her and patted her hair. It felt strange to be comforting a naked woman. "No, no, Leda, I think you're beautiful."

Then her mouth was on mine. One hand went to my hair and the other one to my belt.

I'm not proud of what happened next. She tore at my clothes, frantic, and I helped push my shorts down and pull off my shirt. I stood, and she took my stiff dick deep into her mouth.

Maybe Tyler had taught her a few things, because this blow job felt much better than the last one. Her lips slid all the way down, and her cheeks caved in as she came up again. I ran my hands through her hair, enjoying the slurping sounds and the amazing feeling all the way up my cock.

"WHAT THE HELL?"

I turned to see a tall man with thick dark hair and a thick black moustache. Thick black eyebrows pulled together till they almost touched. Too late, I realized that my dick pointed straight at him.

"Henry!" Leda shrieked. "What are you doing here?" She crossed her arms over her breasts and crossed her legs.

"I live here! Who is this son of a bitch!"

I realized he was holding a bouquet of flowers. Shit shit shit! "I thought you had broken up!" I whined. Did I have to sound like such a weasel?

Henry took two big steps toward me, fist rising behind him. "Who the *fuck* is this?"

Henry swung and I dove. I rolled past him, grabbed my shorts and ran for the door. Henry growled and swung again, but I dodged and tore the door open. Naked, I ran for my car, my dick flapping against my thighs with every step.

Inside, I couldn't fish my keys out of the pocket of my shorts fast enough, because (as I found out then), it's more awkward to get something out of the pocket of pants that you're not actually wearing. I managed to lock the doors before Henry got there to pound the hood with two massive fists. The tires squealed as I backed out of the driveway. And then I was down the street. In the rear-view mirror, I could see Henry waving a fist, while Leda, now in her bathing cover-up, pulled him back into the house.

I managed to pull my pants on at the next red light. I drove straight home, looking over my shoulder as I crossed the parking lot to the building door.

I flopped onto my old sofa. Maybe I should go stay at my parents for a few days, I thought. But I'd rather stay with Alexis.

Leda Casales. What a fucked-up bitch. Sucking off pool boys. What the hell was the matter with her?

Alexis had told me that Leda's marriage had ended. So what was her husband doing there? And did he have to arrive just before I was about to come in his wife's mouth?

Why am I thinking things like this?

I tried to process the events of the afternoon. Leda Casales calls me up, demands that I come over; she presents herself to me, asking for sex, and bursts into tears when I say no. Okay, I didn't actually *say* no. I backed away.

That was more from surprise than refusal, said part of my brain.

Okay. Then I tried to comfort her.

Sure. Comforting. When she was nude. Let's go with that.

I *was* comforting her.

Until she stuck her tongue into my mouth. And ripped my clothes off. And practically swallowed my cock.

Don't forget, that cock was hard before her mouth got to it. In fact, to be honest, I'd have to admit that I was hard when I saw her in that cover-up.

I'd have to admit that I was hard driving up to the house. As soon as I heard her voice on the phone, I knew what would happen when we were together.

I heard a noise in the apartment hallway, and all I could think of was Henry with a baseball bat in his huge fists. I fished my phone out of my pocket and hit speed dial.

"It's me. Damian."

"I know it's you, Damian. Are you all right?" Alexis' voice sounded reassuring. "You sound funny."

"How well do you know Mrs. Casales? Her husband, actually."

"Henry? Not that well. He's kind of a hothead."

"Has he ever killed anyone?"

"What! Damian, what are you talking about?" Her tone down-shifted. "What have you done?"

"I fucked his wife. Mrs. Casales. Leda."

There was a pause, and then a shriek. It took me several seconds to figure out that Alexis was laughing.

"Oh, I should have seen that coming!" She shrieked again. I could picture her, lying on her side on the sofa, the phone against her face, eyes closed, head thrown back. I actually heard her gasping. "Some people never change!"

"You said their marriage broke up!"

Alexis laughed and laughed. "Sorry, sweetie." She gasped a few more times, taking control of herself. "Oh, dear. Yes, Leda and Henry have a history of breaking up, mostly because of Leda's history of sleeping around. Did Henry catch you in bed with her? It wouldn't be the first time."

"Not exactly in bed. She was blowing me in the family room." That sent Alexis into another storm of laughter.

When she controlled herself, she managed to say, "Damian, that's the most entertaining thing I've heard all week! But really, what's the reason for your call?"

"I think Henry followed me home. I think he's outside, in my apartment hallway with a baseball bat."

Alexis laughed again. "Oh, my, no, that doesn't sound like Henry. Do you really think he's there? Have you looked?"

"No."

"Well, check!"

I looked out the peep-hole, as far to the left and right as I could see. Nothing.

My brain had a sudden vision of Henry crouching against my door, just below the peep-hole, with an oversize baseball bat in his fists. "I don't think he's here, but I'm not sure," I whispered into the phone.

"Hold on, sweetie. I'll call Leda on the other line." The phone took on that strange suspended feeling as Alexis cut away.

The seconds ticked by. I pushed my ear to the door, listening for ... anything. Breathing, footsteps, muttered curses and descriptions of what an angry cuckold would do to his wife's lover.

Where is Alexis? Is she talking to Leda? Has she forgotten about me?

Maybe she's calling the cops on my behalf. What would the

cops do, though? Probably pin my arms while Henry pummeled me.

I couldn't stand not knowing. I strained my eye and my neck, seeing only empty hallway through that stupid fish-eye lens. I made sure the door-chain was secure, even though I remembered several scenes in movies where the bad guy easily kicks open a door secured by a flimsy brass chain. I braced my shoulder against the door, then opened it.

Just a crack.

Just wide enough to peek through.

Nothing. No one there.

Alexis' voice on my phone startled me. "Nothing to worry about, sweetie. I finally got through. It sounded like Henry and Leda were having sex while I was talking to her."

"What? That makes no sense."

"I sure got the feeling that they were fucking while I spoke to her. Anyway, Leda told me all about the two of you. You naughty boy, you. And you sent over your assistant after she showed you such appreciation the first time. How could you?"

"She fucked Tyler, too, you know. Did she tell you that?"

Alexis howled another laugh. "No wonder you fired him!"

"That wasn't why I fired him! He was a lousy worker! I kept him on for weeks after I found out he was doing Casales!"

"How are you feeling now?" The change in conversation startled me.

"Okay, I guess."

"Not too shaken up?"

"No, no, really. I'm fine."

"Good. Then get your sweet little ass over here. I'm jealous of all the action that Leda Casales is getting."

"I'm sorry, you want —"

"I want you to come over and fuck me right now."

How lucky can one guy get? Two women in one day demand sex.

"I'll be there in ten minutes."

I was there in seven.

Chapter 21

The Limit

I pulled into Alexis' driveway just as the sun set. The days were getting shorter. Pool season would end soon. And the university year would begin sooner.

I wanted to talk to Alexis about cutting back on cleaning pools to make more time for studying and classes. I wasn't a genius like Nick; I needed to concentrate on school work.

I could have called Alexis to ask her questions, or emailed her, or messaged her. But I wanted to see her. Touch her.

The sun had sunk below the rooftops and the sky had taken that grayish-blue hue as I pulled into her driveway. The air still felt sticky and warm, just not stifling as it had been during the afternoon. As I walked toward the fence, I pictured Alexis lying back on the chaise lounge, wearing her red bikini, her cover-up fallen open around her, reading a book and drinking white wine. I thought of her round, wonderful breasts rising and falling with every breath. I would walk up to her and kiss her, and pull off her bikini. I thought of the scent of her skin, the taste of her pussy, the heat of her mouth, the sound of her gasps ...

... and I heard her gasps as I pushed the gate open. I stopped: had I imagined it? Yes; I was thinking about her voice, the way she sounded as I pushed into her, and ...

There it was again.

Her gasp. Then the unmistakable cry Alexis made as she came. "Oooh, Grant," I heard.

Grant?

I came around the corner and saw I had been partly right: Alexis was on the chaise lounge. Instead of lying back, reading a book, she knelt with her naked ass high, outlining the shape of a greeting card heart. Her breasts swung back and forth as a large, naked man ploughed into her from behind.

Her hair bounced with every thrust of the large man's — Grant's — hips. She squeezed her eyes tight and panted through a wide-open mouth as she pushed back against his every thrust.

Grant tilted his head back and clenched his eyes shut, too, until I must have made a sound. He opened his eyes and grinned, not even pausing as he pounded into Alexis.

"Grant!" Alexis screamed when he smashed hard enough to move her knees. Her hand slipped off the lounge. I heard her palm slap onto the pool deck as she opened her eyes and looked right at me. She didn't pause, either. She pushed her ass back at Grant and climbed back onto the chaise lounge. "Hello ... Damian," she said between gasps she made every time Grant slammed into her. "Oh, yes. So (gasp) nice to (pant) see you ... ohhh ... see you again. (pant). This is Grant." She closed her eyes and pressed her ass into Grant's hips.

"Nice to meet you, Damian," Grant said. He gripped her hips more firmly and thrust harder again. It was like a competition between them.

I realized that my mouth was hanging open. I closed it, but didn't move otherwise.

Alexis looked at me again. "Why don't you join us?" Grant started smashing into her faster, as if he were trying to keep her from speaking. From being able to speak.

I still didn't move. Join them? A threesome?

Alexis and I had had a threesome already, with McQuaig. Alexis wanted two men this time. Had she done this before? I wondered. With whom?

Who the hell was Grant, anyway? Would I like him?

Did I like that his dick was in my girl's pussy?

She's not "your girl," said my brain.

"Come over here," Alexis said. "I want to suck your cock."

Who could argue with that?

"Mmm. While Grant ... fucks me ..."

My brain had trouble processing this, so my dick led me to Alexis. Dick took control of my hands and pulled down my short pants. Dick had no questions: it was standing up.

Alexis looked up and smiled as she took Dick into her mouth. Her lips made a delicious O-shape. She let Grant set the rhythm: every time he thrust into her, she slid down Dick, and came up when he drew back. She looked up and laughed, then closed her lips again.

Brain was quiet. Dick was joyous.

Alexis lifted her head from Dick again. I heard a squishy sound as she straightened up. She turned around and took Grant's cock into her mouth.

Her wide-splayed ass rubbed against Dick. I couldn't keep my hands off her beautiful butt. I grabbed and kneaded the flesh. God, she was beautiful.

"Stop fooling around and put your cock in me!" she ordered.

Brain started to make some kind of incoherent objection, but at that point, it was powerless against Dick. Dick pulled my hips forward and slipped into Alexis' pussy.

Dick made my hips move. When I looked up, my eyes met Grant's. "Fuckin' a," he said, smiling from one side of his mouth.

I thrust harder. Alexis moaned, over and over, bobbing her head up and down. I could only see the wild tangle of Alexis' hair, rising and falling, but I could not see her face. And I did not want to see her sucking another man.

I reached around to play with Alexis' clit. I could only tolerate being that much closer to Grant because it made Alexis scream and she let his cock out of her mouth. Her pussy sprayed me.

I kept rubbing while thrusting into her. Alexis screamed over and over again. The best part of that was that she wasn't sucking on Grant's cock.

I straightened and looked at Grant as I slammed into Alexis. Harder, something in me said. Brain? Dick? What did it matter? I slammed into Alexis so that her head bumped Grant's stomach. His hard, flat stomach. Fucker had abs.

Grant tried to guide his penis into Alexis' mouth, so I slammed harder and faster to make Alexis scream again. I could feel her thighs trembling against mine. I reached down again, rolling her nipples between my fingers. She screamed and gushed again.

I banged into her, hard as I could. Furious. She screamed and quaked, arching her back and lifting her head.

She was not sucking Grant.

I gripped her hips, hauling her back and slamming into her. Was I trying to please her or punish her? Or punish Grant?

I don't know. Brain wasn't present then. Dick slammed Brain down as I slammed into Alexis as hard as I could.

I could not hold back any longer. My orgasm erupted out of me, sharp and hot. I thrust one more time, lifting Alexis up. Her ass jiggled and I collapsed on top of her, pushing her down onto the lounge chair.

"Oh, my god, Damian," she murmured. "That was incredible."

I rolled off her and fell onto the deck. Grant looked down on me and laughed. He stepped around behind Alexis, grabbed her hips and plunged into her again. Alexis shrieked and pushed herself up on her arms. "Oh, yes, fuck me!" she yelled. She looked at me. "Come over here!"

I staggered toward her, and she reached out, grabbed my softening penis and pulled me to her face. It had only been seconds since I had climaxed, and I was so sensitive, my whole body jerked when her lips touched the tip. When she sucked me into her mouth, my vision went blank. I couldn't tell if it felt good or bad.

When I opened my eyes, all I could see was Grant fucking Alexis. A grin split his face. Sweat dripped down his sculpted chest. He laughed and then his whole body went stiff. He grunted, growled and pulled away. Alexis squealed and shook in a minor orgasm.

I made her come harder, jerk, I did not say.

Alexis let me go and sat back on the chaise lounge. "Oh, boys, that was terrific."

Grant and I just stood there, panting. After a few minutes, he stepped over to me, arm extended. "Pleased to meet you," he said.

I shook his hand. How do you greet the other guy in an unexpected threesome? My brain was silent, and Dick was exhausted.

"You were an unexpected surprise," Alexis said. "And a

yummy one, too. Get yourself another glass; there's lots of wine."

Fetch another wine glass? The words did not make any sense. I clenched my eyes shut, then opened them, still unable to believe the scene in front of me: Alexis and Grant, both naked in her back yard, drinking wine.

"Uh, no thanks. I don't really want any wine."

"More for us," Grant laughed and drank his wine down.

"What brings you over tonight?" Alexis asked.

"I, uh, I wanted to ask you something. About business."

"What?"

I could not take my eyes off her body, glistening with sweat and other liquids. She was so sexy, but I wasn't responding sexually. How was I responding?

Brain was still quiet. "I — I have to go," I stammered.

"Why? You just came." Grant and Alexis both laughed at her pun.

I picked up my shorts and t-shirt and walked away without another word.

On the way back to my apartment, my mind just wouldn't work. I could not think. I didn't know how I felt.

We met the next morning in the café at the street level of Alexis' office building. Water trickled musically over an installation of rocks and plants. Customers ordered overpriced coffees in soft tones. Baristas answered and served in chipper but muted tones. The air was way too humid even for Toronto in August. But the air conditioning kept the temperature ideal.

I poured what seemed like a gallon of cream just to get my coffee to the right colour. Alexis sipped elegantly on espresso.

Alexis looked sexy sipping espresso.

"What did you want to talk about last night?" she asked. She wore a sleeveless white blouse with a deep neckline and tight white pants that ended half-way down her calves. Women's clothes are weird.

She managed to carry off a look at once powerful and hotter than the coffee I gave up on drinking.

"Who's Grant?"

"Oh, Grant. We're working on a deal. Financial." She leaned

forward. "Just between us, I fucked him yesterday and today I'm going to screw him." She fell back into her chair and laughed at her own joke. I forced a couple of yucks.

"Have you known him long?"

"I've known him for close to a year, but last night was the first time we fucked." I still found it shocking to hear Alexis, a sophisticated woman, saying "fuck" in public in the same tone she said "work."

"I don't know what to think, or even feel about last night," I admitted.

"You're not feeling possessive all of a sudden, are you?" I had seen, I think, every other emotion on her face: angry, horny, passionate, tender — but that was the first time I had ever seen Alexis look unhappy. "I don't like it when men, or women, feel possessive about me."

"Who am I to you, Alexis? What is our relationship?" I cannot believe I said that. I sounded like Kristen.

"I told you before: you are my lover. My favourite lover."

"And Grant?"

"Grant is a very attractive man."

"Do you fuck every attractive man you meet?" I tried, but failed, to keep an angry edge off that question.

"Of course not!" Alexis sounded and looked like she was talking about buying shoes. "I only fuck men when I feel like it. They have to be attractive, of course, and they have to make me feel good. And if they're not good lovers, I certainly won't fuck them again."

I couldn't pass up that compliment. "So, I'm a good lover?"

Alexis smiled and I couldn't feel mad, or hurt, or anything but happy and horny. "You had a certain raw talent, and a lot of passion. And you have to admit, you've been getting a lot of practice. So yes, now, you're a good lover. Very good, in fact. Don't feel threatened by Grant. You didn't feel threatened by Julia McQuaig. You didn't have this kind of reaction when we had a three-way with another woman! And despite your misgivings, you were turned on last night. You fucked me so hard I thought I was going to pass out!"

"I was turned on by *you*. Not by Grant."

"You were turned on seeing two gorgeous people fucking."

"No, by seeing *you* naked." My voice dropped. I just couldn't talk as casually and openly about sex, about fucking, as Alexis did. "By seeing you fucking."

"Well, it's moot now. Damian, are you breaking up with me?"

"God, no! No, Alexis, I ..." what? How *did* I feel? Did I love her?

Dick did. Brain kept sending me images of naked Grant behind naked Alexis' upturned ass. So I sat there with my mouth hanging open.

"Damian, you're so cute, but I have a meeting. What did you come over to talk to me about?"

I shook my head. "Oh, yeah. Um, well, it's close to the end of August, and university is starting soon. I won't have as much time for PoolGeeks. So I wanted to discuss the end of the season with you. How do I tell customers that I won't be able to maintain the same level of service?"

We talked about business for another fifteen minutes before Alexis looked at her watch. "Oh, hell. Damian, I have to go to another meeting..."

I slid off my chair onto one knee in front of Alexis. "Marry me."

What the fuck? said Brain.

Alexis took my outstretched hand and pulled me to my feet. "You're so sweet, I could eat you up right here. But that would get us arrested in Toronto, and I already used up my police favours in Rosedale Park. Come over tonight, okay?"

"Will Grant be there?"

She patted my cheek. "No, sweetie. Just you and me, I promise."

I rushed through cleaning two of the four pools I had on my schedule for that afternoon and texted the other two customers that I would catch up the next day due to "unforeseen circumstances." I pulled on a slightly cleaner shirt as I pulled up in front of my neighbourhood's jewelry store.

The sales lady's eyebrows drew down and her lips thinned as I came in the door. Maybe I should have changed into something other than tattered and stained cut-offs and my Metallica t-shirt. "I need to buy an engagement ring," I said.

As if those words had launched an app, the sales lady's expression morphed from "Don't get my store dirty" to "I love all your money." I stepped up to the counter. "I guess I should go for a diamond, huh?" I looked at her name-tag: Ivana.

Ivana was a short, round woman with a lot of bleached hair and dark eyes that had a strange glitter. I could not be sure, but I thought I saw her lick her lips quickly. "Diamonds are traditional for engagement rings, yes," she said with a slight accent. "Please, sit down." She indicated two seats in front of a part of the counter that was lower to accommodate seated browsing.

I sat and looked at the rings arranged in ranks and rows. I had to move my head back and forth to get around the glare. How do you choose a ring?

"So, who is the special girl?" Ivana asked in the same tone I remembered my kindergarten teacher using.

"A lady, actually," I said, not looking at Ivana but at the rings. "How much is that one?" I pointed to a solitary diamond in the middle of the display.

"Very nice choice," said Ivana, and I swear, she licked her lips again. She unlocked the drawer with a key attached to a plastic coil around her wrist, slid the drawer open and made a show of putting a tray of rings on top of the display case. She put the one I had pointed to half-way up her own index finger, pulled the round tag attached to it to one side with her other hand and squinted at it. "Two caret certified Canadian diamond, excellent quality, no inclusions, brilliant cut on a platinum band. An excellent choice. She will be very happy."

It *was* beautiful, but then, all the diamond rings were. They were almost indistinguishable, in fact, except for their size. Some were different shapes, some had smaller companion stones set in the same ring, and there were several rings that had three identical stones in a row. How could you decide based on beauty?

"How much?" I asked.

Ivana looked into my eyes. "Seventeen thousand, nine hundred ninety-nine dollars." Her smile revealed sharp white teeth.

Something in the back of my mouth went the wrong way down my throat. I could not stop coughing for what felt like five solid minutes. By that time, Ivana had put the offending ring away and had set out three other choices. "May I ask how much you intended to spend?"

"I don't know ..." I had no idea how much diamonds cost. Sure, it's going to be expensive, said part of my brain. But you don't have that much money. Plus, you have tuition and books to pay for.

"Generally speaking, you should spend three months' salary on a diamond engagement ring," Ivana offered. "Does that help?"

Who came up with that one? And based on what? How much money diamond merchants want to make. What did *they* spend their money on?

Focus, Damian. I knew I would have to spend more than I wanted to. There was no way I could hope to impress Alexis, even if I were to give Ivana all the money I had saved, maxed out my credit card and thrown in my car and my right arm, too. I had to find a ring that showed I was sincere, serious.

I looked at rings with successively smaller stones, thinking about how much money I had in my bank account, how much in PoolGeeks', how much credit I had left on my credit card. I ignored my brain when it told me to relax, if Alexis says yes, I will never have to worry about money again.

I will always worry about my own money, I told my brain. I'm not going to sponge off of her.

Of course not, said my brain.

I finally selected a ring. Ivana told me the price. I felt nauseous and dizzy when she presented the invoice, with tax.

"Would you like to take advantage of our easy-payment plan?" said Ivana in a voice like honey. "There's no interest, just an administrative fee of one hundred thirty-five dollars, and you make 24 easy, equal payments."

I thought of my father's advice against payment plans. I could hear his voice: "They make it cost twice as much money in the end." But if I could keep up the easy payments, the only amount over the tag price would be that administrative fee, right?

Part of my brain did not believe that.

Then I thought of my bank account. My mouth was very dry when I said, "All right, I'll do that."

Ivana smiled at that and pulled out a file folder from under the counter. That led to a half-hour of paperwork to set up the account, a phone call to my credit card company and another one to the jewelry store's credit office and signature after signature on long paper that crinkled as the pen moved across it.

Finally, Ivana put the ring into a little box. "Would you like me to wrap it?"

"No." I had to get out of there. I had to see Alexis.

In the evening, Alexis buzzed me in the front door without asking who it was. When I stepped into the house, she called me from upstairs. "Come to the Play Room. Quickly!"

She was nude, lying on the bed. "I couldn't wait and started without you," she said.

I pulled my clothes off as quickly as I could while Alexis rolled a nipple between her fingers.

Dick clobbered Brain and I dove into Alexis' crotch. I slid two fingers into her, curving them up to rub her g-spot until she squirted.

I got up on my knees and pounded her like I had the night before. Alexis lifted her hips to pound me back.

She likes it doggy-style, said Brain or Dick. I couldn't tell. I flipped her over and pulled her hips up.

She screamed and squirmed. I felt her twitch as she climaxed. I held back. When I felt my orgasm coming on, I pulled out and pushed Alexis down onto her side. She pulled her upper knee to her chest, opening for me. I rubbed her clit as I pushed in again, making her wail.

Dick wanted to come, but Brain said "Wait." Hard to believe, but Brain won that time. I turned Alexis on her back again. I grabbed her ankles and lifted her legs high, pushing her thighs as far apart as I could. Alexis groaned as Dick slid into her.

I watched her face as she came. Dick warned me that I was going to come soon. I erupted, hot, my arms spasming and my hips losing control. Jerking, I dropped to the bed. When I could move again, I pulled Alexis closer to me, just to feel her body next to mine.

She kissed me. "Come to my bedroom. Stay the night."

I grabbed my shorts, fumbling in the pockets while my eyes followed Alexis' naked, swaying backside to her bedroom. She stopped by her gigantic bed and looked at me with a puzzled expression as I fell onto my knees in front of her again. "No, I think even I have had enough of your tongue on my clit for a couple of hours, at least."

Dick was tired enough to let Brain stay in control. I pulled the ring out of my pocket. "Marry me," I said again.

"Oh, Damian." And once again, Alexis looked unhappy. She sat on her bed. "Put that away and sit beside me. Let's talk rationally."

Have you ever tried to speak rationally to a beautiful woman while both of you are sitting naked on her bed?

"It doesn't make sense for us to get married," she said.

"Why not?"

"First, I'm ten years older than you."

"So?"

"How would your parents feel about that? Do they even know I exist?"

"Sure they do!"

She shook her head. Her hair bounced around her shoulders. "Do they know you're fucking me regularly?"

"Well..."

"I told you this afternoon that I am no one's property, Damian. My late husband treated me like I belonged to him, but I set him right. No one is going to do that to me, ever again."

"I don't want to own you! I lo—"

"Ssh." She put her finger against my lips, a gesture both aggravating and exciting. I kissed it. "Don't say that." Tears glistened in her eyes. "We are lovers. We do not possess each other. We have no claims on each other but our mutual feelings and respect. Leave it at that."

I could not say anything more. My voice had deserted me. So had Brain and, for all I could tell at the moment, Dick, too. All I could do was to lean closer, feel the warmth of her light brown skin and kiss away her tears, one soft kiss to each eye.

Her tears were salty, her skin soft. She was holding her breath and I held mine as long as I could while I kissed her eyes again, her cheek, her mouth.

We fell back together, slowly, kissing. Alexis reached for me and I wrapped my arms around her. I should have wondered why she was sad, but I did not think at all in that moment. I just breathed in her soft skin, tasted her warmth, felt her breaking sadness. The only desire I had was to take away whatever was hurting her.

We pressed together, tender and tight at the same time. Her fingertips tickled my neck, her lips explored my mouth. Her thighs caressed mine, my hands warmed her back. We were one being, moving closer to each other, making no sound but our own breath. I moved within her, she moved around me. We knew nothing but our mutual hunger. At that moment, I truly lo— no, I won't say it.

The world became nothing but the soft heat of Alexis pressed against, around and within me and I saw nothing but white heat.

I woke to Alexis smiling down at me. "I have to go to work," she whispered. "You know how to let yourself out."

I knew to stay out of Alexis' way as she showered and dressed. I knew to take everything of mine from her house when I left. And I knew not to call her that day, or the next.

Or the next.

She called me three days later. "What, you propose marriage, and then try to hide from me for the rest of your life?"

"Well, I ..." I had absolutely no words for her. I thought about telling her about returning the ring, about the embarrassment that Ivana's phoney sympathy made worse. I thought about telling her that I didn't get a refund on the hundred thirty-five dollar "administrative fee." I thought about telling her the return process was another hour in my life I would never get back.

All those thoughts died when Alexis ordered: "Get your ass over here. We need to talk, and I need you to fuck me."

So I went. Dick drove.

She let me in as usual, buzzing the front lock open without bothering to come to the door. I found her by the pool, stretched out nude on a lounge chair with a business magazine on the table beside her. "Get yourself a beer and take off your clothes," she said.

Dick made me obey. Nude, I sat on the second chaise lounge, sipping overpriced beer from the bottle.

"So, what do you have to say for yourself?" she demanded, and took a sip of white wine.

I shrugged. "I didn't know what to say to you. I've never had a marriage proposal rejected before."

"Don't be a smart ass. You knew I wasn't going to marry you. And you were relieved when I said 'no.'"

She wasn't wrong.

But this was not a fair discussion, not with her boobs staring at me like that. I fought back the only way I could think of. "So, how's Grant?"

"Grant? What has Grant to do with anything?"

"Well, the last time I came to your pool, I found you ... fucking him." Why was it so easy for Alexis to say "fuck," and so hard for me? When referring to sex, that is.

"Don't worry about Grant. I told you, we were working on a business deal."

"That was a business deal?"

"Men play golf when they work out business deals. I fuck. Anyway, I've taken everything I can use from Grant. He's finished, now."

"What do you mean?"

"I mean, he came out on the losing end of that deal. While he was fucking me, he was trying to screw me. But in another day, I'll control ninety percent of his capital. He's going home broke and drained of a significant amount of body fluid." She smiled and sipped her wine.

She dripped some on her chest. I could see it was deliberate. She looked at me as she rubbed the wine into her nipple and then put the tip of her finger in her mouth. "What are you waiting for?"

Dick was ready to go. Brain, though, damn it, brought up an image of Alexis kneeling on that same lounge chair, ass high in the air, and Grant naked behind her.

As if she could read my mind, Alexis sucked her finger, made it really wet, and then trailed it down her naked body, over her nipple, down, over her belly, lower. Her fingertip traveled to her thigh, lower still, then reversed direction, climbing, climbing.

I let out a breath.

Brain realized that I was kneeling between her thighs only when my tongue reached her clit, pushing her finger away. She was so wet, so hot. I looked up to see my hands on her breasts.

Making love to Alexis had become so easy, so natural. I knew what she liked and I loved to do it. I slid my tongue inside her as I tweaked her nipples with my fingertips. The sound of her moans sent vibration through my body.

Alexis slid lower. She lifted her legs higher in the air and shook and squirmed. The next thing I knew, she wrapped her arms and legs around me and tried to pull all of me into her.

I was moving purely by instinct, guided solely by Alexis's reactions. I watched her face, and when she threw back her head and screamed out her orgasm, I pulled out, flipped her over and took her from behind. Like I had before. That night.

I grabbed her hips and pulled her to me, smashing into her like a demon. I only thought of how I felt. What felt good. I held back my orgasm just to make myself feel better, longer. I almost didn't hear her screams, her pants, her groans.

Sweat dripped from my face onto Alexis's ass, and then I could not hold back any longer. I growled, I moaned, I yelled as my orgasm flew out of me. I pulled her closer and smashed my hips forward as far as I could, roaring into the summer night.

Conscious thought came back slowly. Were those stars in the blackness overhead? Was that the night breeze caressing my shoulders? Was that Alexis' smooth ass pressed against me? Was that her voice? "Damian, stop digging your fingers into my hips."

I sat back on my heels. Alexis rolled over, leaning back into the lounge chair. She picked up her wine and drank half of what was left. "Mmm, that was interesting," she said. "Do you feel better, getting that out of your system? And into mine?"

The things that woman said would have killed my grandmother.

I did not know what to say, so I drank beer.

"Damian, we make each other feel good. I love having hot sex with you. And you love having hot sex with me. There's no use denying it at this point. Let's not play games, and let's not pretend this is any more than what it is. You come over here and I'll fuck your brains out. Deal?"

Dick would not let me turn this down. "No more Grant?"

"Are you asking me to be exclusive to you? I told you, I won't be anyone's possession."

"I don't want to possess you. I just want ... you."

Alexis smiled her indulgent smile. "You really don't get it, do you? Damian, I love sex. Lots of it. And I have no illusions about it. I like fucking men and women, and I will not be exclusive to anyone. But I also won't fuck anyone if it makes them uncomfortable. Are you uncomfortable fucking me? Do I need to find a new favourite young lover?"

I actually thought about that. Dick was tired enough that it let me use my brain for a few minutes. "No, you don't need to find another lover," I said, finally.

What did I have to lose? This beautiful woman was offering me what every man fantasized about: no-strings, enthusiastic sex, whenever I wanted it.

But high-school lectures about STDs and promiscuity kept echoing in my mind. I struck for a compromise. "But, when I'm here, it's just the two of us from now on. Okay?"

Alexis smiled the most genuine smile I have ever seen. She sat up and kissed me. She touched my face and said, "All right. You have a deal."

Then she reached down and took Dick in both hands. She rubbed it gently and softly, and then bent forward and took it into her mouth.

I could not believe that I was hard already. Alexis moved steadily until I came again. She sat up and finished her wine. "Okay, lover-boy. Time for you to go home. We both have work in the morning."

As I drove home, I realized that I still understood Alexis no better than I had that first day I saw her in that incredible bikini.

Chapter 22

School Begins Again

Summer had to end. The rain started on September 1 and continued all week.

It was time to end the pool-cleaning business. Heavy, cool rain makes cleaning pools not only miserable, but more difficult, too, with more leaves, debris and dirt washing into the pools. Customers weren't swimming much and didn't mind when I cut back the cleaning schedule to once every ten days. It meant less money for me, but I had to find some way to accommodate the start of classes. I knew that third year would be a lot harder.

I skipped the orientation week activities; I had done them before, and I wasn't interested in hanging around with frosh anymore. I spent the time shopping for used books. Of course, most of my professors insisted on the latest editions, so I ended up in long line-ups in the bookstore, trying to hold onto about a hundred pounds, and several hundred dollars worth of textbooks.

"That economics book is close to two hundred dollars," said a voice behind my shoulder. I turned to see a tall, slim girl with straight blonde hair and big brown eyes.

"Mary-Anne Krupa," I said. "We were in Microeconomics together last year." Her hair was lighter than I remembered it had been last winter, and she had a deep tan. She must have worked outdoors through the summer, like me. I wondered how different I looked, myself.

"We were in the same project team! Did you forget that?" she laughed.

When she smiled, she pushed her tongue up behind her top teeth. It struck me as somehow innocent and sexy at the same time. How do women do these things?

"I didn't forget."

"Have you seen the prices of these books? They've gone up since last year," she said. She leaned closer. "I can't afford all these new books. You wanna split on the cost of a couple? We could be study-buddies."

Study buddies with a gorgeous blonde sounded too good to be true — especially since she was already acting friendlier than my old girlfriend.

I paid for the economics book, and she promised to give me half the price later. To impress her, I carried her books as well as mine to one of the campus' cafés. I told her about my summer as a PoolGeek. She told me about her summer job in northern Ontario, planting trees for the paper companies. That explained the sun-bleached hair and the tan. I tried not to look like I was looking at her trim body. I could see the muscles in her bare arms. I wondered about her legs under those boots and pants. Then I wondered about the rest of her under those clothes.

To slow down my brain, I asked her "Does tree-planting make much money?"

"Tons," she said. "I bought a whole new wardrobe." She showed off her new high boots. "But you still gotta be careful with money, right? 'Specially with the tuition increase."

We compared schedules: we shared three classes together. "My major is a little different from yours," she said.

"Maybe they'll complement each other. That can help us, as study buddies."

"Gotta go," she said, gathering her new books. "Call me tomorrow?"

"You know it." Don't sound sleazy, said my brain.

Call her, call her, call her! said Dick.

I called her the next morning. "Where are you?" she asked.

"Just came out of the subway. Heading for the first Financial Accounting lecture."

"I'm there, already. Jaffer's lecture theatre, third row from the back. I'll save you a seat."

I found her almost dead-centre in the lecture theatre. Professor Jaffer, a very small, very fat man, had already started droning at the podium. It was going to be a dull, tough year.

When she saw me, Mary-Anne surprised me with a wide smile that lit up the whole lecture theatre. I stumbled past a huge guy on the aisle seat and a girl who seemed to be all legs, made of pipe cleaners.

"Geez, I thought third-year lectures would be smaller," I said.

"Did you bring the textbook?" she asked, leaning close and putting her hand on my arm.

"To the lecture? No."

"You have your computer?"

I slid my brand-new Macbook out of my backpack. "Go to his website, quick. He's not going to project his lecture notes; he expects you to follow the PowerPoint on the Web."

What a dweeb, I thought.

At the end of the lecture, Mary-Anne and I managed to sign onto the same tutorial group. Then we had to part for separate classes. "Meet for lunch?" I asked.

We met and endured a university cafeteria lunch. I didn't even notice the food: I looked into Mary-Anne's deep brown eyes and watched her lips as she spoke.

"Wanna hang out next Saturday night?" I managed to stammer when she finished her coffee.

"Sure!" she said with a wide smile. She looked at her watch. "Gotta go!" She squeezed my shoulder and skipped once as she hopped from her high chair. I watched her ass sway as she walked away.

Mary-Anne and I met every day through the rest of the week. In addition to sharing three classes, we managed to get into the same tutorial groups for each one. She seemed as happy as I when we discovered the same interest in a lecture that was coming at the end of September.

As we walked out of our last class together Friday afternoon, she stopped in the hallway and pulled three twenty-dollar bills from her pocket.

"What's this for?"

"The economics textbook. The one we split on, that we're sharing, remember?" She pulled it from under my arm, and I could see her muscles ripple as she tucked the book under her own arm. "I'm paying for my half now, because I'm using it this weekend. I'll let you have it Monday."

She stood on tiptoe and stretched up to kiss my cheek. "See you then." She walked away, turning once to look over her shoulder, wave and give me that smile that was both wicked and innocent.

For the first time in my life, I wished the weekend would go by quickly.

Chapter 23

Hello, Mary-Anne

My new routine set itself so easily during the second week of classes. Lectures, tutorial groups, visits to the library. Mary-Anne seemed to feel sitting together with me in every class and tutorial we shared was also a part of her natural routine.

She brought back the economics textbook as she had promised on Monday. I spent the whole week looking for her on the campus, breathing in her presence when she was beside me in classes and tutorials, missing her in the evening.

On Friday, Mary-Anne surprised me as we walked out of the last class we had together. "So we're hanging out tomorrow night, right?"

I felt surprised, delighted, *amazed* that she still wanted to hang out. It was a date.

Like my old Friday night dates with Kristen. Only ... maybe it could be much more.

Shut up, Dick, I thought. I had one more lecture to get to.

I woke up Saturday at noon, thinking of Mary-Anne. I showered, shaved — I was up to shaving twice a week by that time — and while gulping down instant coffee and Cheerios, texted her. Want to go 2 movie 2nite? Cliché, but sometimes, a standard approach is best.

We went to something completely forgettable. I forgot the point and the plot immediately.

I walked her to her dorm room. "No guests inside after 11:00," she said.

"Wanna come to my place? I live on my own, off campus."

"Maybe next time." And then she tilted her head back and closed her eyes. I leaned closer and we kissed. Deeply. When she pulled away, I swayed on my feet. I felt dizzy.

"See you on Monday?" she said as she pushed the lobby door open.

"Why not tomorrow?"

"Okay."

Morning could not come fast enough. I woke up insanely early and paced my apartment, waiting for a decent hour to call someone. When I picked up my cell phone, the Message icon flashed.

Mary-Anne K.: Want 2 go 2 ROM?

The Royal Ontario Museum? I texted: YES.

Meet there 1 hr.

She wanted to see an exhibit of First Nations textiles. I learned a few interesting tidbits about our own history. I wanted to see the bats, but Mary-Anne absolutely refused. "I hate bats!"

"What about Batman?" I pulled her toward the Bat Cave. "He has a Bat Cave, full of computers and the coolest car in history. Maybe that's what's here."

Mary-Anne took my arm in both hands and swung me into a side corridor. She pushed my back against a wall, pressed her body against mine and kissed me.

Her tongue pushed into my mouth and her hands roved up and down my sides. She kissed my throat and pulled away. Her brown eyes, I swear, shone. Her breasts heaved and her mouth was open.

My mouth felt dry when hers parted from it. "Come home with me," I croaked.

"Way ahead of you," she said, running to the entrance.

We pushed our way through the crowds into the station. We couldn't stop kissing all the way on the subway. An older lady, sitting beside my knees, made that "tsk" noise every thirty seconds until we reached Pape station.

I scrambled to lock my apartment door while Mary-Anne tore at my clothes. I pulled too hard on hers and her eyes flashed angry when her t-shirt ripped. "Damn it! I like that shirt!"

I fell on her, shoving my tongue into her mouth and pulling her pants down. Somehow, we made it to my bedroom. Somehow, we were both naked.

I kissed down Mary-Anne's neck, sliding my tongue down her breasts. I sucked her nipple into my mouth and swirled my tongue around it. Mary-Anne's hands wrapped around my penis, sliding up and down.

I moved my mouth to her other breast and sucked it deep. She cried out, then swivelled on the bed so that she was on top of me. She pressed her narrow hips down, smothering my face, and licked the length of my penis.

I slid my tongue in between her pussy lips, tasting her. Her lips slid up and down me, wet, hot.

I grabbed her, flipped her onto her back and lifted her long legs up over her head. She squealed, delight on her face as I drove into her. I pressed as deep as I could, over and over, and she screamed my name again and again.

I roared as my life flowed out of me into her. She quaked, clutched at me, pulled me deeper.

I fell on her and slowly relaxed. When I rolled onto my side, Mary-Anne melted into me. I breathed in her scent, her sweat, her exhalations. And we fell asleep.

I woke in the dark, Mary-Anne pressing her naked ass into my cock. I don't know what point she was between sleep and consciousness, but my lust was urgent.

I kissed the back of her neck and slid my hand under her knee. I lifted her leg and slipped into her. She was wet, so wet, and hot. She moaned a little, turning her head against mine. I kissed her cheek and pushed into her. One hand reached around and took her breast. We slid against each other like that for a beautiful, long time. She shook and cried out once. I felt her spasm around me, and I climaxed quietly and sweetly inside her.

We slept again.

I woke with sunlight streaming through the window. I had forgotten to close the blinds last night. I wondered if anyone had been able to see us making love the night before.

Who cares, I decided. We're two young, good-looking people doing what comes naturally. Fuck you, Kristen.

I got up on one elbow and looked at Mary-Anne, stretched out naked on my bed. A beautiful girl, sleeping naked on *my* bed. Fuck you, Tyler.

Her skin, so smooth and tight, made my mouth water. The soft curve of her shoulder echoed her cheek. Her lips parted a little. The curve of her chin took my eyes down her throat to her arm, which blocked my view of her naked breast. Lower, her ass rounded so smoothly to her thigh, to her knee. I felt a sudden urge to kiss her whole body, to taste her, to eat her up.

Her face looked as innocent as a child's. I brushed her blond hair away from her shoulder and kissed it.

Mary-Anne stirred a little. I kissed lower, kissed her nipple, kissed her stomach, kissed her thigh.

She rolled onto her back and made a little noise. I looked at her lovely face: her eyes were closed, but a tiny hint of a smile touched the corners of her lips.

I kissed her navel, then lower, and again lower. She squirmed under me. Her slim legs parted. I kissed lower and breathed her in. Musk, sweat, another smell: myself.

I kissed my way down her wet pussy. She raised a knee and her lips parted. My tongue slipped in between.

God, she tasted good. Or was that me? Or both of us? My tongue slid up and found her clit. I flicked it until Mary-Anne arched her back and moaned.

I slid my tongue as deep as I could, claiming her. God, she was so hot. She trembled and shook and as I sucked her clit into my mouth again, she screamed.

Someone in the apartment next door banged on the wall.

I rose over her in time to see Mary-Anne open her eyes. She almost killed me with her smile. She raised her knees along my sides and I slid into her.

I leaned forward to kiss her. She opened her mouth wide and lifted her knees higher, opening herself wider at the same time.

I pushed my hips into her, pressing and grinding. She pushed back, licking my tongue at the same time. I had to break the kiss, though. I needed air. I gasped and panted, feeling sweat slide down my back.

I kissed Mary-Anne's throat. She was sweating, too. I drank her in as I shifted my hips. We pressed together as tight as we could. I felt different types of pressure all down my penis as she clenched at it, pulled it in deeper.

This time, I came like a river, a smooth flow that didn't rock me so much as draw all of me through the tip of my penis and into Mary-Anne. I heard a strange noise and realized it was my own breath. I fell beside her on the narrow bed.

She kissed my face. "Good morning," she giggled.

"Wow," was all I could manage to say.

We lay in bed, cuddling and nibbling on each other until we could no longer tolerate its confines. "Ever think about getting a double bed?" Mary-Anne asked.

The morning light gave me a good look at her nude body as she went to my closet. I had never seen such a fit looking woman naked before. Her shoulders were broad and muscular, her breasts high. Her butt twitched with every step and the long muscles on her narrow thighs stood out.

She put on one of my button-down shirts, one that Alexis had bought for me to wear to meet with new clients. When Mary-Anne did up just one button in the middle and padded to the kitchen to look for breakfast, I realized something: I hadn't thought of Alexis once in two days — even as I made love to Mary-Anne using some of the techniques that Alexis had taught me.

You're not supposed to think of one woman and fuck another one, said my brain.

You're right this time, brain.

I pulled on pajama bottoms and followed Mary-Anne. "Don't you eat breakfast?" she asked.

"Of course." I took out the instant coffee and put the kettle on.

"Instant coffee?"

"What's wrong?"

"Don't you have real coffee?"

I shrugged. "No coffee-maker. This is okay for getting you going in the morning."

She touched my face. "I thought I already did that."

The morning sunlight filtered through her long blonde hair from behind, leaving enticing shadows down her neck. I could not pull my eyes away from the border between sunlight and shadow on her skin just above the button on my shirt. I kissed her.

"Come on, I'm starving. Sex always makes me hungry and I haven't had anything to eat since supper last night!"

"Where do you want to go?"

She found her clothes in the hall, where I had dropped them the night before. It was a thrill to watch her take off my shirt and move, nude until she pulled her sweater on. But it was a disappointment to watch her pants slide up her legs.

I pulled on some clothes and we went to a café for a good breakfast. All I could think until her food arrived was that Mary-Anne was not wearing any underwear. Then I watched her open her mouth wide and scoop in crepes stuffed with cream cheese and blueberry syrup. I could not take my eyes off her mouth as she chewed, or from her throat as she swallowed. When a tiny drop of syrup mixed with cheese dripped from her lips and down her chin, I thought I would come right there.

She saw me staring and smiled, trying to keep her lips together. She swallowed again, then while looking right into my eyes, licked her lip and made a show of swallowing. She touched her finger to my forehead. "Dirty mind," she laughed.

All too soon, she stood. "Gotta get to class. See you tonight." I watched her stride out the door, her ass twitching with every long stride. Only when the door had closed did I realize that my mouth was open.

I knew I had a problem. There was only one way to deal with it.

I took the subway to Alexis' place before supper. She wasn't home; I keyed in the passcode on the security keypad and hung out by her pool for two solid hours before she slid the walkout open and handed me one of her expensive beers.

"I've met someone," I said. No preamble.

Alexis sat on her chaise lounge and sipped her wine. "Someone other than your silly childhood girlfriend?"

"My relationship with Kristen is over. I've met someone new, at university. I didn't plan it. It just happened."

"Congratulations. So what are you trying to tell me: no more sex?"

I could not bring myself to say "yes." Not with Alexis sitting there in her perfect white blouse and tight beige pants.

"Relax, lover-boy. It's fine. I understand. Oh, you're so cute when you try to be noble!" She smiled, but there was something about her eyes that told me she was lying.

"I'm sorry ..."

"You're not planning to marry her already, are you?"

Fear stabbed through me. I could not move. "Close your mouth, Damian," Alexis added with a humourless laugh. "You can be impetuous, you know." She turned away suddenly, blinking repeatedly. "I think you had better go. I have a busy day, tomorrow, and some things to take care of tonight." Her voice was low, rough, not musical at all.

On the way home, I thought of the people I had left over the summer: Kristen. Tyler. Patrick. And now, Alexis. She had only come into my life four months ago, and now, she was gone.

I was going through some kind of passage. How does the old saying go, or is it a song: leave childish things behind.

Chapter 24

Make-up Kristen

Kristen found me on the way to the St. George subway late Friday afternoon during that first week of classes. Had she been waiting for me?

No, that's ridiculous, I thought. She knows where I live. She'd wait there.

Still, I could not shake the feeling that Kristen had been pacing St. George Street for hours, waiting for me to come along, on my way to or from classes, so that she could make it look like a chance encounter.

Stop over-thinking it, my brain said.

"Well, hello," said Kristen, smiling broader and brighter than I had seen her in ... well, years.

"Hello, yourself," I said, and I could not help smiling back. She hooked her arm into mine and fell into step beside me. "What brings you here?"

Instead of answering me, she asked "Where are you going?"

"Class," I said.

"Me, too!"

Coincidence, said part of my brain. You're in the same university, same year, same faculty. You're bound to run into each other.

"We haven't seen each other for a long time," she said.

"No, not since—"

"Why don't you come over tonight?" she interrupted. "You know, our regular Friday night date."

Date sounded forced. In fact, her whole cheery attitude and conversation sounded forced. "We can talk, and make popcorn. And my brother got a bunch of horror movie DVDs. Some zombie movies. We can make popcorn!" she repeated. She looked up at me from beside my shoulder, beaming.

"I don't know if that's such a good—"

"It'll be fun!"

She stopped, and since she had a death-grip on my upper arm, I stopped, too. "Please come over. My parents will be out."

Dick heard that.

She looked at her toes; one foot scraped at a spot on the sidewalk. "We need to talk. I need to talk. To you. About ... what I need from you."

Yes! Yes! Say yes! Dick yelled.

I should have said, "I think you said it all the last time you were at my place."

I should have said, "Why? Have you changed your mind?"

I should have said, "I'm involved with someone else."

I should have said "No."

Or, I should have remembered what my mother said, just a couple of weeks earlier in the back yard, and adjusted my expectations.

Dick took charge while Brain dithered.

"Okay," came out of my mouth.

"Great!" Kristen chirped. Her smile brightened her face again and she skipped back toward the subway station. "Come over around 8:30, okay? We'll have the place to ourselves." Dick liked the sound of that. "My parents will be out by then."

"Where are they going?"

She looked at me with her head tilted. "Out with your parents, silly! Boy, are you out of it! See you then."

Her parents, out with my parents. So we can be alone together. Shit.

I parked in my parents' driveway at 8:28. I had a bunch of flowers I had bought for half-price just before the florist on Pape closed, and a package of gourmet popping corn. I knew there was no use bringing wine.

Kristen opened the door before I could ring the doorbell, grinning even wider than she had in the afternoon. I couldn't even speak: she looked so completely different.

She had had her hair done at some point during the day. It was big and fluffy and looked two shades brighter. She was wearing tight pants, the kind that women like, the ones that end half-way down the calves. She must have borrowed them from her mother. And her top, or blouse, too: no sleeves, low neck. It was the first time I had seen a glimpse of Kristen's cleavage.

I was struck, for the first time in a long time, by just how lovely she was, with her delicate features and big blue eyes. She didn't smile very often, but when she did, like now, she could make you forget everything else.

"Well, don't just stand there, silly! Come in!" We sat on the sagging sofa in the family room. The open blinds let in the last of the sunset, giving the room a cozy, romantic appeal.

Oh, this is gonna be good! said Dick.

Shut up, Dick, Brain and I said together.

Kristen surprised me again by pressing a can of beer into my hand. "It's okay," she said, and I figured I must have looked shocked. That made sense, because I felt shocked. "Daddy said I should offer you a beer."

I cracked the beer and Kristen put the popcorn in the microwave. She put one of her brother's Blu-Ray disks into the player and we settled down for Dead Alive. Like we had never had any disagreement, Kristen settled her body against mine. She fit against me like an old baseball glove.

I'd seen Dead Alive twice before, but anyone who likes zombie movies as much as I do can watch it over and over. "Gotta commend your brother's choice in movies," I said.

Kristen tilted her head up at me, and Dick made me kiss her, like our fight had never happened, like I had never pressured Kristen to have sex. Like we were 14 again.

Her lips parted, and mine did, and our tongues wrestled. We had never done that before. Kristen's arms went around me and she leaned back, and I followed her down on the sofa.

"No pressure!" my mother's voice echoed in my head, and even Dick listened. We made out for a long time while dwindling numbers of humans sliced their way through zombies and spilled swimming pools-ful of gore. I kept my hands on Kristen's back and sides. She moaned ever so slightly, so I kissed her more deeply. I moved to her neck, her throat.

Kristen kissed my neck. Her hands roved down my back and I nearly jumped out of my skin when she grabbed my ass. I kissed that little spot where her collar-bones met, just under her chin.

"Damian, I ... want you," she whispered.

I kept my lips on her throat. She was so soft. So familiar. "I want you, too, Kristen," I murmured against her skin.

"I want you, Damian," she repeated. She pulled away and looked me in the eyes. "I want you to ... to make love with me."

The whole world stopped. I looked into her wide-open eyes. She was scared, but there was something else, as well. "I want you, and I don't want to lose you." She kissed me on the mouth again, then said "I've missed you so much. I want to make you happy."

I remembered that first time we had made out. We were both 14 years old and were used to spending long hours together, doing homework or chores or just teenager stuff. We were used to our bodies being close together. I remembered thinking that we had been together, friends, for nearly a decade. And I remember that I had noticed her sweet smell and flawless skin a long time before that night.

I remembered that summer evening six years earlier, how we were lying in my back yard, on the grass, looking at the sky as it went from blue to purple to black. I don't remember what we were talking about — some TV show, probably — and I turned to her at the same time she turned to me, and we looked the same question into each other's eyes. I moved forward for a kiss, tentative. I had no idea what to do. We mashed lips together for a few minutes until Kristen pushed me away. "We can't let our parents find out," she said.

"No," I agreed, but I wondered why not. It seemed to me that both her parents and mine expected us to be boyfriend and girlfriend, to make out.

We used to make out a lot, I remembered, but Kristen early and firmly put any sexual activity, even petting, absolutely beyond her limits. "Not until we're married," she had said.

It wasn't until now, this night that I thought of how our parents' expectations about us paralleled Kristen's expectation that we would marry.

I pushed those thoughts away and kissed her gently. "It's okay," I said. She was trembling. "It's okay. How long will your parents be out?"

"Long enough." She stood and took my hand. We went up to her bedroom, where we stood beside her bed, holding hands. She looked down from her toes to the bed and back again. I kissed her where her neck met her shoulder and took her soft little body into my arms. I lowered her to the bed, kissing her throat, moving up to her mouth.

"Make love with me, Damian," she whispered. Slowly, gently, I raised the bottom of her blouse. She sighed, but when I looked at her face, her eyes were wide and her lips pressed together so tightly, they were almost invisible.

I kissed her eyes, kissed her lips. I broke away just long enough to pull her blouse off. "Are you sure?" I asked. She nodded her head. I kissed her again, unhooked her bra and slid it off. I looked in wonder at her girlish breasts, so much smaller than Alexis', but still beautiful. Perfect, pointed, tipped pink. A pinker blush spread from her face, down her neck and over her breasts.

I lifted her hips and pulled her pants and underwear off together. I kissed her naked stomach and caressed her skinny thighs. She still looked terrified.

I took off my shirt and kissed Kristen again. I stood to lower my pants.

When I turned to Kristen, Dick was hard already, pointing at her.

"No! I can't!" Kristen sat up on the bed and turned away, closing her eyes. "No, go away!"

I tried to keep my voice level. "Kristen, if we're going to make love, we kind of have to be naked."

"No! It's disgusting! Put your pants back on!" She pulled her blouse in front of herself and ran to the bathroom. I heard the door lock.

I had never felt as ridiculous as the moment when, with my naked erection wilting, I knocked on Kristen's bathroom door. "Kristen, it's all right. We don't have to do anything. Come out, let's watch the rest of the movie."

"Go away!" she snapped. "Just go home, Damian. I don't want to see you anymore."

On the drive back to my apartment, I let my anger surface. I raged incoherently inside my car, wishing my voice could break the windshield. I threw my apartment door open and kicked my shoes across the living room so they made marks on the far wall.

I had three beers left and I drank them fast. I found some porn and relieved my aching balls, and then watched zombie videos on YouTube until I fell asleep.

When I woke up the next morning, I brushed my teeth for fifteen minutes, trying to scour the taste of beer and anger out of my mouth. I thought of Mary-Anne, of her body on my bed just a week earlier. But there was something I had to do before I called her.

I dialled Kristen's cell. While listening to her phone ring, I planned what I would say: I was moving on; she should, too; our respective parents were friends and neighbours; we can still be friends; all those stupid clichés from movies and TV shows.

Her cell rang and rang, but she didn't pick up. Her mother answered when I called her parents' house. "Hello, Mrs. Petri. Can I speak with Kristen?"

"Oh, hello Damian." There was an odd, uncharacteristic stammer in her voice. Then a pause, long enough for me to wonder if my cell had dropped the call. "She's not home right now ... can you call again?" I heard Kristen's unmistakable snap at that one: "Mom!"

What do you say in a situation like that? "Okay. I'll try in the evening."

"In the evening, dear. Goodbye."

I called Mary-Anne. She met me at the Eaton Centre. "I need a new fall jacket." I groaned silently, but with Mary-Anne, shopping wasn't boring. We talked, we laughed, we kissed.

I tried Alexis' idea at a clothing store, but Mary-Anne wouldn't even think of it. "Get the fuck out of my changing room before security catches you!"

I had to wait until evening to get her home. She fell into my bed under me, laughing even while I pushed my tongue into her mouth.

I left her naked in my bed long enough to pick up shawarmas on the Danforth. On the walk back, I called Kristen's house again. She still wouldn't come to the phone, so I sent a text:

Meet me for coffee Mnda? Sid's 9 am?

No response. And she didn't show up at the café Monday morning. I waited until I was late for my class. Mary-Anne had saved a seat for me and looked a question at me, but I ignored it.

I kept sending texts, twice a day for the rest of the week — of course, when Mary-Anne wasn't around. I dreaded getting the Inbox chime when I was with Mary-Anne, but that never happened.

Brain and Dick agreed with each other for once: it's over with Kristen. You tried to do the honourable thing. She doesn't want to hear it. But she doesn't want anything to do with you. You became free in August, and now you've dodged a bullet.

Chapter 25

Hockey Night

Disaster struck in the middle of September: the NHL locked out the players.

"Greedy jerks," my Dad said.

"Which ones? The owners or the players?"

"Both. How many billions of dollars are they arguing over? What more could either side want? Solid-gold toilets instead of just gold-plated?"

He handed me a beer, our Sunday afternoon tradition. By September, we were usually watching hockey. But not this year — not big-league hockey, anyway. Dad flipped through the sports channels. We found a broadcast of a European university game and settled in.

"Your Mom tells me you and Kristen broke up," he said.

Dad. Subtle.

"Yah, a couple weeks ago."

"I'm sorry, son. You two have been going out for years. I thought ... well ..."

"You thought I'd marry the girl next door. Look, Dad, I know that you and the Petris are close friends, but ... I just don't think that Kristen and I are compatible."

"You've been friends since you were little. Kindergarten, wasn't it? Seems like you took an awfully long time to figure out that you're not compatible."

I took a long drink of beer. Dad's serious talks usually exhausted and embarrassed me.

"What I'm getting at is, are you sure that you're really not right for each other? You know each other better than anyone else. You've been close all through growing up. Are you really certain that you want to break up? Maybe you just need a short break *from* each other."

Geez, now he was sounding like Oprah. Okay, I've never watched Oprah, but that comment sounded like something she would say. "We just have some mutually exclusive ideas, Dad. I don't see how we can agree, ever."

"You mean, about sex?" Oh my god, my dad wanted to talk about my sex life! I drank more beer. "You know, girls must feel so much conflicting pressure about sex these days: do it, don't do it. You ever seen women's magazines?"

"They're not my thing, Dad."

"Nor mine, but they're in your face every time you go to the store. Like Cosmopolitan: every cover has a headline like 'New sex tricks to drive your man wild.' And TV shows and movies make all women seem sexually insatiable.

"Then you get the churches and feminists and experts talking about how sex can be so ... traumatic for young girls. There are a lot of conflicting messages, but they're all extreme: be a whore, or be a virgin."

"Yah, but ... Kristen has become so religious in the last couple of years. It's weird."

"Strange. Her parents aren't particularly religious. I mean, they go to church more often than we do ..."

"That's easy. We only go three times a year."

Dad nodded and drank his beer. We watched European hockey for a while in silence. It wasn't bad: lots of speed, and much cleaner play than in Canadian games. Still, I missed the hitting.

Dad spoke up during a commercial. "Why do you think religions are so terrified of sex?"

"Terrified? Why do you think they're terrified of it?"

"Because every religion tries to control it. 'Sex must only occur within marriage.' Adultery is a sin. Pre-marital sex is a sin. Homosexuality is a sin. Every religion controls sex as much as it can. That goes for Christians, Jews and Muslims. And as far as I'm concerned, they're all dead wrong."

"I think the Hindus are more open about sex," I said.

"I don't know much about that," Dad said. "But the three religions from the Holy Land are all against sex. People try to control things they're afraid of. Like fire: we need it, but it's dangerous, so we control it carefully."

"Is sex dangerous?" I asked. My dad had never spoken to me like this before. I felt like I was in the middle of the ocean without a paddle.

"Of course not! Not in itself. Okay, there are STDs — you've learned about those, right, son?"

"Yah." I hoped I wasn't blushing.

"Okay, those can be dangerous, but you can protect yourself against them. And there is risky sex — you've heard of the 'choking game'?"

"Where people choke themselves while ..." I could not bring myself to say "masturbating" to my father.

"Choke themselves or their partner. I hope you're not doing that!"

"No!" Now, I knew my face was red.

Dad just nodded and gestured with his beer bottle. "Good. People have died doing that. David Carradine, and that singer a few years back ..."

"Michael Hutchense from INXS?"

"I think so ... the point is, it's a fucking stupid thing. Choking yourself."

"I know, Dad." Fortunately, the game came back on then. We watched and drank beer and stayed quiet until the next commercial break. Then Dad just had to pipe up again.

"Maybe, as far as Kristen goes, take it slow. Let her think about things. Putting pressure on her to have sex will only drive her away. Only make things worse."

When Dad was right, he was right — even though his advice at this point was moot. "Okay, Dad. No pressure. I'll let her think things through."

Conversation returned to hockey. Dad even gave me a second beer. I guess he thought I was growing up that much more.

But more beer equals a looser tongue. Before the end of the game, I admitted to Dad: "We tried, you know. Kristen invited me over and we tried to make love."

"Uh ..." Dad looked uncomfortable.

"You know, that night you and Mom went out with the Petris?"

"Yes, I know." He drank more beer and choked. When he stopped coughing, he said "It was your mother's idea."

"For Kristen to agree to try sex?"

"No, no," Dad said, still choking on beer. After some more wheezing and pounding his fist against his chest, he managed to say "It was her idea to give you two some time together where Kristen would be most comfortable."

"Geez, are our parents trying to plan out our sex lives?"

"No, no, of course not!" Dad moved like he was going to sip his beer again but thought better of it. "No. Your mother and I spoke about you and Kristen, of course, but we didn't talk about it with the Petris! Not in those terms, that is. What do you think I said to them? 'So, Tony, let's clear out of the house so your daughter feels more comfortable about letting my son fuck her.'"

I had to laugh.

"No, no. The Petris were upset about the two of you breaking up. We all thought that we'd give you an opportunity to make up, and that meant leaving you a wide berth for the night. What you did with it was completely up to you two."

I had been caught in a web woven by Kristen, her parents and my parents. I had known Kristen had planned it from the second I saw her at the subway station. I guess I also should have known that our parents were complicit.

"But, I guess it didn't work out, anyway," Dad concluded.

"No. I mean, we tried. Kristen tried. I think she wanted to, but ..." I needed more beer. I polished off my second bottle and got a third from the beer fridge. "You know what Kristen said? 'It's disgusting.' She thinks sex is disgusting." I swallowed a good third of the beer and felt my anger grow. "I think she has a problem. A psychological problem."

"With what?"

"With the male body and the idea of sex."

Dad shook his head. "Well, I don't know where she got that idea. Her parents never struck me as prudes. Certainly not

Barbara."

I laughed. "When we were kids, me and my friends thought she was the hottest mom in the neighbourhood."

Dad threw back his head and laughed. "Yah, Barbara certainly knows how to attract attention!"

The hockey game ended. We finished our beers and I got ready to go home. "Thanks, Dad, for the talk."

"Anytime, son. Anything you ever want to talk about. I have to admit, it was pretty damn awkward talking with your son about his sex life, at first. But I want you to know, you can ask me anything."

"Ask an expert, right?" He laughed at that.

At the door, he put his hand on my shoulder and looked me in the eye. "Give her some time, son. A relationship is more than sex. You have to ask yourself: do you love her. Do you?"

I left without answering, but the question haunted me all night. Did I love Kristen?

Did I love Mary-Anne?

Kristen was the obvious choice for me, literally the girl next door. We had known each other for so long, had gone through things together.

Kristen was not willing to go through an important rite of passage with me. I had gone through it ahead of her. I had not wanted to wait. Did that make me a bad person?

What if Kristen never wanted to take that rite, take that important step? What if we got married like everyone expected us to, and Kristen never got past her disgust? How long could I live with someone I disgusted?

Did I love Kristen? At home, I cracked another beer, and then in that drunken state when you can convince yourself you're actually thinking more clearly than ever before, I made a list. I drew a line down a sheet of paper. On one side, I wrote Things I Love About Kristen. On the other, Things About Kristen I Hate.

Love: face — cute.

Nice smile.

Smart (in school)

Cute ass.

Nice tits (saw 'em, finally!)

Kind to animals (cats)
Cooks own pasta
Knows everything about me — ALMOST

Hate: Disgusted by ME
Disgusted by SEX
Judgemental
Opinionated
Talks too much WAY TOO MUCH
Narrow-minded
Hates sex
Too religious

Back to Love:
Can drive
Can be designated driver any time

Back again to Hate:
Won't drink alcohol
Doesn't want me to drink alcohol

I realized I needed more beer after that.

Still with Hate:
Dragged me to church retreat last yr.
Smart-ass
Show-off
Know-it-all

I wrote that down for the way she always had her hand up for every question in every class, for all four years in high school. And in junior high. And in elementary school.

I underlined Know-it-all. And Smart-ass.

I went back to Love and wrote Smart. Then I realized I had already written it and crossed it off. More beer.

I sat back and looked at my list, but by this time I was far too drunk to count which side had more entries. I blinked at the sheet, and the lines started to cross.

When I came to, the sun was shining. It was time to get to class.

As I pulled on my shirt, a piece of lined paper on my desk caught my eye. I looked at the scrawling, smeared ink and vaguely remembered making a list the night before. What was it?

I then noticed the horrible taste in my mouth. Must never drink that much at one time, ever again! said my brain. I squinted at the list: what the hell had I written?

The first words that I could decipher were nice smile. The next thought: Mary-Anne.

I sat on my bed and thought about Mary-Anne until I noticed the time. I had to scramble to get to class.

Chapter 26

Nick Returns

I nearly dropped the hundred pounds of textbooks on my own feet when I came into my apartment. "Nick! You're back!"

He sat on the sofa like he was doing it a favour, suitcases strewn around him. Designer jeans and new shoes practically screamed their price tags. A brand-new Macbook Air sat open on the coffee table. And a very expensive-looking leather jacket hung on the coat-tree. His hair had been precisely mussed to accentuate the planes of his face, and a 5-o'clock shadow on his chin ended in a precise line just under his jaw, as if he had painted it on. Even his full lips looked like someone in London had worked on them, somehow, to make them look their plump, girl-swooning best.

"The internship was for three months," he said in his aggravating, superior way. "Then they offered me an extension and a raise. I made a shit-load of money. They offered a contract, but I wanted to finish my degree."

"When did you get back?"

"About an hour ago. I helped myself to your beer."

I grabbed a beer and flopped into the chair across from Nick. "You shoulda called and told me you were coming."

"I only announced my whole itinerary on Facebook."

I shrugged. "I almost never look at Facebook."

"I know. I got almost no info from you all summer. So, how did my business work out?"

"*Your* business? You mean, PoolGeeks? Pretty good. I made some money, too. Thirty regular customers." Thirty-one if you included the Casales. But I hadn't gone back there. Whether they had reconciled or not, I liked having my balls under my cock, not hanging from Henry's rear-view mirror.

"Not bad, not bad at all, mate," he said. Was he trying to affect a British accent? Or was that coming naturally after five months in the UK? "So, we should work out what we're going to do for a business through the winter."

"Look, man, I don't have time for another business. I'm going to concentrate on ..." My phone went off. The call display showed Mary-Anne. "Hi, beautiful!" I answered.

"Did you take the book by Krugman from the library?"

"Um, yah, I think so." I went to my room and sifted through the pile of books I had dumped on the bed. "*The Self-Organizing Economy*?"

"You have it?"

"Yes, I'm holding it in my hands right now."

"Then how are you talking to me?"

"On the phone!" What the hell was she getting at?

"If both hands are holding the book, what's holding your phone to your head?"

"Okay, I'm holding the book in one hand, and the phone in the other."

Silence. Then a long gasp. Laughter. She was laughing. "What's so funny?"

"Oh, Damian, it's so easy to get you." She laughed some more. "I kept picturing you in ridiculous positions, holding a bunch of books and trying to keep your mouth by the phone at the same time."

"I'll bring the book to your place tonight," I said to steer the conversation away from my ridiculousness.

"Why don't I just come over there? We'll be alone."

"No, we won't. Nick's back." He coughed and I jumped — I hadn't realized he had followed me into my bedroom.

"Nick, the business genius?" Mary-Anne bubbled. "Great — I've been dying to meet him!"

That didn't sound good, but what could I say to Mary-Anne, especially with Nick standing right there? "Oh, okay. See you later."

"Get some good snacks!" She broke the connection.

The phone beeped immediately: a message was coming in.

"Who was that?" Nick asked as if it were any of his business.

"Mary-Anne," I answered while opening the Messages app.

"Who's Mary-Anne?"

"She's my study partner." I know, I should have said "girlfriend." Or "lover." I *know.*

The message was from Kristen. "I can meet U 2morro," it said.

"Kristen. Now you get back to me. Weeks later." I only realized I had spoken that out loud when Nick's jaw dropped.

"Dude, who are you and what have you done with Damian?" Nick said.

"What are you talking about?"

"Well, for one thing, you've got a lot more confidence in your body language now."

"So now you're an expert in body language, as well as contract negotiation?"

"There was a two-day seminar. You gotta know body language if you're going to be a half-decent negotiator. And you bought a new phone, and not a cheap one, either. And it requires a data plan, which is still way overpriced in this country."

"Yah, I get it, you were in England for five months."

"But the biggest thing of all: you got two different women calling you? I know, one is Kristen, you've been engaged since you were both babies, but — is your 'study partner' Mary-Anne *Krupa*?"

"Shit. Do you know her?"

"She was in a couple of my classes last year," he shrugged. "Dude, she is seriously *hot!* Her, and Kristen, too — like I said, who the fuck are you? Damian Serr ain't no playah."

"Fuck off. Anyway, she's coming over tonight. She says she wants to meet you." Fuck: Nick already knew her, and she wanted to meet him. This was not going to be a good thing.

"I bet she does," said Nick. "But I can't stay."

I tried to hide my relief. "Why not?"

"Dude, I just got home after five months away! If I don't have supper with my mom tonight, she'll die of unhappiness! Sorry. We can catch up later. So tell me, did Kristen finally come to her senses and dump you, or did you get tired of the no-sex girlfriend?"

"Both."

Nick laughed so hard, he nearly spilled his beer. "Dog! This is just too good! Oh, man, I gotta talk to Tyler and Patrick ..."

No, please! I thought. "Look, about Tyler ... it'd probably be better if you didn't mention me when you talk to him."

Nick froze in the hallway. "Why? What happened?"

I took a deep breath. "I hired Tyler to help me with the pools, and I had to fire him less than a month later."

Nick shook his head. "Dude, that was a mistake I could have warned you away from. I would never hire him in the first place. He's always been lazy."

"I got a lot of complaints about the lousy jobs he did."

"I can imagine. Did you give him a chance to improve?"

"Was that something you learned in your internship? Of course I did. Lots of chances."

"When you hire a friend, it's tough to fire him. I mean, what did he do that was so bad that you had to let him go?"

I hesitated. How much did Nick need to know?

"Come on, Dam. It's pretty cold to fire a buddy like Tyler."

"Buddy! Friends like him, I don't need!" What the fuck did Nick know? Nick, ever superior, always smarter than everybody else in the room, always with a plan?

"Shit, man, what did he do? Steal from you?"

"No, nothing like that. Just too many complaints."

"Complaints? For what? How bad? Come on, tell me."

My mouth opened, but nothing came out. There were so many thoughts going through my head at one time, I didn't know what to say first. It was like they were all crowding into my mouth, trying to get out at the same time: Why should I tell him? It wasn't his business, not really, all he did was set up a bank account and a lousy website, and I had had to spend hours, days, fixing it and making it work and look good; and cleaning pools during the hottest summer in Toronto's history is no fun; and he always stole all the glamour and dumped his shit on everyone else, me especially, ever since we were kids; and Tyler didn't make my life easier, he just made more work for me —

"Come on, what did he do? Piss in the customer's pools?"

— and what did I know about running a business before Nick left this all on my shoulders; and what did I know about managing people, or hiring the right people; but now, now I had learned so much, I knew more about running a real business and dealing with actual customers than Nick learned in his glamour job in London —

"Did he steal from the customers?"

"He fucked the customer's wife!" I shouted.

Nick just stood there with his mouth open for a full minute. Finally, he said "Tyler?"

"Yes, Tyler. He had sex with the third customer that I got."

"Woah. I never believed his bullshit about getting all those girls ... wow."

"Yah. 'Wow.'"

Nick got two more beers for us. "So, he's still pissed at you?"

"Why should he be pissed at me? I should be pissed at him! And I am!"

I had almost forgotten the truth of it: that I had let Tyler continue banging Mrs. Casales — Leda — for two weeks after I found out about it, and it really was just a matter of the complaints that kept on coming.

Nick flopped onto the sofa again. "Shit, you go out of the country for five months, and everything falls apart. Your friends all turn into sluts and don't speak to each other." He gulped down half the beer. "Well, Romeo, I gotta get cleaned up before I go see my Mom for dinner. Have fun with Hot Mary-Anne tonight. Hey, you gonna put a tie on the doorknob, or something, if you're going at it when I get home?"

"Fuck off, Nick."

He grinned and went for a shower, humming a tune I couldn't recognize.

I returned Kristen's text as the shower began. "Campus Café, 10 a.m.?" She responded in less than a minute: "OK. CU."

I organized my books and notes while Nick got dressed, still humming that same insipid tune.

Mary-Anne came over after her late-afternoon class. We shared pizza and swapped books after highlighting them. She showed me how to solve a tricky equation and how it fit into a graph in Krugman's book. I made her some coffee in my new coffee-maker, like the one Alexis had.

We sat at the kitchen table. She pulled her chair until it touched mine so that we could both look at the laptop screen. Our fingers touched on the keyboard and she leaned her shoulder against mine. She felt warm. I faced the screen, but my eyes traced the curve where her breast pressed against the back of her hand as she leaned forward.

"So, what time does the famous Nick get home?"

"Dunno. He's visiting his mother. I guess he won't be that late."

"If he won't be late, we better get started."

I turned to her, puzzled, and her lips met mine. Her arms went around my back. She explored my mouth as she pulled my shirt up, and only broke the kiss to pull it over my head.

She leaned forward to kiss my neck, but I stood up. Before she could say anything, I picked her up, one arm under her back and the other under her knees. She squealed when I straightened, so I smothered her with my mouth. Keeping my lips clamped on hers, I carried her to my bedroom.

I had to place her carefully at the head of my bed and sweep the books onto the floor, so it wasn't quite the romantic move I had hoped for. Mary-Anne stretched out on the mattress, smiling up at me. "How long do you think we have?"

I started undoing tiny buttons on her blouse, kissing down as I exposed her skin. I was surprised and delighted to see that she wasn't wearing a bra, and I wondered about her underwear as I pulled the blouse out from her pants.

Her downy pubic hair puffed out when I pulled down the zipper. Mary-Anne lifted her hips so I could slide the jeans off her.

I stood to rip my own pants off, taking in the glory of a beautiful young woman stretched naked on my own bed. Her blonde hair sprayed across my pillow like a bursting star. I watched her pink nipples rise and fall with her breath. A tiny shadow curved below her navel like a smile as she raised one knee. She parted her slim, muscular thighs and reached her hands to me.

I just could not hold back any longer. I fell on her body. I pasted her soft, warm skin with kisses, licking down from her neck, over each nipple, across her belly, lower. I slobbered on her clit and gasped when Mary-Anne's hand wrapped, soft and hot, around my penis.

I rolled us so that she was on top. I pursed my lips and sucked in, pulling her clit a little into my mouth. Downy hair tickled my nostrils.

Mary-Anne responded, slobbering wet and hot up and down my length. I kept on licking her while enjoying the torture she was giving me.

Her breath accelerated. When she moaned, I rolled again so that I was on top, spread her pussy lips with my fingers and attacked her clit with my tongue. I felt dampness, tasted sharp sweetness as I pushed my tongue inside her. Her pussy parted and I could not tell whether moisture came from her or from my tongue. She cried out when I slid a finger into her and pushed her hips upward, cried again and pushed my face away from her. "Too much, too sensitive," she panted.

I smiled at her. I kissed her cheek and lifted one leg high in the air. She looked puzzled until Dick found its way into her, and then she smiled wide as her eyes closed.

I stroked in and out of her and after a few minutes touched her clit again. She reached for my head, so I leaned down and kissed her mouth while I slid in and out. There was no way I could keep that up for very long. When I came, so did Mary-Anne. I pressed my lips onto hers and she screamed into my mouth.

We just held each other for a long time. We must have fallen asleep, because the next thing I knew, I heard the front door open. "Nick?" I called out.

Footsteps came down the hall. "Yah, it's me, Dam. Went to bed early, did you?" He came around the corner with a stupid grin on his face and jumped back when he saw Mary-Anne in my bed.

She sat up, holding the sheet in front of herself, completely at ease. "You must be Nick." She held out her hand toward him. Her smile could have melted bricks.

Nick just stood there with his mouth open.

"Nick, this is Mary-Anne. My study partner. We've been studying. Hard." Mary-Anne elbowed me in the ribs. Hard. "And girlfriend." I coughed.

Nick stepped to the bed and shook Mary-Anne's hand. "Pleased to meet you," he mumbled.

"We've actually met before," Mary-Anne said as cheerily as if she were fully dressed, sitting in a library or something, not sitting on my bed, naked except for a moist sheet in front of her. In that moment, I felt proud to know that Nick could see the outline of her left nipple pressed against the sheet. "In a tutorial section."

"Yah. I remember," he mumbled. I could not believe it: Nick was actually blushing! "I, uh, I gotta go ... study," he said. "Nice to meet you. Again."

When he left the room, Mary-Anne and I laughed.

Chapter 27

Collision

Mary-Anne didn't bother dressing; she pulled on one of my shirts, but left it unbuttoned. I admired her long legs as she slipped into the bathroom to brush her teeth. When she came out, she dropped the shirt on my floor and stood for a moment, showing off her trim body, high breasts and flat stomach before she slid into bed, pressed her soft skin against mine and kissed me on the cheek. "Good night."

I luxuriated in the warmth of her naked back against my body. I pushed my hips forward a little so that my damp penis pressed against her skin. I felt a tingle, a quiet thrill, but I was exhausted.

I woke in the middle of the night, Mary-Anne's back cuddled against me. I moved my hand up and rubbed her breast with my palm. She moaned, so I slid my other arm under her neck and reached for her other nipple.

She turned her head and I craned my own to kiss her. I slid into her again, wet and smooth. We moved together slowly, quietly in the dark until Mary-Anne's whole body shook, stiffened, shook again. She pressed her hips down and squeezed my penis until I climaxed.

We held each other, just breathing, until we fell asleep again. When the sun lit the shades, my hands were still on her breasts.

"No time for that," she said, sliding away from me. "Shit, where are my pants? Oh, yeah. Hey, can I borrow a pair of your underwear for today?"

"Sure."

"Great. I gotta get to class. See you after?"

"Sure thing."

She stood in the sunlight, nude and glorious. I could not take my eyes from her butt, where the muscles flexed as she rooted in my underwear drawer. She had to hold her them up with one hand as she pulled on her pants, and then she let met stare at her breasts as she opened her purse, pulled out a brush and bent forward. Her breasts pointed to her chin and her hair fell in a golden cascade toward the floor. She flicked the brush through it, twice, thrice and then straightened fast, flinging the whole mane into place behind her. She smiled at me and made a kissing motion with her lips before pulling on her blouse.

"Don't you want some breakfast?" I asked when she pulled open my bedroom door.

"I'll grab something. I'll have to eat it in class." She strode to the front door with bouncing steps as Nick's bedroom door opened. "Morning, Nick. See you later, 'kay? I wanna talk to you about Krugman."

She paused only long enough to shove her bare feet into shoes, and she was gone.

Nick looked at me as if he didn't quite believe I existed. He shook his head. "Dog, I wish you'd tell me where the real Damian is." He shut his door again.

I looked at my watch: I had time to wash and shave before meeting Kristen at the café in the middle of the campus. When I got there, she was sitting at a table by the window, both hands wrapped around a steaming mug. Tea, her usual. The bag was still floating in it. She hated the mess when she took it out.

"I'm glad you finally agreed to talk with me," I said as I slid into the chair opposite her.

She just looked at me, lips pressed together. Her eyes were so sad. She did not say anything. Oh boy, said my brain. This is going to be awful.

"Look, we shouldn't be enemies. We've known each other all our lives," I said. I thought about taking her hand in mine, but the tight line of her lips told me it was a bad idea. How could she look so delicate and so hard at the same time?

"Is this the 'let's be friends' speech?" she snapped quietly. She did not want anyone in the café to hear.

"Well... I guess so."

"Damian, you're such a cliché, it's pathetic."

"No, really, Kristen! We should at least be on speaking terms."

"We're speaking."

I tried to remember all those sentences I had rehearsed over the past several weeks. Months, actually. But my stupid mouth kept screwing them up. "Our parents are friends. Let's try to get along."

Kristen leaned across the table. "I miss you," she mumbled. "Can't we go back to the way we were?"

"What, watching a movie once a week, and continual pressure to go to a church retreat?"

"That's not as bad as continual pressure to have sex!" She put her hand on mine, surprising me. "No, no pressure either way. Just let's go back to where we were."

"Why are you pressuring her to have sex?" said the voice from the worst-case scenario.

Mary-Anne stood beside the table, smiling at her own joke. Brain was spinning, trying to think of a way to disappear. Dick already had.

Mary-Anne bent and kissed my cheek. "Who's your friend?" she asked.

"I'm his *girlfriend*," Kristen said. "Since we were fourteen. Who are *you*?"

Mary-Anne stared at Kristen, her smile frozen. As she turned to me, her expression thawed into accusation.

Kristen slapped me across the cheek and fled. Mary-Anne watched her until the café door closed behind her and turned to me. "Jerk."

"Look, Mary-Anne ..."

"Fuck off. Forever." Her long legs only needed two steps to take her to the café door. Her long arm whipped the door against the wall and everyone in the café jumped at the crash. Those muscular legs, the legs that only a few hours ago had slid up my own like silk, took her away from me.

And all I could do was stand there.

Chapter 28

Answers

There was only one person to turn to. I got to her house when I knew she would be home, right after 5. I rang the doorbell and she buzzed me in, as usual. Or what used to be usual.

"I'm in the kitchen!" I followed her musical voice and a complex aroma. The hangar of a refrigerator gaped open. With a big knife, she pushed a heap of chopped vegetables into a pot. As usual, a large glass of wine stood on the counter near her elbow.

"Long time, no see," she said cheerfully, but she did not look at me. "What brings this unexpected pleasure?"

I had not anticipated how I would feel when I saw Alexis again. Even though a white apron embroidered with pink flowers covered her casual clothes, I saw her nude as she had been that day after the first time we had made love ... fucked.

Made love.

I saw her hair flowing over her naked shoulders, her big dark nipples. I could almost taste her skin, feel it against my cheek.

I collapsed into a high chair before I remembered to breathe again.

My mouth opened and poured out my mind. I told her everything: about Kristen, about trying to get into her pants even when I was getting mind-blowing sex from Alexis; about Mary-Anne and that amazing first weekend in my apartment; about how she was uninhibited around Nick (but of course nowhere near as uninhibited as Alexis); about Kristen's weird, abortive attempt to make love to me; and then about the disaster in the coffee shop that afternoon.

And I ended it like the schoolboy I was inside: "What do I do, now?"

Alexis looked at me without expression. "You're asking your former lover, with whom you broke off the relationship, about how to get your two girlfriends back?"

"No! Just one." I stared at the hand that held the long spoon, stirring the pot and thought about how it had slid down my bare chest.

Alexis shook her head and poured herself more wine. She sat down beside me, and when our knees touched, my heart pounded in my ears. "Let's look at this strategically," she said. "First, what do you want to do? What outcome do you want?"

"I want Mary-Anne back."

"What about Kristen?"

"That will never work."

"So, you want her out of your life forever?"

"No! No, that won't work, either. Our parents are friends. We've known each other for years. I would like us to be friends. I know that sounds like a TV cliché, but it happens to be true. I just wish she weren't always disgusted by me."

"And what's the situation now?"

"They're both disgusted by me."

"Good. We have a starting point and a goal. What do you want to do next?"

"That's what I came to you for! I have no idea how girls think!" My voice took on that pathetic pleading note that I had tried to keep out. "Maybe, you could talk to her? To Mary-Anne?"

Alexis laughed. "And tell her what? 'My former lover has tired of me and now he wants you?'"

"No! That's not true!" The way things were going, all women in the world would soon hate me. "Maybe you could make her see things the way I do."

Alexis shook her head again. "When it comes to emotions and women, you are as dumb as shit." It still shocked me when she swore. "In case you haven't noticed, my dear, sweet dumbass, I am not a typical woman. I don't think the same way most women in society today do. It's one of the reasons that I am successful.

"To me, sex is like a sport. Other people play tennis or golf or run, to stay in shape and work out stress. I run, too, but to me, nothing gets rid of stress like good fucking. And while I believe in love and hope to find it someday, I don't think it necessary for good sex. When I fuck someone, I keep emotion out of it. As you know, at this stage of my life, I relish a good three-way. I think you'll have a very hard time finding someone else, particularly a young woman, who looks at sex that way."

Dick sprang up as soon as Alexis said "fucking." I had to shift in my chair because it was pressing against my pants. My mouth felt dry.

Brain told me Alexis was right. "So, what do I do about Mary-Anne? She's pretty open about sex."

"Yes, but I think that it's still an emotional matter for her. She was attracted to you in a big way, but she obviously has other feelings for you, too. She probably has had these sorts of feelings for quite some time, even before this school year."

Mary-Anne liked me last year? Had she liked me when we were in that project group last year, and I hadn't noticed?

Wow. I was thinking like a stereotypical junior-high girl.

"What do I do?" I repeated.

"You know what to do. What you know you should have done right away, instead of coming over here."

Again, she was right.

Alexis kissed me on the cheek. Heat spread from the touch of her lips, across my face and all down my neck and throat. I could not breathe, and Dick jumped again.

But Alexis was in charge, and Brain listened to her. Alexis stood and went back to stir her pot. Time to go, said Brain.

I listened to Brain.

Chapter 29

What I Knew I Had to Do

I knocked twice on Mary-Anne's door. Not too hard, my panicky brain said. You don't want to come across as aggressive.

She whipped the door open. "Took you long enough," she said.

"Can I come in?"

She stepped away from the door. I came in, but she left the door open. "Look, I'm sorry about that." Mary-Anne had a private dorm room like most third-year students. The Krugman book sat on the desk beside her open Macbook. A green quilt covered the narrow bed, reminding me of her tree-planting summer job.

Bob Marley in mosaic form looked down from his poster. I heard him say, "Mon, you're screwed."

"About what? Cheating or lying?" Mary-Anne asked.

"I didn't do either! I'm just sorry you had to get involved in all that. *See* all that." I realized I hadn't thought this through at all. Come on, brain, think up something fast.

"You didn't lie about having another girlfriend?"

"She's not my girlfriend!"

"She said she has been since you were fourteen." Mary-Anne's combination of calm and anger made my panic worse. "You should have told me that you were involved with someone when we first started going out. You should have broken it off with one of us."

"I did break it off! She told me during the summer that she never wanted to see me again!"

"And yet, there she was, sitting with you, looking at you, talking about sex."

"I wanted to talk things over. We broke up in a bad way. I wanted to set things right. This was just a meeting to settle the relationship, hopefully so we could remain friends."

Okay, I know I left out the abortive attempt at sex, which technically happened after Mary-Anne and I got together. Okay, more than technically. Mary-Anne and I had already had sex. Lots of sex when my old girlfriend tried to seduce me.

I couldn't tell her that.

"Why is it important to be friends with her? That's such a TV cliché."

"She lives next door to my parents, for god's sake. And the last thing she said to me was that I was disgusting." Oops, that was from the time when I had actually gotten her naked, *after* I had started sleeping with — making love to — fucking — okay, let's just sum it up as "going out with" — Mary-Anne.

"Was that when you were pressuring her into having sex?"

I looked at my feet. "Yah."

Mary-Anne sat on her bed. "Is that why you broke up with her? No sex?"

"Partly ... but it's just part of her whole attitude. We were only boyfriend and girlfriend because it seemed expected of us. She's actually the girl next door. I lived a cliché. But I don't think I actually like her all that much. She's ..." Admit it, said my brain. "She's kind of a bitch."

"And what does that make me? A slut?"

"No!"

"Well then — what am I?"

I sat beside her and took her hands in mine. "You're the most wonderful girl in the world."

"Oh, shove the bullshit! You're just going out with me so you can fuck me!"

"No, no, Mary-Anne! That's not it! Not all of it! The sex is ... fantastic." I realized only at that moment that making love to Mary-Anne was better than with Alexis, despite Alexis' techniques and experience.

Fortunately, Brain was in control. "You're smart, smarter than

I am. I love that about you. And you're beautiful —" that brought the beginning of a smile "— and you're a lot of fun to be around." You should have been saying these things all along, dumbass, my brain said to me.

Keep going, Brain. "I feel happy with you. I never felt happy with Kristen. Not since I was six, anyway, and I got to eat her mother's baking."

"Her mother's baking?"

"I told you, she's the girl next door. When I was six, I used to go to her house after school and have home-made cookies." Mary-Anne smiled, really smiled at that.

Cuteness. Stick with cuteness, said my brain. I think it was my brain.

Mary-Anne's eyes narrowed. "When did you say you broke up with her?"

"In August," I lied. "Before you and I met at the bookstore. It was over."

"Then, why did it take two months for the 'let's still be friends' talk?"

"I've been calling her and texting her since then! She ignored me until a few days ago. I don't understand it, either!"

"What did you say a minute ago?"

Brain's wheels started spinning like my Suzuki Swift's in mud. "Umm..."

"You were talking about me." The hint of another smile played around her lips.

"It's fun hanging out with you?"

"Before that."

How do women remember conversations verbatim? "You're beautiful."

"Before that. You said I was smart." She couldn't stop smiling now.

"Yes. Smarter than me."

"That's not very impressive."

Ouch. But she was still smiling.

"You said you ..." she prompted.

My wheels slipped again, making that slippery, whining sound. This was worse than mud; this was black ice.

"... loved that about me." She looked into my eyes, and Brain shut right off. The wheels stopped spinning, stopped whining, just stopped.

"How do you feel about me?" she asked.

Oh no! Now car alarms, horns blaring.

"How do you feel? About me?" Mary-Anne repeated, her smile fading.

You know what she wants to hear, said Brain. Tell her! Or was that Dick?

"I ..."

Mary-Anne's smile vanished. She stood. "You should go," she said.

"Mary-Anne, hold on. What about us? We're cool, right?"

"Is that how you feel? 'Cool'?"

"I think you're cool. And hot." I tried to smile.

Say it! said something inside my head.

Mary-Anne just looked at me. She wasn't happy. I knew this was my last chance.

My eyes flicked past the laptop. Bob Marley was no help. We were alone. I opened my mouth, but there was a war in my throat. My brain and my dick were pushing, fighting to get the words out, but something else, some tiny, fearful thing fought back, pushing down with all its might.

"I ..." I pushed, the words came higher. "...think..." The tiny fearful thing dug its heels in. The three of us, me, my brain and my dick, all got together and rammed against the blockage. It started to move. "No. I feel, I know ..." Damn it, why can't I get past this?

Mary-Anne tilted her head. I could not interpret her expression. Yes: impatience. I had about two seconds left before she threw me ...

"Get out." She stood and pointed to the door. "Get the fuck out of here."

Time to grow up. I got down on one knee, like I had before, for Alexis. I took her hand, the one that wasn't pointing out the door, between both of mine. "I'm falling in love with you."

Mary-Anne's pointing hand dropped, and her head along with it. "Stop it."

"Stop what? I just started." I stood and looked down into her eyes. "I am falling—" I collapsed to the floor, careful not to hit my head. "Oops! Yup, it happened! I just fell in love with you."

Mary-Anne could not stop herself from smiling. "Damian Serr, you are the cheesiest man I have ever met! Get up!"

"I'm really sorry about Kristen. I was just trying ..."

"Cheesy, and full of shit."

"What?"

"I cannot trust you, Damian. You say you and Kristen never had sex, but you obviously weren't a virgin the first time we did it. You're hiding something, you're carrying a shit-load of baggage. No. You and I are through."

"Please, Mary-Anne ..."

"No. Don't worry, we'll still be project partners. It's too late in the term to start looking for new study buddies. But no more sex, no more romance between us. Our relationship now is strictly business."

I swallowed. "Is this the 'let's be friends' talk? Because I've never had one," I lied.

Baggage. Somehow, Mary-Anne had sensed Alexis. Female intuition, my father would have said. She didn't know the details, couldn't have known, but she knew there was something I wasn't telling her.

"I'd like you to go now," she said.

"We have a tutorial group tomorrow," I whined.

"Then I'll see you tomorrow." She put her hand on the door. I felt cold, heavy. I shuffled into the hallway, into the glares of the other girls in the dorm. The sisterhood stood shoulder-to-shoulder.

Somehow, I made it out of the dormitory. Only when I reached the sidewalk did I realize the fog in my eyes was tears.

Chapter 30

A Strategy for Missing

I missed Mary-Anne. Every time I saw her in a class, tutorial or project group, my throat tightened and my eyes burned. My stomach ached when I saw her walk away.

She treated me exactly like everyone else, like another member of the team. Nothing in her words, her voice, her face showed that she had any thought, any memory of those incredible nights together. How could she just turn off whatever feelings she had?

Sometimes, I thought I saw something in her eyes: a shimmer, a cloud, something indefinable. My brain told me it was just wishful thinking.

She's dropped you. Move on.

Some other part of me, not my brain, not my dick, no, something else, would not move on.

So I relished her cold shoulder, hung on to her every word about curves and ratios and eco-fucking-nomics. I endured the music of her voice, I suffered the rippling of her hair, I cherished the pain I felt in the back of my sternum whenever I looked at her face across a study carrel or a cafeteria or a classroom.

Alexis sent me a text message the day after I had gone to Mary-Anne's room. "Did U make up?"

I texted back just one word: "No."

She replied with some kind of sad emoticon. I could not bring myself to call her.

The next day, she texted again: "Come over?"

"Cant" I texted back. "Midterm 2moro." Not a lie, but I didn't study that night. I just stared out my bedroom window at grey, drizzly Toronto.

I blew the midterm. On the way home, I walked past the café, that café where Kristen had torpedoed my relationship with Mary-Anne. And there she was: Mary-Anne, sitting in the same fucking chair as Kristen had, opposite some jerk who was so much more fucking better-looking than me. I recognized him from some of my classes. I knew he was on the basketball team, but could not think of his name.

The only thing I could think of was how the glass top of the table they were sitting at, sipping coffee over, laughing over, making each other feel happy over, the glass table top Mr. Basketball Team Economics Whiz was trying to pick up my girl over, how it would break into such interesting patterns as I smashed his face into it.

I cut my next two classes for some therapeutic staring at the ceiling over my bed. I thought about Mary-Anne, her eyes when she was happy, the look on her face when she drank coffee with Mr. Basketball Jerk. I thought about the silky skin on the inside of her thigh and the pink colour of her nipples.

I closed my eyes and jerked off, remembering Mary-Anne's nipples in my mouth, her mouth wrapped around my cock. After I came, I felt worse: lonely and disgusted with myself.

Then I thought of Alexis and her advice: you have a starting point, you have a goal, said my brain. Now you just have to figure out how to get from one to the other.

My cell-phone beeped as I got out of the subway station the next evening. I dug it out of my pocket and hit the green button as I walked up the steps to my building.

"I have to go to New York in the morning," said Alexis. "Want to come with me for a few days?" she purred.

"Shit, Alexis, I'd love to, but tomorrow I have two midterms." A few days in New York with Alexis, nothing to do but see the sights, eat great food and fuck? What's the matter with you? said my brain. Yes, my brain said that.

"Oh, that's too bad. Julia McQuaig is coming, too. I remembered how much you enjoyed her in the summer, and I thought how long it's been since we had a really good three-way."

Go! Go! said Dick.

The answer came to me at that moment, delivered to me and my brain by that other part of me, that smart part that usually hides so well. It reminded of Alexis' advice: where I was, and what I wanted. Alexis Rosse and Julia McQuaig were not on the path between those two points.

I opened my door and ran up the stairs to the apartment. "Geez, Alexis, that sounds nearly ... irresistible. I'd love to come." I fumbled my keys out and somehow got the door open while holding the phone to my ear with my shoulder. "But these midterms ... they're really important. If I miss them, I won't get my year, and that means I won't graduate next year."

"Oh, that's too bad. Well, do you think you could join us for the weekend?"

I dropped my books on the floor and pulled the door shut behind me, heading back to the street. "The weekend? Like, Friday?" I was stalling, and I knew that Alexis knew it.

"Yes, Damian, the weekend is Friday evening till Sunday. I can email you a plane ticket."

I broke the connection, hoping Alexis would think the phone had dropped the call.

She didn't call back.

I ran to the florist and fidgeted as she wrapped a dozen roses and ran the blade of scissors along a ribbon to make it curly. Then I ran to the subway, cradling the paper wrapping.

I bounced on my toes on the subway platform for an endless five minutes. Finally, the train came. Seven stations. Eternity. People stared at me, made annoyed clicking noises with their tongues and teeth as I paced up and down the half-empty car.

At last, my heart hammered as I stood, shaking and sweaty, in front of Mary-Anne's dorm. I pressed the buzzer.

I could not think, could not plan what to say. I only knew one thing: I was going to get Mary-Anne back.

The door buzzed and clicked. I went in.

FIN

About the Author

Scott Bury is a journalist, editor and novelist based in Ottawa, Canada. His articles have appeared in magazines in Canada, the US, the UK and Australia, including *Macworld*, the *Financial Post, Applied Arts*, the *Globe and Mail* and *Graphic Arts Monthly*.

One Shade of Red is his second novel to be published.

His first published novel is *The Bones of the Earth*, a fantasy set in the real time and place of eastern Europe of the sixth century. He has also published a short story, "Sam, the Strawb Part" (proceeds of which are donated to an autism charity), and a paranormal story, "Dark Clouds." His work in progress is tentatively titled *Out of the USSR*, and tells the true story of a Canadian drafted into the Red Army during the Second World War, his escape from a German POW camp and his journey home.

Scott Bury lives in Ottawa with his lovely, supportive and long-suffering wife, two mighty sons and the orangest cat in history.

He can be found online at www.writtenword.ca, on his blog, Written Words, and on Twitter @ScottTheWriter.